THE CHOWDER HOUSE MURDER

Books by Lee Hollis

Hayley Powell Mysteries
DEATH OF A KITCHEN DIVA
DEATH OF A COUNTRY FRIED REDNECK
DEATH OF A COUPON CLIPPER
DEATH OF A CHOCOHOLIC
DEATH OF A CHRISTMAS CATERER
DEATH OF A CUPCAKE QUEEN
DEATH OF A BACON HEIRESS
DEATH OF A PUMPKIN CARVER
DEATH OF A LOBSTER LOVER
DEATH OF A COOKBOOK AUTHOR
DEATH OF A WEDDING CAKE BAKER
DEATH OF A BLUEBERRY TART
DEATH OF A WICKED WITCH
DEATH OF AN ITALIAN CHEF
DEATH OF AN ICE CREAM SCOOPER
DEATH OF A CLAM DIGGER
DEATH OF A GINGERBREAD MAN
DEATH OF A TOM TURKEY

Collections
EGGNOG MURDER
(with Leslie Meier and Barbara Ross)
YULE LOG MURDER
(with Leslie Meier and Barbara Ross)
HAUNTED HOUSE MURDER
(with Leslie Meier and Barbara Ross)
CHRISTMAS CARD MURDER
(with Leslie Meier and Peggy Ehrhart)
HALLOWEEN PARTY MURDER
(with Leslie Meier and Barbara Ross)
IRISH COFFEE MURDER
(with Leslie Meier and Barbara Ross)
CHRISTMAS MITTENS MURDER
(with Lynn Cahoon and Maddie Day)
EASTER BASKET MURDER
(with Leslie Meier and Barbara Ross)
HALLOWEEN NIGHT MURDER
(with Leslie Meier and Liz Ireland)
EASTER EGG MURDER
(with Leslie Meier and Peggy Ehrhart)

Poppy Harmon Mysteries
POPPY HARMON INVESTIGATES
POPPY HARMON AND THE HUNG JURY
POPPY HARMON AND THE PILLOW TALK KILLER
POPPY HARMON AND THE BACKSTABBING BACHELOR
POPPY HARMON AND THE SHOOTING STAR

Maya & Sandra Mysteries
MURDER AT THE PTA
MURDER AT THE BAKE SALE
MURDER ON THE CLASS TRIP
MURDER AT THE SPELLING BEE
MURDER AT THE HIGH SCHOOL REUNION

Downeast Maine Mysteries
THE CHOWDER HOUSE MURDER

Stand-Alones
MY FATHER ALWAYS FINDS CORPSES

Published by Kensington Publishing Corp.

THE CHOWDER HOUSE MURDER

Lee Hollis

KENSINGTON PUBLISHING CORP.
kensingtonbooks.com

This book is a work of fiction. Names, characters, businesses, organizations, places, events, and incidents either are the product of the author's imagination or are used fictitiously. Any resemblance to actual persons, living or dead, events, or locales is entirely coincidental.

To the extent that the image or images on the cover of this book depict a person or persons, such person or persons are merely models, and are not intended to portray any character or characters featured in the book.

KENSINGTON BOOKS are published by

Kensington Publishing Corp.
900 Third Avenue
New York, NY 10018

All Kensington titles, imprints, and distributed lines are available at special quantity discounts for bulk purchases for sales promotion, premiums, fund-raising, educational, or institutional use. Special book excerpts or customized printings can also be created to fit specific needs. For details, write or phone the office of the Kensington Special Sales Manager: Attn. Special Sales Department, Kensington Publishing Corp., 900 Third Ave., New York, NY 10022. Phone: 1-800-221-2647.

Library of Congress Control Number: 2026931867

ISBN: 978-1-4967-5505-6
First Kensington Hardcover Edition: June 2026

ISBN-13: 978-1-4967-5507-0 (ebook)

10 9 8 7 6 5 4 3 2 1

Printed in the United States of America

The authorized representative in the EU for product safety and compliance
is eucomply OU, Parnu mnt 139b-14, Apt 123
Tallinn, Berlin 11317, hello@eucompliancepartner.com

THE CHOWDER HOUSE MURDER

Chapter One

Audrey Holbrook balanced a tray laden with steaming bowls. The Chowder House in Halibut Cove, Maine, was bustling tonight. Audrey had been on her feet for hours, and every muscle in her body ached. She loved the familiar hum of the diner, the clatter of dishes, and the low murmur of conversations, but tonight felt endless.

Her phone buzzed on the counter near the register. A glance at the screen revealed a familiar name: Nana. With a resigned sigh, Audrey snagged the phone and pressed it to her ear, propping the tray on her hip.

"Hi, Nana," she said, trying to sound cheerful.

"Audrey, darling, I hope you haven't forgotten about Sunday dinner tonight," Maggie Holbrook's voice came through, as sharp and determined as ever. "I've been baking your favorite dessert all afternoon. Bread pudding with vanilla sauce."

Audrey closed her eyes briefly. "I didn't forget, but I'm working a double today, Nana. Ethel's out sick, and someone has to close up. I might be too wiped out to make it."

"Nonsense," Maggie cut her off. "You're young. You'll find the energy. You don't want to disappoint your old grandmother, do you?"

Audrey could practically see Maggie's raised eyebrow through the phone.

"Of course not," Audrey said with a smile, conceding defeat. "I'll be there."

"Good girl. Dinner's at six. Don't be late." Maggie hung up without waiting for a response, leaving Audrey shaking her head with a fond smile.

As she resumed her rounds, her thoughts drifted to Maggie and the life she and Wes, Audrey's late grandfather, had built. Halibut Cove was a small picturesque fishing village, nestled along the rugged coast of Downeast Maine. Colorful boats bobbed in the harbor, and wooden boardwalks crisscrossed the shore. The Holbrook home sat perched on a cliffside, overlooking the Atlantic. Its sprawling land, dotted with wildflowers and framed by golden autumn leaves, was as much a part of the Holbrook legacy as the seafood and real estate empire Maggie and Wes had built together. Audrey's childhood was filled with days spent playing in those fields and evenings watching the sun dip into the ocean with her grandparents.

Her phone buzzed again, this time with a text from her best friend and coworker Isabella. Audrey glanced at the message.

SOS. Jimmy incoming.

Audrey smirked and looked up just in time to see Jimmy Beckett, the busboy in his late teens, shuffling toward her, red-faced and avoiding eye contact.

"Hey, Jimmy," she greeted, setting down her tray. "Everything okay?"

"Uh, yeah, sure," Jimmy stammered, his voice cracking slightly. "I was just wondering if maybe you—"

Her phone buzzed again. Her eyes flicked to the screen. Audrey held up her phone. "Sorry, Jimmy, I have to take this." She dashed into the kitchen, where Isabella was grinning mischievously.

"You looked like you needed rescuing," Isabella said, leaning against the counter with a smirk.

"You're a lifesaver," Audrey replied, setting her phone down. "Poor kid's got it bad."

"Too bad he's not your type," Isabella teased. "But let me guess—you're still hung up on older guys. Like Mason Dooley."

Audrey blushed furiously. "Come on, he works with my mom. I'd never go there."

Isabella laughed, tossing her curls. "I'm sure that's the only thing stopping you."

Before Audrey could retort, the bell above the door jingled again, and Isabella groaned. "Ugh, closing time. Guess who's here." She peeked out into the dining room and sighed. "Yup. Chips Hogan. Right on schedule."

Audrey chuckled. Chips was a regular, always arriving minutes before closing to order his nightly bowl of clam chowder. He was grouchy and obstinate, claiming he was too busy to come earlier, though everyone knew he just liked the quiet of the empty diner and the undivided attention of the staff.

Audrey grabbed a fresh bowl and filled it with steaming soup.

She was about to carry it out to him when she stopped. "Wait, he likes extra oyster crackers. Where are they?"

"We're out of the homemade ones, but maybe there's a box of store-bought in the pantry."

Audrey set the soup down on the counter, and she and Isabella headed into the pantry in search of crackers. There was one half-empty box stuffed in the corner of the top shelf.

Audrey turned to Isabella. "Do you think he'll notice the difference?"

"Of course he will. Gird your loins. He's not going to be happy tonight."

"When is he ever?" Audrey snorted.

They emerged from the pantry, and Audrey sprinkled a few on top of the chowder, pouring some more into a small bowl to serve on the side since she anticipated him wanting more.

She carried both bowls out to Chips's usual table with a smile. "Here you go, Chips. Just in time."

Isabella trailed behind her, unable to resist chiming in. "You know, you could make it easier on yourself and come in an hour earlier. Just a thought."

Chips scowled but didn't argue. "I'm a busy man," he grumbled, though they both knew better.

Audrey smiled politely and turned to clean up as Isabella locked the front door behind Jimmy, who had just clocked out.

"These oyster crackers taste stale. How long ago did Ethel make these?"

"She had a little help tonight. From Nabisco," Isabella cracked.

Chips mumbled something unintelligible and then shrugged and slurped his soup.

As Audrey wiped down the counter, her gaze lingered on Chips for a moment. Something about him seemed different tonight, but she chalked it up to his usual cantankerous mood.

It wasn't until much later, as the lights of the diner dimmed and the quiet of the night settled over Halibut Cove, that she would recall this meal as his last. For now, she simply finished her shift, blissfully unaware of the storm that was about to brew.

Chapter Two

Maggie Holbrook stood in the expansive kitchen of her hilltop home, surveying the chaos of her family's Sunday dinner preparations. Through the wide windows, the view of the harbor below was breathtaking: fishing boats bobbing in the water and the vibrant hues of fall leaves painting the town in fiery reds and golds. This was the heart of the Holbrook family legacy, the land her late husband, Wes, had cherished and the home they had built together from scratch.

At her feet, Flounder, her scruffy, aging Golden Retriever, sat attentively, his tail wagging expectantly as he waited for any stray morsels to fall from the counter. Maggie bent down to scratch behind his ears. "Patience, boy," she murmured with a smile.

"Maggie, where do you keep the extra napkins?" called out Katie, her oldest son Oliver's bubbly and petite wife, her cheerful voice cutting through the noise.

"Bottom drawer near the pantry, dear," Maggie replied, glancing over her shoulder. She wiped her hands on her apron and turned back to the stove, where a bubbling pot of her signature seafood stew competed for space with roasted vegetables and a freshly baked apple pie cooling on the counter. The house smelled heavenly, a mix of savory and sweet that always seemed to calm her nerves.

Oliver, dark-haired with an air of authority, was leaning against the kitchen island, recounting details of a recent case to anyone who would listen. As a defense attorney, he was always full of stories, though tonight's seemed particularly thorny.

"The evidence isn't great," Oliver admitted, adjusting his glasses. "Clyde Peterson may be a lousy neighbor, but aggravated assault is a serious charge. And those vandalism accusations? Circumstantial at best. The prosecution's case is hanging by a thread."

"Come on," Maggie's youngest son, Sandy, said from across the room, his voice quiet but firm. Sensitive and exceedingly handsome, Sandy rarely jumped into debates, but when he did, his words carried weight. "The guy's a known troublemaker. Half the town thinks he's guilty. Why waste your energy?"

"Because it's my job," Oliver replied, his tone edged with exasperation. "Everyone deserves a fair trial, Sandy. Even Clyde Peterson."

Katie, always eager to steer the conversation to lighter topics, interjected with a teasing grin. "Speaking of notable men in town, has anyone met Dr. Bradley Comstock yet? He's the new dentist. Handsome, tall, and with the softest hands."

Maggie raised an eyebrow. "What about Dr. Lawry?"

Katie shrugged. "Lawry's nice, but how old is he now? Last time I went for a cleaning, his hands were so shaky, he stabbed my lip with that scaler thing he uses. He drew blood!"

"He is getting on in years, but he's been my dentist since I was a teenager," Maggie said wistfully.

"Maybe it's time he retired," Katie said. "You know, to make room for a new generation . . . someone whose gorgeous blue eyes instantly put you in a trance." She chuckled. "Honestly, Oliver, I might need another appointment soon. I may have a loose filling. Or something."

Oliver rolled his eyes but didn't take the bait. "I'm sure you'll think of something. Glad to know dental hygiene is alive and well in Halibut Cove."

Katie's laughter was infectious, and for a moment, the room was filled with warmth and easy conversation. Maggie smiled to herself. These gatherings were her favorite, even when they came with their share of complications.

Jill, Maggie's only daughter and the town's police chief, was unusually quiet tonight. She sat at the far end of the table, her sharp gaze occasionally darting toward the window as if expecting something to go wrong. Maggie's heart ached for her. Since Jill's divorce, the tension between her and her only child, Audrey, had only grown. Maggie suspected Jill worried that Audrey blamed her for the breakup. Maggie, however, understood both sides. She knew how hard it was for Jill to watch her ex-husband's new life in Portland, complete with a young wife and baby boy. And Maggie's close relationship with her granddaughter certainly didn't help matters. Audrey had recently decided to live with her grandmother instead of at her mother's house in town. Maggie suspected Jill might feel like the odd man out.

Audrey arrived late, her cheeks flushed from the cool evening air. "Sorry, Nana," she said, planting a kiss on her cheek. "The diner was a madhouse. And of course Chips Hogan showed up just as we were trying to close."

"You're here now, sweetheart. That's what matters," Maggie said, squeezing her hand.

Jill's eyes flicked to Audrey, her expression guarded. Maggie decided to step in before things turned tense. "Audrey, help your mom set the table, will you? The sooner we eat, the happier everyone will be."

Audrey nodded, though the interaction was brief.

Maggie sighed inwardly. She wished Jill and Audrey could find the same ease with each other that she shared with her granddaughter.

The sound of the front door opening cut through the bustle. Cord, Maggie's middle son, burst in, his boisterous energy filling the room.

"Sorry I'm late," he announced. "You all know Phoebe . . ."

He gestured to the young woman beside him, her bright red hair catching the light, an eager smile fixed in place. Phoebe Barker. Maggie's eyes immediately landed on the glint of a diamond ring on her finger.

Cord cleared his throat dramatically. "She said yes. We're engaged."

A stunned silence rippled through the room.

Phoebe lifted her hand with theatrical flair, flashing the ring. "Surprise!"

Oliver looked like he was gearing up for an objection, but Maggie raised a hand to stop him before he could get a word out.

"Welcome, Phoebe," she said warmly, though her spine straightened just a little. "We're glad you could join us. Congratulations."

"Thank you, Mrs. Holbrook," Phoebe said, sidling closer to Cord, who proudly slipped an arm around her waist.

Maggie crossed to them, offering a kiss on Phoebe's cheek before adding, "How are your parents? Bert and Rhonda still down at the marina?"

Phoebe nodded, clearly pleased. "They are. Busy as ever."

Despite the cordial words, Maggie could feel the temperature shift behind her. The skepticism from her other children wasn't subtle. Everyone had heard of Phoebe—her name floated around town often enough, not always with flattering context—but few had actually spent time with her. Maggie suspected this was the first time most of them were seeing her in the flesh.

She turned and clapped her hands. "Well, come in, both of you. Dinner's almost ready."

Katie, ever the diplomat, broke the ice. "Phoebe, that's a lovely sweater. Is it cashmere?"

"Yes," Phoebe beamed. "Cord bought it for me."

Sandy ambled over to give his brother Cord a hug. "Never thought I'd see the day you'd convince some poor unsuspecting girl to marry you."

Cord erupted in a loud laugh and slapped his brother on the back as they embraced. Sandy then turned to Phoebe. "I hope you know what you're getting into marrying into this family."

"I certainly do," Phoebe chirped, grabbing Sandy by the shirtsleeves and pulling him into her, his chest crushing against her ample bosom. Sandy's eyes widened in surprise as Phoebe tried to kiss him on the lips. He quickly turned his head, avoiding a direct hit. Her lips pressed against his left cheek instead, leaving a slight lipstick stain.

Maggie noted the inappropriate gesture but kept mum, especially since Cord did not seem to notice. Still, she worried about the pace of this surprise engagement. They had only been dating a few months on the down-low, but Cord could be impulsive and pigheaded. It would be the wrong move to register any disapproval at this point.

As the conversation moved forward, Maggie noticed

Jill's phone buzzing on the table. Jill glanced at the screen, her expression tightening. "Excuse me," she said, rising from her chair. "Work."

Maggie watched as Jill stepped into the hallway, her voice low but urgent. When she returned a few moments later, her expression was grim.

"I have to go," Jill announced. "There's been an incident."

Audrey's eyes widened. "What happened?"

"Chips Hogan," Jill said, grabbing her coat. "He's been found dead outside the pub."

"*What*?" Audrey gasped.

A shocked silence fell over the room. Maggie felt a chill run down her spine. Chips had been at the heart of Halibut Cove for years, a gruff but lovable fixture of the town. She crossed herself instinctively, murmuring a quiet prayer for his soul.

Jill's voice broke through the stillness. "I'll keep you updated," she said, already heading for the door.

As the front door closed behind her, Maggie's gaze drifted to the window, where the lights of the harbor twinkled in the distance. An uneasy feeling settled in her chest. Tonight's dinner had begun with warmth and laughter, but it had ended with a shadow cast over them all.

And Maggie couldn't shake the sense that this was just the beginning.

Chapter Three

Jill Holbrook arrived at the scene to find Mason Dooley leaning against the hood of his squad car, phone pressed to his ear. From the exaggerated expressions and occasional muttered apologies, it was clear he was immersed in a personal conversation—one entirely unsuited for the proximity of a crime scene. Jill's sharp eyes darted to the victim sprawled on the cobblestone street: Chips Hogan lay motionless. The only sound apart from Mason's murmurs was the distant cry of seagulls and the low murmur of onlookers.

As Jill approached, fragments of Mason's conversation floated over. "Mom, I've told you a hundred times, Amy didn't like me being a cop. That's all I've ever wanted to do. No, I'm not going to work for her dad's construction company . . . Yes, I know you liked her . . . No, I'm not seeing anyone else, jeez . . ."

Jill crossed her arms and cleared her throat. Mason's head snapped up, his expression shifting from sheepishness to panic. He shoved his phone into his pocket, turning toward her so abruptly that his foot caught on Chips's lifeless hand. Mason's eyes widened as he stumbled and landed unceremoniously on his rear, inches from the body.

"For the love of . . . Mason!" Jill groaned, extending a hand to help him up. "This is a crime scene, not a therapy session with your mom."

Blushing furiously, Mason scrambled to his feet, brushing off dirt. "Sorry, Chief. Won't happen again."

"It better not. Now, what do we know?"

Mason straightened, adopting a more professional demeanor. "Witness says Chips was staggering and fell face-first onto the cobblestones. No sign of an attacker, no evidence of foul play at first glance." He gestured to a small gash on Chips's forehead. "The cut looks like it's from the fall."

Jill crouched beside the body, her gaze sharp and clinical. Her attention lingered on Chips's lips, where a faint, fizzy residue clung to the corners of his mouth. She made a mental note.

"What's that?" Mason asked, squinting.

"Could be nothing," Jill said carefully. "Or it could mean poison." She kept her voice low, glancing toward the growing crowd. "Let's not jump to conclusions yet."

Before Mason could respond, Lou Grady, the *Halibut Cove Chronicle*'s resident bulldog of a reporter, barged through the crowd. His unlit cigar bobbed in the corner of his mouth as he bellowed, "Hey, Holbrook! Got a comment for the *Chronicle*? Did Chips's ticker finally give out?"

Jill rose, fixing Lou with a steely glare. "No comment, Lou. Not until the autopsy's in."

Lou snorted. "Chips had a heart condition. Bet you dollars to donuts that's what finally got him."

"We'll see," Jill said curtly, motioning for Mason to follow her. "Let's wrap this up here."

The following morning, Jill sat at her desk at the Halibut Cove Police Station, scanning the autopsy report. Her stomach churned as she reached the conclusion: Chips Hogan hadn't died of a heart attack. The culprit was poison—deadly nightshade, ingested not long before his death.

Mason entered, a steaming cup of coffee in hand. "Anything new?"

Jill handed him the report. "It was poison. Deadly nightshade."

Mason's eyes widened. "Poison? Who would . . . ?"

"That's what we need to figure out. First stop: The Chowder House. Chips had their clam chowder pretty much every night of the week, including holidays. Let's see what they can tell us."

The Chowder House was bustling when Jill and Mason arrived. Through the window, Jill saw Ethel Primrose perched on a stool at the counter, chatting animatedly with Audrey and Isabella. As they stepped inside, Jill caught Ethel's voice mid-monologue.

"I'm feeling much better, but now my arthritis is acting up something fierce. Can't even shuffle the cards properly at game night with the girls anymore." She noticed Jill and Mason entering the diner. "Good morning, Chief. Just in time for the breakfast rush. Mason, I was just telling the girls about the terrible pain I have to endure due to my arthritis."

Mason gave her a confused look. "I'm sorry to hear that, Mrs. Primrose."

"Your mother knows all about it. She will tell you—we play cards every Wednesday. She's got the patience of a saint, putting up with my constant complaints."

Mason gave her a polite smile. "She always speaks very highly of you, Mrs. Primrose."

Ethel beamed. "Well, she's a gem, that woman. And

you—looking more handsome every time I see you. Isn't he, girls?"

Audrey rolled her eyes but stayed silent, while Isabella smirked.

"I have a table in the back. I'll get you some menus," Ethel said.

Jill cleared her throat, stepping forward. "We're not here to eat, Ethel. I was hoping we could have a chat."

The warmth drained from Ethel's face. "This about Chips? Poor man. Meaner than a junkyard dog but a loyal customer. What happened?"

"He was poisoned," Jill said, watching Audrey's reaction. Her daughter's eyes widened, and she paled visibly. "We need to know about the chowder he had for dinner here. According to the autopsy report, it was the last thing he ate. Who served him?"

Audrey's voice trembled. "I did. But . . . I didn't do anything to it, I swear!"

Jill's eyes narrowed. "Did anyone else have access to the chowder before you served him, Audrey?"

Audrey shook her head. "No. Isabella and I were the only ones working, and most of the customers had already cleared out by the time Chips arrived."

"He's always doing that, showing up at the last minute just before we're supposed to close!" Isabella sniffed.

"Can you walk me through it, please?" Jill asked.

Audrey nodded. "Chips came in. I didn't even bother giving him a menu because he always orders the same thing. I went into the kitchen and ladled some from the pot into a bowl, and I served him."

Audrey headed into the kitchen followed by Jill, Mason, Isabella, and Ethel.

"So the poison had to have been put in the pot," Jill surmised.

"Yes!" Isabella gasped, but then she scrunched up her face. "Wait, no, it couldn't have been in the pot because I had a bowl before I left. My fridge was empty at home, and Ethel doesn't mind us eating what's left here after closing and I was starving. But I feel fine!"

"So if the autopsy report is correct, and he ingested the poison shortly before he died, and this was the only thing he ate, someone had to have slipped it in the bowl."

"Well, that's impossible, unless it was one of us who did it," Isabella declared before realizing what she was suggesting. "Which is ridiculous! I mean Chips was an annoying, grumpy old man who didn't care one whit about keeping us here late when we wanted to clock out, but we didn't want to kill him, right, Audrey?"

Audrey didn't answer. Jill could see her mind racing. "Hold on a sec. We did leave the bowl unattended for a minute or two, remember? We were out of Ethel's homemade oyster crackers, and Isabella and I both went into the pantry to find some."

"Oh, dear, I knew I should've made an extra batch the night before, but my migraine was raging and I just didn't have the energy. Chips loves my oyster crackers. I'm sure he noticed!" Ethel wailed.

"He did," Isabella confirmed. "He wasn't too happy the ones we gave him were store bought."

"So someone could have slipped into the kitchen and put the nightshade in the bowl during the time you were out of the room," Jill concluded.

"Yes, I left it on the counter for a minute while Isabella and I grabbed crackers from the pantry."

Isabella nodded. "It was less than a minute. Maybe a few seconds."

Jill glanced around, noticing a back door that led out to

a back alley. "Do you keep this door locked when the restaurant is open?"

"Yes, of course," Ethel confirmed. "The garbage bins are out there, and we have a lot of waste we need to clear out to keep the kitchen spic and span. I don't need any health inspectors downgrading me from my A rating!"

Mason wandered over and opened the door, poking his head out into the alley. "Someone could have been lurking outside, watching, waiting for the right opportunity."

Jill's mind raced. "Isabella, did you see anyone when you left before Audrey?"

"No, nobody, I . . ." She stopped.

A lightbulb seemed to go off in her head.

Jill noticed immediately. "What? Did you remember something?"

Isabella hesitated, then nodded slowly. "Waldo Duggan. He was loitering outside when I left. I said hello, but he didn't respond. He just turned his back on me. He's always had it out for us."

"I know Waldo well," Jill remarked ruefully, shaking her head.

Ethel's eyes narrowed. "That man's been claiming for years that we stole his family's chowder recipe. But everyone knows your mother Maggie gave me that recipe. It's been in the Holbrook family for generations. He's just bitter."

Jill exchanged a glance with Mason. "We'll look into it," she said. Turning to Audrey, she softened her tone. "Audrey, this isn't your fault."

But Audrey was already spiraling, her eyes brimming with tears. "I served him. I didn't notice anything. What if . . . what if I . . . ?"

Jill reached out, awkwardly placing a hand on her daughter's shoulder. "Audrey, listen to me. We'll find out who did this. You couldn't have known. None of this is on you."

Audrey nodded, but her expression remained distant. Jill's heart ached, knowing that her words could only do so much. As the tension in the diner hung heavy, Jill resolved to uncover the truth—for Chips, for Halibut Cove, and for her daughter.

Chapter Four

The cobblestone streets of Holbrook's Wharf gleamed in the morning light, still slick from the previous night's rain. Seagulls circled overhead, their cries mingling with the sound of waves lapping against the docks. Fishermen bustled about, loading crates of the morning's catch onto trucks, while the faint scent of saltwater filled the crisp air. Maggie tightened her wool coat against the brisk sea breeze as she stood at the corner where Chips Hogan had been found, slumped and lifeless. Her sharp eyes darted over the scene as though daring it to reveal its secrets.

"Ma! What are you doing here?" Cord's deep voice broke through the crisp air. Maggie turned to see her two younger sons, born within a year of each other, Cord and Sandy, striding toward her, their work boots clapping against the stones. Both wore heavy flannel jackets over their sweaters, ready for a morning on their lobster boat.

"Good morning, boys!" Maggie greeted cheerfully, though her expression held the unmistakable determination they'd come to recognize over the years.

Cord exchanged a wary glance with Sandy before fixing

his gaze on his mother. "You're not seriously poking around the crime scene, are you?"

"And why shouldn't I?" Maggie countered, hands on her hips. "You two aren't the only ones in this family with a nose for seafood and trouble. Chips Hogan didn't just keel over from bad luck. Someone poisoned him, and I intend to find out why."

"Ma, this is Jill's investigation," Sandy pointed out, rubbing the back of his neck. "You know how she gets when people—more specifically, *you*—tend to butt in."

"Jill may wear the badge, but I've got the experience," Maggie retorted, her eyes twinkling with mischief. "And don't you two worry about me. I've raised three sons, a headstrong daughter, managed a seafood empire, and outlasted a hurricane or two. A little murder mystery isn't going to do me in."

Cord sighed and glanced toward the dock, where their boat bobbed impatiently in the water. "Just don't get yourself in over your head, Ma."

"You're sweet to worry, but I've got this handled. Now go check your traps before I start wondering if you're slacking." Maggie waved them off with a brisk motion and turned her attention back to the cobblestones, inspecting the area for any clues. The boys hesitated a moment before heading off, shaking their heads.

By noon, Maggie had made her way to her eldest son Oliver's office. The building was a no-nonsense affair, much like Oliver himself. Inside, the steady hum of activity filled the air, punctuated by the ringing of phones and the shuffle of papers.

Oliver, his shirtsleeves rolled up, glanced at his phone, reading a text from Sandy. His brow furrowed slightly as he set the phone down and looked up just as Maggie entered. "Mom, what are you up to now?" he asked with a sigh.

"Can't a mother visit her busy son without an ulterior motive?" Maggie teased, setting down a paper bag filled with sandwiches and fresh-baked cookies.

"Not when that mother is Maggie Holbrook," Oliver replied with a smirk before opening the bag on his desk. "What did you bring me?"

Maggie snatched the bag away from him. "Those are for your staff. You're taking me to lunch."

"I just got a text from Sandy. He says you're channeling Angela Lansbury, playing amateur detective again?"

"Angela Lansbury was known for many more roles than just Jessica Fletcher. She won an Honorary Oscar, five Tonys . . ."

"You're avoiding the issue, Mother," Oliver pressed.

The door suddenly opened, and Oliver's secretary stepped in, a tentative smile on her face.

"Mr. Peterson is here," she began, but before she could finish, Clyde Peterson pushed past her, flashing a greasy smile.

"Great outfit today, Kimmy," Clyde said, his voice dripping with insincerity. "Really compliments . . ." His eyes fell to her bosom. "Your figure."

The secretary cringed slightly and stepped out, closing the door behind her.

"Afternoon, Mrs. Holbrook," Clyde said, nodding politely.

"Clyde," Maggie replied coolly.

"I'm sorry, did we have an appointment, Clyde?" Oliver asked, scratching his head.

"Nope, but since you're charging me by the hour, I

don't see why you'd mind me just dropping by." Clyde sneered.

"Fair enough," Oliver muttered.

"So tell me, Oliver, are we still cutting that deal, or are we going to trial?"

Oliver glanced at his mother and sighed. "I believe we should make a deal, Clyde. But we'll discuss the case after lunch. I'm taking my mother out."

Clyde shrugged, unbothered.

"Your poor mother must be worried sick about you," Maggie interjected. "You know, if you'd stop drinking, you might spare her some of that worry."

Clyde shifted uncomfortably. "She's always worried about me. My older brother. My sister. That's just how she is. Always worried about her family. Speaking of family, though, I saw Cord down at the bar the other night, drinking up a storm, celebrating his engagement."

"Yes, that's right. Cord's getting married," Maggie said with a tight smile.

"Phoebe Barker, seriously?" Clyde scoffed.

Maggie adopted a stern tone. "Why do you say it like that?"

"Well, as a mother, I'd think you'd be worried too." He leaned back with a smirk. "You know, I went out with Phoebe once. Nice enough girl. Easy, if you know what I mean."

Maggie's eyes narrowed, her tone sharp. "That's enough gossip, Clyde. Phoebe is going to be part of this family, and I'll not have you sullying her name."

Clyde threw his hands up in mock surrender. "Easy on the eyes. That's all I meant to say."

Maggie knew he was lying, confronting him with a steady gaze.

"All right, Clyde, why don't you come back around two and we'll discuss next steps?" Oliver said, standing up.

"Sure, no problem. You have a nice day, Mrs. Holbrook," he said, backing out of the office. Maggie nodded but didn't say anything.

When Clyde left, Oliver closed the door and pinched the bridge of his nose. "I'll never understand Cord's taste in women."

"It's his life," Maggie said firmly. "He has to make his own decisions, even if they aren't ones you or I would necessarily make."

"Why does he always have to be so impulsive? Cord's track record isn't exactly inspiring," Oliver muttered.

"They all can't be your Katie," Maggie said with a smile, then she folded her arms. "Obviously, you're all talking behind my back. So Sandy is unhappy with my involvement in the Chips Hogan case too?"

Oliver sighed. "Mom, you've got to let this go. Think about what people are going to say if you're obsessively running around town trying to solve a murder!"

Maggie scoffed. "First of all, I take umbrage with the word *obsessively*. And secondly, people have been trashing the Holbrook name for generations, and I've never once cared. But now that the Holbrook family chowder recipe has been dragged into it, well, that's sacred."

A few minutes later, they found themselves at The Chowder House where the usual warmth was dampened by an undercurrent of tension. Ethel, the owner, greeted them with a weak smile.

"Business has been slow since the news broke," Ethel admitted as she poured them each a cup of coffee. "People are spooked."

Audrey appeared from the kitchen. Her cheeks were flushed, and her eyes betrayed her anxiety. "I've been scrubbing every inch of that kitchen," she said. "I can't bear the thought that our chowder—Great-Great-Grandma's recipe—was used to kill someone."

Maggie reached across the table and placed a reassuring hand on Audrey's. "We'll figure this out," she said firmly. "You and I, together."

Audrey blinked in surprise. "You mean it?"

"Absolutely. If there's one thing I can't abide, it's injustice. And this? This is personal."

"Mom, are you serious?" Oliver interjected. "Jill will already be mad enough that you're stepping on her toes. Now you're pulling Audrey into this too?"

Audrey hesitated, glancing between them, but a customer's arrival pulled her attention. She trotted off to attend to them, leaving Maggie and Oliver alone.

"Audrey is consumed with guilt," Maggie said softly. "This will help her. If she's actively working to clear her name, it'll give her something to focus on. Trust me on this, Oliver."

Oliver sighed, knowing better than to argue. Maggie's resolve was as unshakable as the tides.

Chapter Five

Jill Holbrook's office at the Holbrook Police Department was cluttered but functional. Stacks of files teetered on the corners of her desk, and a corkboard on the wall displayed a chaotic patchwork of case notes and photos.

Jill tried to focus on the paperwork for the Chips Hogan case.

A knock at the door interrupted her thoughts.

Mason stepped in, ushering in a young couple. "Chief, Gary and Andrea Kirklys are here. They'd like to speak with you." Their hyper terrier mix darted into the room, tail wagging furiously.

"Please, come in, take a seat," Jill corrected, eyeing the dog's rapid exploration of her office. "And who's this?"

"That's Millie," Andrea said with a nervous laugh, gripping the leash tightly. "She's . . . friendly."

Gary looked uncomfortable, shifting from foot to foot. "Look, we're not sure if this is even important," he muttered.

"Go on," Jill said, gesturing for them to sit. She glanced at Mason. "Wait at your desk."

Mason hesitated. "Hey, I was wondering, can I head to lunch early?"

"No," Jill replied. "Go back to your desk. I'll call you if I need you."

Mason sighed and backed out of the office, closing the door behind him.

Andrea cleared her throat. "Gary was reading about Chips Hogan's murder on the *Chronicle* website. It . . . sparked something. We were out walking Millie that night, and we saw something that might help."

Millie leaped up, pawing at Jill's desk. Jill opened a drawer and pulled out a small bag of dog treats. "Here, Millie. Let's calm you down." She tossed a treat to the dog, who eagerly pounced on it.

"We were near The Chowder House," Andrea began, "and Millie stopped to do her business by the alley behind the restaurant. That's when we saw a man loitering outside the back door."

Jill leaned forward. "Can you describe him?"

"Older," Andrea said. "Sixty-five or seventy, maybe. He was wearing a cap and bundled up. It was cold that night, so it was hard to tell much else. Normal height. We didn't recognize him. But we did see him slip in through the back door of the diner—like he didn't want anyone to notice."

Jill jotted down notes. "Did you see anyone else?"

Andrea hesitated. "There was another dog walker. She had a really big dog, and Millie was scared at first. But the other dog was friendly, and they got along after a minute."

"Do you remember what kind of dog it was?" Jill asked.

Andrea's face brightened. "Yes, it was a Newfoundland."

Jill's mind clicked into gear. "That must be Katty Caulfield. She works at the Seaview Diner and is always walking her Newfoundland around town. Thank you for coming in. This could be helpful."

She walked the couple and Millie out, giving the dog one last pat. Turning to Mason, who was at his desk, scrolling on his computer, she said, "We're heading to the Seaview Diner. Let's go."

"Great! I'm so hungry I feel light-headed. Can we stop at the vending machine on our way out so I can nibble on something on the ride over there?"

"No!" Jill barked, charging off with Mason chasing after her like a puppy dog.

The Seaview Diner was bustling with its usual lunch crowd. Jill and Mason slid into a booth near the window. Katty Caulfield, a cheerful woman in her mid-thirties, approached them with a notepad in hand.

"Hey there, Chief, Mason! What can I get for you?" she asked, her smile bright.

"We'll just have coffee," Jill said.

Mason's stomach grumbled audibly. "Just coffee?"

Jill ignored him. "How's Boris?"

Katty laughed. "Boris is his usual high-maintenance self."

"Is Boris your boyfriend?" Mason asked innocently.

Katty howled. "No, he's my Newfoundland. But he might as well be. He's just as demanding of my time as my last boyfriend but much more loyal. I don't have to worry about Boris sneaking off behind my back to see that pretty new yoga instructor who teaches at the YWCA on Mondays."

"I'd take a dog over a boyfriend any day," Jill said. "By the way, were you walking him near The Chowder House on Sunday night?"

Katty hesitated. "Uh, yes. We were out for our usual nighttime walk."

"Did you see anyone else in the alley besides the young couple, Gary and Andrea Kirklys?" Jill asked.

Katty's smile faded. "I—I did see someone. But I don't want to get anyone in trouble."

Jill pressed. "Katty, this is serious. We need to know who it was."

After a long pause, Katty sighed. "It was Waldo Duggan. He works here. He can be moody, sure, but he's not a bad guy. He'd never hurt anyone."

"Everyone in town knows Waldo has a problem with The Chowder House," Jill said somberly.

Katty hesitated again. "Well, he claims their clam chowder recipe was stolen from his family. But . . . I'm sorry, Jill. I know you're a Holbrook."

Jill waved it off. "Don't worry about it. What time is Waldo's shift today?"

"Today's his day off," Katty said.

Mason picked up a menu. "In that case, I'll have a double cheeseburger, fries, and . . . Jill, want to split some fried clams?"

Jill snatched the menu out of his hands and gave it back to Katty. "Cancel those coffees, Katty." Then she turned to Mason and frowned. "A murder investigation doesn't stop just because you're hungry. Let's go."

Waldo Duggan's house was modest but well-kept, with neatly trimmed hedges and a freshly painted porch. Jill knocked firmly on the door. Waldo answered, looking annoyed.

"If you're here about my neighbors blasting their music, I've already called twice," Waldo said.

"We'll look into it," Jill said. "But we're here about Chips Hogan."

Waldo stiffened. "I don't have time for this. I've got a shift at the diner. I need to go."

"That's odd," Jill replied. "Katty told us today was your day off."

Waldo glared. "Since when has Katty started memorizing my work schedule?"

"Mind if we come in?" Jill asked.

"Do you have a warrant?" Waldo snapped.

"Why? Do we need one?" Jill shot back.

After a tense moment, Waldo sighed and stepped aside. "Fine. Come in."

The living room was small but tidy, with an old plaid couch and a coffee table stacked with newspapers. Jill noticed Waldo's face was shiny with sweat. His hands trembled slightly as he gestured for them to sit.

"You all right?" Jill asked.

"Yes, I'm all right!" Waldo snapped. "Is that why you're here, is this some kind of wellness check?"

Jill leaned forward, locking eyes with Waldo. "As I mentioned, we're here to talk about Chips Hogan."

A bead of sweat trickled down his forehead, and he started wringing his hands, then in as casual a tone as he could muster, asked, "Uh, can I get you some coffee or something?"

"We're good, thanks," Jill said firmly.

"I'll take some," Mason chimed in, earning a glare from Jill. Mason took his cue and shook his head. "Thanks, anyway."

Jill didn't waste time. "Two witnesses saw you loitering in the alley behind The Chowder House Sunday night. What were you doing there?"

"That's a lie," Waldo said. "I was just walking by."

"They saw you go inside," Jill countered.

He opened his mouth but hesitated to speak.

Waldo paused. "Fine. I popped in to say hello to Ethel, but she wasn't there. I've got nothing against Ethel." He looked pointedly at Jill. "My beef is with your family. The Holbrooks stole that recipe from my family."

Mason's stomach growled loudly, breaking the tension.

Waldo barked, "Help yourself to the pantry, if you're that hungry."

Mason glanced at Jill for approval.

Jill sighed. "Fine. But make it quick."

Mason disappeared into the kitchen.

Jill's expression hardened. "Maybe Chips was collateral damage from you trying to exact your revenge on my family and The Chowder House for supposedly stealing your family's recipe?"

"Like I said, Ethel's a good egg. A real sweetheart. If I decided to go after your family, Chief, I wouldn't endanger Ethel's business, her livelihood, not in a million years!"

"So the door was unlocked?"

Waldo nodded.

"The staff says the back door is always locked."

"Then I guess the staff is wrong. Somebody left it unlocked."

Jill considered this curious detail.

Moments later, Mason returned from the pantry, pale and holding a plant. "Jill, look at this. It was in the pantry behind some crackers. It looked strange, like why would anyone keep a plant in a dark place with no light, so I took a photo and looked it up online. It's a belladonna plant."

Jill's eyes narrowed. "Deadly nightshade. The same poison found in Chips Hogan's system."

She stood, pulling out her handcuffs. "Waldo Duggan, you're under arrest for the murder of Chips Hogan."

Mason's eyes widened as Jill added, "Mason, be careful with that. Don't touch it. The whole plant is toxic. The root, the stem, the leaves . . . everything. It can kill you."

Mason yelped and dropped the plant on the floor, stepping back quickly.

Waldo stood frozen in shock as Jill cuffed him, her tone icy. "You're coming with us."

Chapter Six

Maggie stormed into the Halibut Cove Police Station, her coat still damp from the drizzle outside. The receptionist, a young officer named Terry, barely had time to lift his head before she was past him, heading for Chief Jill Holbrook's office.

"Mom," Jill said, glancing up from the paperwork on her desk, "what are you doing here?"

"What's this I hear about you arresting Waldo Duggan?" Maggie demanded, shutting the door behind her.

Jill sighed and leaned back in her chair. "Mom, I don't have time for this right now."

"You'll make time," Maggie said, planting her hands on her hips. "I've known Waldo for years. Ever since your father and I were young and just starting out and trying to scrape by. He may hold a grudge about that silly clam chowder recipe feud, but there's no way he'd do something so reckless and stupid as to tamper with Ethel's chowder. Maybe with a little hot sauce as a prank but not a deadly poison!"

"How did you hear about the belladonna plant?"

Maggie sighed. "This is Halibut Cove, dear. I suspect

the whole town knew about it before you even had a chance to read him his rights. Now, where is he?"

Jill's patience was visibly wearing thin. "Mom, I understand you want to help, but this is an official police investigation. I need you to respect that."

"I do respect your job," Maggie countered. "But I know this town better than anyone. I know its people, and I know Waldo didn't kill Chips Hogan."

Jill took a deep breath. "Okay. I'll take it under advisement."

Maggie softened her tone. "Can I see him?"

"No." Jill's reply was firm.

"What law prevents someone arrested from having visitors?" Maggie pressed.

Mason, Jill's deputy, popped his head into the office. "Actually, Chief, I don't think there is one."

Jill shot him a glare. "Fine. Mason, take her down. Ten minutes. Not a minute longer."

As Mason led Maggie to the small visiting room near the holding cells, she gave him a once-over. "You're looking thin, Mason. Are you eating enough?"

Mason chuckled. "I think your daughter's on a mission to starve me to death."

Maggie smirked. "I'll bring you some lobster rolls next time. My clam chowder might be out of favor right now, given the circumstances."

Mason laughed ruefully as he led her to the cramped visiting room before leaving her. Maggie sat down at the small table, her hands folded in front of her. A few minutes later, Mason escorted Waldo Duggan in. He looked equal parts surprised and annoyed. Mason stepped out of the room and shut the door behind him.

"Well, now, Maggie Holbrook," he sneered. "This is a surprise. Here to gloat?"

"Waldo, sit down," Maggie said firmly. "We need to talk."

Waldo sat but kept his arms crossed defensively. Maggie leaned forward. "I know there's been bad blood between our families over the years, Waldo, but I don't believe you killed Chips Hogan."

"Hmph." Waldo snorted. "Tell that to your daughter. She certainly thinks I did."

"Jill's just doing her job," Maggie said. "But I want to help you, Waldo. Whether you like it or not."

Waldo's eyes narrowed. "Help me? Why?"

"Because Cecile was my friend. She never cared about the feud, and I owe it to her memory to make sure you get a fair shake."

At the mention of his late wife, Waldo's posture softened. He sighed and rubbed his face. "I didn't kill Chips," he muttered. "Yeah, I was at The Chowder House that night, but only because I was hoping to run into Ethel. I . . ." He hesitated, then admitted, "I've got a little crush on her."

Maggie's eyebrows shot up. "Oh?"

"Don't make a thing of it, Maggie," Waldo snapped. "She wasn't there, so I left. That's it. I swear I didn't touch the chowder."

"And the belladonna plant Mason found in your pantry?" Maggie asked.

Waldo looked genuinely baffled. "I don't know how it got there. Someone's framing me."

Maggie looked down to take all of this in, then glanced up at Waldo. "Do you have bail money for after the arraignment?"

Waldo shook his head. "Cecile handled the money

when she was alive. After she passed, I let things slide, so I'm pretty much going from paycheck to paycheck."

"I'll cover your bail," Maggie said.

"You don't have to do that, Maggie," Waldo whispered.

"I'm not going to let you rot in jail while you await trial, especially since I believe you're innocent. Now, what about a lawyer?"

Waldo shrugged. "I guess they'll just assign me a public defender."

Maggie raised an eyebrow. "Whip Butler? He's a baby. He probably writes his legal briefs in crayon. No, you need someone more experienced, more dynamic in a courtroom."

Waldo's brow furrowed. "Like who?"

Maggie smiled. "I have just the right man for the job."

An hour later, Maggie was sitting in her son Oliver's office. The walls were lined with shelves of law books, and his desk was covered in neatly stacked files. Oliver listened as Maggie explained the situation, his expression neutral but his eyes betraying a hint of weariness.

"Mom, I can't take this case," Oliver said finally. "The Clyde Peterson trial is coming up. It's going to eat up all my time."

Maggie leaned forward, her tone cajoling. "Oliver, you're a brilliant lawyer. You can handle two cases at once. And let's be honest, the Peterson trial is a slam dunk for the prosecutor. Everyone knows he's guilty."

Oliver frowned. "He still has the right to a defense. It's my job to give him that."

"I know, I know," Maggie said, waving her hand. "But Waldo needs you more. Whip Butler is barely out of law school. He's going to get eaten alive in court."

"Whip is finding his footing," Oliver said. "He's not as bad as you think."

Maggie crossed her arms. "Maybe not, but Waldo can't afford a rookie mistake. You've been in high-pressure cases before. You're the best chance he has."

"And you expect me to do this pro bono?"

"Either that, or I pay for it."

"In what world would I ever agree to allow my own mother to bankroll a client's case?"

"Then pro bono it is," Maggie said with a sly smile.

Oliver sighed heavily, leaning back in his chair. "You're not going to let this go, are you?"

Maggie grinned. "You know me better than that."

He rubbed his temples. "Fine. I'll do it. But I'm only agreeing because I trust your instincts."

"That's all I ask," Maggie said, patting his hand. "Now, let's talk about strategy."

Back at the Holbrook house, the kitchen was alive with the sound of chopping and the smell of frying onions. Maggie stood at the counter, expertly preparing a batch of haddock chowder. Cord sat at the table, flipping through a newspaper, while Sandy leaned against the fridge, arms crossed.

"I still think Jill has the right guy," Cord said. "Waldo's been a pain for years. He's always had a nasty temper."

"That doesn't make him a killer," Maggie said, stirring the pot. "And tampering with chowder? That's not just murder, it's sacrilege."

Sandy snorted. "Maybe, but they found the belladonna in his pantry. That's hard to ignore."

"I admit, it's damning evidence. But someone obviously planted it," Maggie countered.

At that moment, the door swung open, and Audrey breezed in with Flounder, trotting at her side. Flounder's thick coat gleamed, and his tail wagged happily as he sniffed the air.

"There's my good boy," Maggie cooed, reaching down to scratch his ears. "Audrey, I'm so glad you're home. I need your help."

Audrey raised an eyebrow. "What kind of help?"

"Computer help," Maggie said, nodding toward the table. "You know I'm hopeless in that department. Grab your laptop. We need to dig up information on Chips Hogan."

Audrey grinned. "Sounds like fun. Give me a minute."

Maggie turned to her two sons. "I suppose you're both staying for dinner, so why don't you go wash up?"

"Ma, we're grown men in our twenties. You don't have to remind us to wash ourselves," Cord groaned.

"Yes, I do. You both smell like you wrestled a sea lion and lost. Go on, you're stinking up my kitchen."

Cord and Sandy shuffled out as Maggie joined Audrey at the table. Audrey was pulling her laptop from its bag. Within moments, her fingers were flying over the keyboard. Flounder lay at her feet, his head resting on her sneakers.

"What do we have here?" Audrey muttered, scrolling through search results. "Hmm, a DUI from the '80s, some mentions of his business dealings . . . Oh, here's something. Back in the '70s, a guy named Griffin Mead tried to sue him for fraud."

Maggie's ears perked up. "Griffin Mead? I remember that! He and Chips were supposed to open a hardware store together here in town, but it all fell apart. Griffin lost everything."

Sandy frowned. "Why would Griffin wait this long to act?"

"His wife, Felicia, kept him grounded," Maggie said. "But she passed away recently. Maybe old wounds have reopened."

Audrey looked up. "So, what's the plan?"

Maggie smiled. "We're going to pay Griffin a visit."

Chapter Seven

The steady beep of the grocery store's registers provided the backdrop as Maggie stepped into the small but bustling market. The fluorescent lights overhead highlighted the faded linoleum floor and shelves stocked with everything from canned soups to fishing lures. Audrey trailed behind her, curiosity lighting her expression.

"There he is," Maggie murmured, spotting Griffin Mead at the far end of the store. The tall, wiry man, now in his late sixties, was diligently bagging groceries with the kind of care one might expect from someone crafting a masterpiece. His thin shoulders were slightly hunched, and he wore the bright red vest that marked him as an employee. Maggie's heart twinged at the sight of her old friend in such a humble position.

"Griffin Mead," Maggie called as she approached.

He looked up, startled, his face breaking into a warm, if tired, smile.

"Maggie Holbrook," he said, straightening. "I'll be right with you."

Before Griffin could say another word, a sharp voice cut through the air. "Mead! What do you think you're doing?"

Maggie turned to see a young man in a crisp polo shirt striding toward them. The store manager, judging by his badge. He couldn't have been older than twenty-five, and he carried himself with the overconfidence of someone untested by life's harsher realities.

"Taking a break *already*?" the manager said, his tone condescending. "You know we're short-handed today."

Griffin's jaw tightened, but he nodded. "Just for a minute. I've got someone to see."

The manager sighed theatrically, loud enough for the cashiers and nearby customers to hear. "Fine. Make it quick. But let me remind you, Griffie, you're already skating on thin ice."

"I'm working a double shift with no break so far. Give me fifteen minutes. Your buddy Ralph took a forty-five minute break this morning, and you didn't say squat."

"It's not your job to tell me how to handle my employees," the manager snapped. "But go ahead, take a break, but I want you back here at three on the dot, got it?"

Maggie could see Griffin seething on the inside before he nodded, turned to her, and said calmly, "Be with you in a sec. I'm just going to hang up my vest." He scuttled toward the back of the store where the break room was located.

Maggie stepped forward, her eyes narrowing. "Excuse me, young man. Are you the manager here?"

The boy blinked, caught off guard. "Uh, yes. Why?"

"Because I've known Griffin Mead longer than you've been alive, and let me tell you something. If you can't treat him with the respect he deserves, you have no business being in a position of authority."

The young man's face flushed. "I didn't mean—"

"I'll be speaking to your father about this," Maggie

added, her voice low and steady. "You're Carey Birch's boy, aren't you?"

He nodded warily.

"Jack, the oldest?"

"No, I'm Peter, the youngest."

"The youngest are always tricky. Tend to get spoiled. Well, Peter, your father's a good friend of mine, and I'm sure he'd be interested to know how you treat your employees."

The manager swallowed hard. "Of course, Mrs. Holbrook. I didn't realize . . . I mean, I'll make sure Griffin gets the time with you he needs."

"Good," Maggie said briskly.

Griffin returned from the break room, sans vest. He glanced between Maggie and the now visibly chastened manager. "What did you say to him?"

Maggie smiled innocently. "Just gave him a little reminder to respect his elders."

Griffin chuckled. "Nobody crosses Maggie Holbrook."

"Nana, you're so badass," Audrey marveled.

The three of them strolled down Halibut Cove's main street, a brisk wind nipping at their faces. Audrey wrapped her scarf tighter around her neck, while Maggie and Griffin walked side by side, their steps in sync like old times.

Griffin was still hung up on his run-in with his boss. "Never thought I'd wind up with a boss young enough to be my grandson. The funny thing is, I don't really need the job. I got my social security, my savings. I'm not exactly blowing it on European cruises. I live a simple, quiet life. But it keeps me busy, gets me out of the house."

"How have you been holding up?" Maggie asked gently.

Griffin's face softened. "It's been hard, Maggie. Losing

Felicia . . . I always thought I'd go first. She was my rock. The house feels so empty without her."

Maggie placed a comforting hand on his arm. "I'm so sorry. She was one of the best."

Griffin nodded, his voice thick. "Our kids are great, but they're so far away. Seattle, Anchorage, even Brussels. I'm proud of them, but it gets lonely."

Maggie's voice turned wistful. "I remember when the four of us were thick as thieves, you, me, Felicia, and Wes, running around Halibut Cove like we owned the place."

Audrey raised an eyebrow. "You, causing trouble? Hard to imagine."

Maggie winked. "You'd be surprised."

Griffin chuckled, but his gaze grew shrewd. "You didn't come here to talk about the old days, did you?"

Maggie's expression sobered. "No. I wanted to ask you about Chips Hogan."

Griffin sighed deeply, as though he'd been expecting this. "I figured someone would bring it up sooner or later. Thought it'd be Jill, though."

"Well, Jill doesn't have a crack researcher like Audrey here down at the station," Maggie said.

"I found an article about you and Chips in the *Chronicle*'s archives," Audrey said.

"Yeah, I remember our royal screwup made the papers," Griffin said ruefully.

"What really happened between you two?" Maggie asked.

Griffin's jaw tightened. "I'm not ashamed to admit I hated the man. He ruined me."

As they walked, Griffin recounted the story. "We were young and stupid. Chips convinced me to open a hardware store to compete with the Carters. We despised that whole family with their high prices and highfalutin' attitude, like they were better than everybody else. We foolishly thought we could run them out of business, but it was all about spite. Nothing good ever comes from that."

"What went wrong?" Audrey asked.

Griffin's face darkened. "Chips went behind my back, gave all our money to a contractor who skipped town. I was left holding the bag. Most of the money was from a loan I'd taken out that Chips conveniently didn't cosign. Took me decades to pay it off. Meanwhile, Chips got bailed out by a rich uncle. Never faced any consequences."

"According to the article, you sued him for fraud," Audrey noted.

"Yeah, but you can't sue if you can't afford a lawyer, so I had to drop the suit."

They paused in front of the cemetery across from the church. Griffin's eyes lingered on Felicia's gravestone, and he walked over, placing a hand on the cool marble.

"Felicia kept me grounded," he said quietly. "She stopped me from doing something stupid, from letting my anger consume me. I owe her everything."

Maggie and Audrey stood in respectful silence as Griffin composed himself. Finally, he turned back to them. "I should head back before my manager loses his mind."

As they walked back toward the store, Griffin's tone turned thoughtful. "I won't deny my resentment, but I wouldn't have killed Chips. I've moved on, as best I can."

"Then who do you think did it?" Maggie asked.

Griffin hesitated. "If you ask me, your daughter Jill arrested the right man. There was bad blood between Chips and Waldo. I know people are buzzing about that chowder recipe nonsense between your families, but nobody's talking about what was really going on between those two."

"What do you mean?" Maggie pressed.

Griffin glanced at Audrey. "You work at The Chowder House, don't you?"

Audrey nodded. "I do. Why?"

Griffin's voice lowered. "There were rumors about Chips, Waldo, and Ethel Primrose. Some kind of romantic triangle. Feuding over her, if you believe the gossip."

Audrey's jaw dropped. "What? Ethel never said anything about that."

Maggie's mind raced. "Well, that's certainly a wrinkle."

Griffin shrugged. "People do crazy things when emotions run high. Might be worth looking into."

They reached the store, and Griffin gave them a small smile. "Thanks for the walk. It was good to see you, Maggie. You too, Audrey."

As he disappeared back inside, Maggie turned to Audrey. "Ethel Primrose?"

Audrey shook her head in disbelief. "I know! I've worked for the woman for two years and didn't have a clue. Who knew Ethel was such a temptress, Halibut Cove's very own femme fatale? I need to get the scoop, like now!"

"Let's go," Maggie said, slipping her arm through her granddaughter's and hustling off down the street to Maggie's car.

Chapter Eight

The lunch rush at The Chowder House was just tapering off when Maggie and Audrey walked through the door. Behind the counter, Ethel Primrose was a whirl of energy, directing her staff and charming her customers in equal measure.

Audrey couldn't help but wonder if there had even been a lunch rush today, given the circumstances. She had been noticing a considerable decline in business during her shifts ever since Chips Hogan keeled over after eating a bowl of the restaurant's signature clam chowder.

Maggie made her way to the counter and caught Ethel's attention with a wave. Ethel's face lit up as she walked over.

"Maggie! Just in time for my lunch special. I think I have a few orders left," she said, her voice bright. She then noticed Audrey hovering behind her grandmother. "Audrey, what on earth are you doing here on your day off?"

"Would you believe me if I said I just miss you?" Audrey asked with a sly smile.

"Although that's a perfectly reasonable answer, dear, I'd have to say no, I don't believe you."

Maggie leaned in slightly. "Ethel, we need to talk. Privately."

Ethel's eyebrows shot up, but she nodded. "Follow me." She led them to a small booth in the back corner of the restaurant, away from the prying ears of the lunch crowd.

As soon as they sat, Maggie didn't waste any time. "We've heard some rumors, Ethel. About a supposed . . . love triangle involving you, Chips Hogan, and Waldo Duggan."

Ethel's jaw dropped. Before she could respond, there was a loud crash from across the room. All three women turned to see Isabella standing in the middle of the dining area, a shattered plate of fried haddock and onion rings and coleslaw at her feet. Isabella's face was a mix of embarrassment and shock.

"Isabella!" Ethel called, her tone both amused and exasperated. "What on earth are you doing?"

"Sorry! I just overheard what you were talking about and—" Isabella stammered, quickly grabbing a rag and starting to clean up.

"Well, let's not share what you heard all over town, okay, Isabella?" Ethel said sharply.

Isabella continued picking up bits of food as Jimmy the busboy raced over with a mop and bucket. "Of course not, Ethel, it's just . . . I mean . . . who knew . . . ?"

Ethel rolled her eyes. "Go on, say it."

"Who knew you were such a seductress!" Isabella blurted out, cackling.

Ethel shook her head and turned back to Maggie and Audrey. "Good grief. And I thought it was obvious to everyone. I mean, look at me." Her voice dripped with sarcasm, but her eyes twinkled. "So, what exactly are people saying?"

Audrey leaned forward. "That you were romantically involved with both Chips and Waldo."

Ethel snorted. "Oh, please. Let me set the record straight. Waldo did hang around here from time to time, trying to get my attention, but I never encouraged him. As for Chips, I had no idea he was interested in me until he asked me out once."

Maggie folded her hands and set them down on the table. "When was that, Ethel?"

Ethel thought about it. "Let's see. Maybe six, seven months ago. I said no, and that was that." She shrugged. "I have no idea how the rumor started, and I doubt Waldo even knew Chips tried to date me, so I can't imagine that's why Waldo put the poison in the chowder."

"Allegedly," Audrey reminded her.

"Oh, come now, dear, everyone knows it was Waldo. According to your mother, they've got him dead to rights."

Maggie tilted her head. "So truthfully, Ethel, you had no romantic interest in either of them, Chips or Waldo?"

Ethel leaned in conspiratorially. "Let me tell you something, Maggie. I have zero interest in doddering older men with wrinkled skin and sagging butts. Never been my thing."

Audrey coughed to hide a laugh, while Maggie's lips twitched. Ethel grinned at their reactions. "No offense, Mags, but I like the young bucks. So full of youth and vigor."

Maggie couldn't help herself. "How young?"

Ethel's eyes sparkled mischievously. "Well, not to make you uncomfortable, but your son Sandy is quite a looker. Fine young man. Good head on his shoulders. And with abs to boot."

"He's twenty-six!" Maggie exclaimed.

Ethel nodded appreciatively. "Exactly. Young enough to be virile, old enough to know what they're doing."

Audrey burst out laughing. "He *is* single," she teased.

Maggie cut in quickly. "Well, to be frank, I'm sure he's more interested in girls closer to his own age, Ethel."

Audrey held her tongue, choosing not to share her suspicion that Uncle Sandy might not be interested in girls at all. It wasn't her place to out him, especially to her grandmother.

Ethel chuckled at Maggie's flustered expression. "Now don't worry, Mags. I promise I won't make a move on him. He was just an example. Truth is, I've got my eye on someone else."

Maggie raised an eyebrow. "Oh?"

Ethel leaned back in her seat with a satisfied smile. "The new manager at the grocery store. Carey Birch's youngest boy."

"The twenty-five-year-old?" Maggie gasped.

"That's the one!" Ethel said, her grin widening. "He winked at me when he ran my Lotto ticket through the machine to see if I won anything. There was definitely chemistry between us. It was obvious to everyone. I just hope he's not allergic to cats. That would be a deal breaker."

Maggie stared at her, speechless. "I didn't think anything could surprise me at this point in my life. Points for you, Ethel."

Audrey, still laughing, added, "Maybe consider Peter Birch's personality before you move forward on that prospect."

"Why? What's wrong with his personality?" Ethel asked.

"I don't think he has one," Audrey cracked.

Before Ethel could respond, Clyde Peterson walked up to the counter where Isabella was ringing him up. "For the record," Clyde said, loudly enough for them to hear, "I'm single and available."

Ethel turned in her seat. "How old are you, Clyde?"

"Thirty-six," he replied, puffing out his chest.

Ethel shook her head. "Ancient."

Clyde's face fell. "I'm a young thirty-six," he protested.

Ethel waved a hand dismissively. "Sorry, Clyde. I prefer a man who is not on trial for aggravated assault."

Clyde chuckled as he grabbed his change and sauntered out the door.

Once he was gone, Ethel's tone grew serious. "Chips and Waldo definitely had a contentious relationship. Chips loved to tease Waldo, always putting him down for something." She sighed. "The sooner Waldo goes to trial and gets convicted, the sooner things can get back to normal around here."

Maggie shook her head gently. "I'm just not convinced Waldo poisoned the chowder, Ethel."

Ethel's expression turned worried. "If he didn't, then what does that mean for my restaurant? People already think The Chowder House is cursed. If we don't figure this out, nobody will ever trust my food again." Her voice cracked slightly as she added, "Maggie, please. Help me restore The Chowder House's good name."

Chapter Nine

Back at the Holbrook home, Maggie set her purse on the counter and glanced at Audrey. "What do you think about dinner? I could make us something quick."

Audrey shook her head, grabbing a spoon from the drawer.

"Thanks, Nana, but I'm meeting Isabella for drinks at the hotel bar. She's got this thing for the new waiter. Supposedly, he's from Greece. You know how she's obsessed with dark and swarthy. She's very excited."

Maggie smirked. "Sounds riveting."

"Oh, it is," Audrey replied sarcastically, pouring herself a bowl of cereal. "She's planning to wear a cocktail dress, flirt with him, and post selfies on Instagram for her dozens of followers."

Maggie shook her head. "It's always nice to have a goal."

Maggie climbed the stairs to her room, already thinking about the book she'd started the night before. But as she reached her bedroom door, she stopped short. Phoebe Barker was just stepping out of her room.

Phoebe jumped at the sight of Maggie. "Oh! Maggie, I didn't hear you come in."

Maggie's eyes narrowed. "What were you doing in my room?"

Phoebe's smile wavered. "I—I was downstairs, Cord and I dropped by for a visit, and I was waiting in the kitchen, but I had to use the bathroom and came up here and got all turned around. I must've wandered in by mistake."

"Where is Cord?"

"He, uh, he went out to the garage to take a look at your car. You mentioned it was making a strange noise when we were over for dinner last Sunday?"

"Yes, I did," Maggie said evenly, still staring at Phoebe, in a way designed to make her extremely uncomfortable. Then Maggie forced a tight smile. "The bathroom's that way," she said, pointing down the hall.

Phoebe nodded quickly. "Of course. Thank you." She hurried off, leaving Maggie staring after her.

Inside her room, Maggie's eyes scanned for anything amiss. Nothing seemed out of place, but her jewelry drawer was slightly ajar. She opened it, carefully checking its contents. Everything appeared to be accounted for, but the unsettling feeling lingered. Was Phoebe just poking around? Perhaps trying to see what someday might be hers? Maggie didn't trust her as far as she could throw her.

Back in the kitchen, Audrey was perched on a stool, shoveling cereal into her mouth, as Maggie returned from her room and leaned on the counter. "Is that your dinner?"

Audrey shrugged. "They have a great bar menu at the hotel, but Isabella doesn't want the bartender to see her eating. Makes her self-conscious."

Maggie shook her head with a chuckle. She lowered her voice. "Phoebe's here."

Audrey froze, spoon halfway to her mouth. "Where?"

"Upstairs," Maggie replied.

Audrey's brow furrowed. "What's she doing upstairs?"

"Looking for the bathroom."

"She didn't see the two we have down here?" Audrey's skepticism mirrored Maggie's.

Maggie shrugged. "Apparently not."

Audrey's expression turned serious. "What do you really think about Cord marrying Phoebe?"

Before Maggie could answer, Cord strode in, brushing his hands on his jeans. "Your car's all set, Ma. It was just a loose belt. I tightened it up."

Maggie smiled. "Thank you, Cord. That noise was driving me crazy."

"No problem," Cord said. "Phoebe and I actually came by to talk wedding plans."

Maggie managed a polite smile. "What are you thinking?"

Phoebe reappeared, her enthusiasm evident. "We were hoping to have the wedding here, at the Holbrook house. The grounds are so beautiful with the ocean view and the islands in the distance. It's picture-perfect, and it's where Cord grew up. It would mean so much to him."

Maggie turned to Cord. "I didn't know you were such a romantic."

Cord shrugged, his face indifferent. "It's whatever Phoebe wants. I just want to make her happy."

Audrey rolled her eyes, tossing her empty bowl into the dishwasher. "I'm heading upstairs to change," she said, brushing past them.

Phoebe then launched into a detailed monologue, her hands gesturing animatedly. "I'm envisioning a soft, romantic palette—pale pinks, creamy whites, maybe a touch of lavender. The flowers would cascade down the trellis, and we could line the aisle with lanterns. For the seating arrangements, I'm thinking long farmhouse tables under a canopy of string lights. It would be so elegant, but still have that cozy, intimate feel."

Maggie nodded politely, but she couldn't help noticing how Phoebe's plans seemed more about aesthetics than sentiment. "It sounds lovely," she said, her tone neutral.

As Phoebe started to describe her dream wedding cake in painstaking detail, Sandy walked in, his clothes streaked with dirt. His sudden appearance made Phoebe falter mid-sentence, her words trailing off as her eyes fixed on him.

"What have you been up to?" Maggie asked, raising an eyebrow.

"In the garden, pulling those weeds you've been complaining about," Sandy replied.

"I could've hired someone to do that," Maggie said.

"I figured if I'm moving back in, I should pull my weight."

Maggie blinked. "Moving back in?"

Sandy nodded. "Cord and I share a house, but now that he's engaged, he needs his own place. I'll stay here until I figure something out, if that's okay with you."

Maggie's face lit up, thrilled. "Of course it's okay!"

Phoebe chimed in, her tone almost too friendly. "Hate to break up the dynamic duo. You're more than welcome to stay with us, Sandy. For as long as you want." Her gaze lingered on him, and her cheeks flushed as he peeled off his dirty shirt, revealing his muscular chest. Maggie caught the look and felt her unease deepen.

"I'm going to toss this in the washer," Sandy said, ambling out, apparently made a little uncomfortable by Phoebe's longing expression.

Cord, oblivious, added, "Phoebe and I also wanted to talk about keeping the wedding small."

"Yes, I always dreamed of having a big wedding, but unfortunately my parents have been going through a tough time lately financially, so I don't want to burden them."

Cord gently rubbed her back. "I told you, honey, don't worry about the cost. We'll handle it, right, Ma?"

Maggie cleared her throat. "Yes, I'm sure we can work something out."

Phoebe shook her head. "No, my dad would never hear of it. He's too proud. He said it's the tradition that the bride's parents pay for the wedding, and that's how it's going to be. He's told me, 'I won't accept a handout.' "

In Maggie's opinion, Phoebe appeared annoyed that her father was sticking to his guns, his sense of duty.

"You want me to talk to him, sweetheart?" Cord asked, taking her hand.

She kissed his hand softly. "No, it won't do any good. You've met him. You know how stubborn he can be."

Maggie's curiosity was piqued. "I thought your dad retired with a nice pension and your mom still worked at the bank?"

Phoebe hesitated, but Cord answered for her. "They've been in a legal battle with Chips Hogan over a disputed piece of land. It's been going on for years, and recently, Chips decided to sue them. The legal fees have drained their savings."

Maggie's mind raced. "Really? I had no idea. That sounds . . . stressful."

Phoebe nodded tightly. "It's been hard on them." She paused, and then, with a renewed sense of hope, added, "Maybe now that Chips . . . Well, now that he's no longer in the picture, maybe things will finally settle down."

As the conversation shifted back to wedding details, Maggie couldn't shake her suspicions. The land dispute with Chips added another layer to the mystery, and she couldn't help but wonder if Phoebe's family had a motive for murder.

Chapter Ten

The buzz of gossip was thick in the air as Maggie stepped into the town library, a canvas tote of books slung over her shoulder. As she approached the front desk, Mrs. Whishaw, the librarian, smiled warmly. "Afternoon, Maggie! Returning some mysteries?" Mrs. Whishaw announced, her booming voice louder than you would expect from a librarian.

"You know me too well, Sylvia," Maggie said, sliding a small stack of novels across the counter. "Any new recommendations?"

Mrs. Whishaw's eyes lit up. "I just got the latest James Patterson. It's got a serial killer, lots of twists . . ."

Maggie wrinkled her nose. "You know, I'm not much for blood and gore. I like something cozier, a mystery set in a quaint little town. Like Halibut Cove."

Mrs. Whishaw chuckled. "You mean where the biggest drama is who's won the clam chowder contest?"

"Or who's poisoned the competition," Maggie muttered, her tone dark.

Mrs. Whishaw raised a curious eyebrow, but before she could ask, voices from behind the counter caught their attention.

"I just don't believe it was Waldo Duggan," whispered Lucy Perkins. "He doesn't have the appetite for murder."

"Then who do you think did it?" Binnie Caldwell replied.

Maggie and Mrs. Whishaw exchanged glances. Mrs. Whishaw opened her mouth to warn the women that Maggie was within earshot, but Maggie shook her head and motioned for her to stay quiet.

"Well," Lucy said, lowering her voice, "I wouldn't be surprised if it turned out to be Maggie Holbrook's granddaughter, Audrey."

Binnie gasped. "Audrey? That sweet girl? I can't believe it."

"Why not?" Lucy replied. "It's no secret she served Chips his last meal. And Maggie spoiled her rotten. She's always been a bit of a wild child."

Maggie's grip on the counter tightened.

"Still," Binnie said hesitantly, "that doesn't mean she'd go as far as kill someone."

"Anything's possible," Lucy whispered. "Phyllis Hoffmann was saying the same thing at the hairdresser's yesterday."

Maggie had heard enough. She turned sharply. "Lucy Perkins."

The women jumped, their faces turning pale.

"Maggie! I didn't see you there," Lucy stammered.

"Clearly," Maggie replied. "Tell me, what evidence do you have that Audrey poisoned Chips Hogan?"

Lucy fumbled. "Well, she served him the chowder . . ."

"In front of witnesses," Maggie said. "If Audrey was a killer, do you think she'd be stupid enough to poison someone in plain sight?"

Lucy's mouth opened and closed, no words coming out.

"And what would her motive be?" Maggie pressed.

Lucy looked at Binnie for help, but Binnie shrank back. "I-I'm not sure," Lucy admitted.

"Exactly. So maybe think twice before spreading baseless accusations," Maggie said, her tone steely.

Lucy mumbled an apology and hurried out.

Binnie lingered awkwardly, twisting her hands together. "Maggie, I just want to say, I don't believe for a minute that Audrey could have done anything like that," she said earnestly. "But Lucy gave me a ride here, so . . ." She gestured helplessly.

Maggie softened slightly. "Thank you, Binnie. You have a nice day and say hello to Charles."

Binnie nodded and scurried out after Lucy.

Mrs. Whishaw sighed. "I'm sorry you had to hear that, Maggie."

Maggie waved it off. "People love to talk. But I'll be damned if I let anyone drag my Audrey's name through the mud."

Maggie dropped her new stack of books in her car and set off on foot to clear her head. The crisp autumn air helped, but she was still fuming when she passed the Thirsty Gull, Halibut Cove's favorite watering hole. Loud voices and the crash of breaking glass made her stop. Peering through the window, she saw a full-blown free-for-all in progress.

Maggie pulled out her phone and called Jill. "You need to get to the Gull. There's a brawl going on."

"Stay out of it, Mom," Jill warned.

"Of course," Maggie lied, pushing open the door.

Inside, the chaos was worse than she'd imagined. Chairs were overturned, glasses smashed, and in the middle of it all, Clyde Peterson and a couple of his hulking drinking buddies squared off against Cord and Sandy. Lester, the bar owner, was crouched behind the counter, shouting, "Stop it! You're wrecking my place!"

"Enough!" Maggie yelled, her voice rising above the din. "Enough!" She grabbed an overturned chair and banged it against the floor. The noise finally cut through the chaos, and the fighters froze mid-swing.

Maggie glared at her sons. "What the hell do you two think you're doing?"

Cord wiped blood from his lip. "Clyde started mouthing off about Audrey, saying some crap about how she's planning her next murder. I told him to shut up, and he kept pushing."

"So you decided to turn this place into a war zone?" Maggie snapped. "You're better than this, Cord. And you too, Sandy. How do you think this looks?" She then turned to Clyde, who was gingerly touching a red welt on the side of his face. "And where did you hear this rumor about my granddaughter, Clyde? Perhaps from your busybody Aunt Lucy?"

Before Clyde could respond, Jill and Mason burst through the door. Jill's voice cut like a whip. "What the hell is going on here?"

Cord gestured toward Clyde. "He started it."

"I don't care who started it," Jill snapped. "You trashed Lester's bar."

Cord sighed. "I'll pay for the damages. And I'll donate to Lester's son's Little League team. They need new uniforms."

Lester peeked over the bar. "I appreciate that, Cord. It's okay . . ."

"No, it's not okay," Jill interjected. "You're all under arrest."

Cord's jaw dropped. "What?"

"Public disturbance, destruction of property, and I'll think of more on the way to the station," Jill said. "Mason, cuff them. And call for backup. We're going to need another patrol car to transport all of them to the station."

Mason nodded then reached for the cuffs attached to his belt. "I only got one pair."

Jill sighed, unhooked her pair, and tossed them to him. "Now you've got two. Tell 'em to bring more when you call for back up." Then she turned to her brothers. "In the meantime, start with those two."

Maggie stepped forward. "Jill, is this really necessary?"

Jill turned to her. "Mom, stay out of it."

Mason began cuffing the brawlers, Cord and Sandy first.

At the station, Maggie paced the waiting area outside Jill's office, where she could hear Jill venting to Mason. "They acted like complete idiots. And now Oliver's going to show up and smooth it all over."

As if on cue, Oliver breezed in, impeccably dressed and exuding calm authority.

Maggie crossed her arms. "What are you doing here?"

"I'm here on behalf of Clyde's parents to bail him out," Oliver said. "They're worried about his trial."

Maggie shook her head. "They're always bailing him out."

Jill scoffed from the doorway. "So are you, Mom. You're here to bail out Cord and Sandy, and Oliver's here to make sure they don't get into any trouble, once again allowing them to escape any responsibility for their actions."

Maggie bristled. "That's not the same thing."

"Isn't it?" Jill shot back.

Cord, led out by Mason, stopped when he saw Oliver. "Don't tell me. You're not here for us, you're here for Peterson. I can't believe you're still representing that piece of scum!"

Oliver's expression remained neutral. "Like I told you, Cord, again and again, everyone deserves a defense. Even Clyde."

"He's trash," Cord snapped.

"Enough," Maggie interjected. "Cord, now's not the time."

Mason led Clyde out. Oliver turned to him. "Keep your mouth shut, Clyde. You're already in deep enough."

Clyde sneered but said nothing.

"Your parents are outside waiting to take you home. Come by to see me first thing in the morning so we can discuss strategy."

"Whatever you say, Counselor," Clyde said, winking at Cord.

Sandy grabbed Cord by the arm to keep him from impulsively lunging at his tormentor and starting the scuffle all over again but this time inside of a police station.

Not the best idea.

Once Clyde was gone, Oliver turned to Jill. "I spoke to the DA. We can sort this out before it becomes a big deal."

Jill shot Maggie a pointed look, her *I told you so* clear without a word.

Maggie sighed. "Let's just get this over with."

Chapter Eleven

The Seaview Diner was alive with the sound of clinking cutlery, muffled conversations, and the occasional hiss of the coffee machine. Jill sat across from Mason in a red leather booth, scanning the room for their witness. Tanya, a slight young woman with long, dark hair that framed a nervous face, slid into the booth without waiting to be invited.

"You must be Tanya," Jill said, smiling warmly.

Tanya rolled her eyes. "Yeah, thanks to my mom, who doesn't know how to mind her own business. Look, I didn't want to get involved in any of this. I didn't even want to call you, but then, of course, like she does, my mother went behind my back and called you anyway. Sometimes I can't stand her!"

"She just wants you to do the right thing," Mason interjected.

Tanya seemed to notice him for the first time. Her eyes brightened. "Hello. Who are you?"

"Officer Mason Dooley," Mason said with a nod.

"You certainly are!" Tanya cooed.

Jill's tone softened. "I understand how you feel, Tanya.

But your mother's right. If you saw or heard anything that could help us solve Chips Hogan's murder, it's important to share it. Justice doesn't work without people like you stepping forward."

Tanya sighed heavily, leaning back. "Fine. Whatever."

As she spoke, Katty Caulfield, the diner's cheerful waitress, approached, flipping open her notepad. "What can I get you all?"

Tanya glanced at the menu and started rattling off items faster than Katty could write them down. "Let's see . . . pancakes, ooh the ones with chocolate chips, a cheeseburger with fries, a grilled cheese sandwich, onion rings, a side of hash browns . . . Oh, and pie. Do you have pecan?"

Katty blinked, her pen hovering over the notepad. "Uh, yeah, we have pecan."

"Great. A slice of that too." She looked at Jill and Mason. "Do you guys want anything?"

Mason raised an eyebrow, and Jill quietly ordered two coffees. As Katty shuffled away, Tanya smirked.

"Stress eating," she explained. "This is your treat, right? I mean, since I'm a key witness and all."

Jill's lips tightened, but she nodded. "Of course."

Tanya turned to Mason, her demeanor instantly more animated. "So, a week before Chips's murder, I saw him arguing with Waldo. They were outside the Thirsty Gull. It was pretty heated."

"What were they arguing about?" Mason asked, leaning forward.

Tanya shrugged. "I don't know. I wasn't really paying attention. I was on the phone with my boyfriend—well, now ex-boyfriend. Caught him cheating on me. Can you believe that? After everything I did for him? I practically emptied my savings to buy him a hot-looking leather jacket last Christmas. What an ingrate. And he gave me mittens! He didn't even buy them. He had his grandmother knit them for him. My friends told me not to trust him, but did I listen? No. I'm always following my heart instead of my head. Stupid, right?"

Jill attempted to redirect. "Tanya, about Chips and Waldo—"

But Tanya waved her off, her eyes glued to Mason. "I'm serious, though. I need to find a guy who's got his act together. Someone with a good head on his shoulders, a decent job . . ." Her gaze lingered on Mason, who visibly blushed, stuttering as he tried to think of a response.

"I, uh . . . well . . ." Mason began, his ears turning bright red.

Tanya leaned in with a playful smile, clearly enjoying his discomfort. "You're cute, but I bet you already know that."

Unable to endure any more flirting, Jill stood abruptly. "Thank you, Tanya. Your information will be very helpful. We'll be in touch if we need anything else."

As they left the diner, Mason groaned. "That was . . . mortifying."

Jill smirked. "What can I say? You're a ladies' man."

"Please stop," Mason muttered, covering his face with his hands. "I'm begging you."

The county courthouse was quiet when they arrived. District Attorney for the County Mark Haskell's office was at the end of the hall, its door slightly ajar. Jill knocked once before stepping inside. Mark, a tall man with sandy hair and a disarming smile, stood behind his desk.

"Jill," he said warmly. "And Mason. Good to see you."

"Mark," Jill said curtly. "We spoke to that witness.

Don't get too excited. She's not exactly a slam dunk. She doesn't even remember what Chips and Waldo were fighting about."

Mark nodded, gesturing for them to sit. "We're going to need a hell of a lot more than that."

Jill raised an eyebrow. "Are you worried about the trial?"

"Yes. Oliver's already working angles for reasonable doubt. And believe me, there's no shortage, and you know how good your brother is."

Jill's jaw tightened. "Don't remind me."

Mark leaned forward. "If you can find more concrete evidence, something irrefutable, it would make my job a whole lot easier."

"We're on it," Mason said eagerly.

Jill's tone turned sharp. "Speaking of jobs, why haven't you filed charges against my brothers for the brawl at the Thirsty Gull?"

Mark looked taken aback. "Lester refused to press charges."

"That's because Cord bribed him with new Little League uniforms," Jill shot back.

Mark sighed. "Jill, it's not favoritism. Without Lester's cooperation, there's no case."

"Convenient," Jill said, her voice dripping with sarcasm. "You've always had a knack for making things easier for Oliver."

Mark's brow furrowed. "I thought you'd be relieved."

"Relieved? That my brothers constantly get to act like they're above the law? Hardly."

Mark leaned back, his arms crossed. "Do you always have to be this stubborn?"

"Do you always have to play favorites?"

Mason shifted uncomfortably as Jill stormed out, and he caught up to her in the hallway.

"I know this is none of my business, but you and the DA, do you two have a history?" he ventured.

Jill shot him a warning glance. "Why would you say something like that? You're way off base."

Mason smirked. "Sure. Right, sorry. But I'm just saying, back there, it sort of felt like sexual tension."

Jill stopped in her tracks, fixing him with a glare. "Let's make a deal. I won't make jokes about you being a chick magnet, and you'll never say the words *sexual tension* in front of me ever again."

Mason held up his hands. "Deal."

Jill nodded firmly. "And for the record, there is none of that with me and Mark. Got it?"

"Yup."

"Good."

Later that evening, Jill stood in front of her bedroom mirror, inspecting her reflection. Her blouse hugged her frame in just the right way, and her dark jeans highlighted her legs. She tilted her head, debating whether to let her hair down or keep it in its usual ponytail.

Her ex's voice echoed in her mind. *You're pretty enough, but not stunning*. The words had burrowed deep, even though she'd tried to shake them off. She squared her shoulders. *He doesn't get to live in my head anymore. I look good. I am good.*

Downstairs, she heard the sound of dishes clinking. Audrey was rummaging through the fridge when Jill entered the kitchen.

"You're here?" Jill asked, surprised.

Audrey shrugged. "Nana's at her book club, even though

she didn't read the book, only the jacket cover, but they're serving Cosmos, so she wasn't going to miss out. Isabella's got a date, and I'm bored. Thought we could have dinner and watch a movie. But you're dressed to go out. You look nice, by the way."

Jill hesitated. "Thank you. I can cancel my plans . . ."

Audrey waved her off. "No, you should go."

"You sure?" Jill pressed. "I don't mind—"

"Mom, go. Seriously. Who are you meeting anyway?"

"Just some friends," Jill said vaguely.

Audrey raised an eyebrow. "Which friends?"

Jill fumbled. "You know, Mary . . . and, uh, Sarah."

"I saw Mary at The Chowder House yesterday. She said she was going to drive down to Portland tonight for some retail therapy," Audrey said flatly.

"Well, I'm not sure who's going to make it," Jill replied quickly. "It's just a casual thing."

Audrey crossed her arms. "Mom, do you have a date?"

"No!" Jill said, a little too loudly. "I don't have a date."

Audrey smirked. "If you did, it'd be fine, you know." She paused. "Awesome, in fact."

Jill gave her a quick kiss on the forehead. "Eat something. Hang out. Watch some Netflix. I'll be back later."

Jill parked her car in front of a charming house just outside of town. It was a classic New England style, with white clapboard siding and dark green shutters. A wraparound porch hugged the front, dotted with Adirondack chairs and hanging flower baskets under the soft radiance of porch lights.

She took a deep breath as she stepped out of the car and walked up the cobblestone path to the front door. The faint sound of music drifted through the air, and there was a scent of wood smoke. Jill hesitated for a moment before knocking on the door.

When it opened, Mark Haskell stood there, a towel slung over his shoulder and a warm smile on his face. "You made it," he said, his voice rich with warmth.

As she stepped inside, the warm glow of candles lit the dining room, and the smell of her favorite dish, shrimp scampi, wafted through the air.

"You've outdone yourself," Jill said, taking in the romantic setup.

Mark grinned. "You deserve it."

Jill's smile faltered. "Audrey's suspicious. She's already asking questions."

Mark set the table and walked over to her. "Why do we have to keep this a secret?"

"You know why," Jill said, pulling away. "My family would make it a circus."

"You worry too much," Mark said, leaning in to kiss her, but she stopped him.

"And this isn't . . . It's not a relationship. We're just . . . dating, " Jill said, trying to sound convincing. "Early stages."

Mark leaned in again. This time she didn't stop him, and he kissed her softly. "If you say so."

"Mark, I'm serious. I'm not ready . . ."

"I know . . ." He kissed her again, cutting her off.

Jill sighed, half-annoyed, half-swayed. "You're impossible."

Mark smirked. "And you're beautiful."

She finally gave in, kissing him back. "Just don't burn the shrimp scampi," she murmured against his lips.

Mark grinned. "Oh, dinner can wait."

Chapter Twelve

The fluorescent hum in the Halibut Cove Police Station was steady, punctuated only by the rustle of papers as Jill scanned the autopsy report once more in front of her. Chips Hogan's cause of death was clear: respiratory failure due to ingestion of a lethal dose of Atropa belladonna, more commonly known as . . .

"Deadly nightshade," Jill murmured, leaning back in her chair. "Not exactly an ingredient you'd expect in your chowder recipe."

Mason, sitting across from her, sipped his coffee and tapped his pen against the desk. "With the plant we found hidden in Waldo's pantry, it seems pretty open and shut. Poisoned chowder, Waldo's deadly nightshade—case closed."

Jill frowned. "But Waldo seemed genuinely shocked when we found it. Like he had no idea it was there."

"Could be a great actor," Mason said with a shrug.

"Maybe." Jill tapped her fingers on the desk. "Where would someone even get their hands on some deadly nightshade? It's not exactly something you find at the local grocery store."

Mason pulled out his phone, typing rapidly. "Let's see . . . aha! Apparently, you can legally buy it in small doses in the

U.S. It's used for all kinds of things: dilating pupils for eye exams, treating stomach cramps, even as a pain reliever. But yeah, it's also supertoxic. Definitely fatal if ingested in large amounts."

"Could it be purchased nearby?"

"The closest place," Mason said, scrolling, "is a nursery about fifty miles away in New Hampshire. Cute name, though—Plant Parenthood."

Jill raised an eyebrow. "Plant Parenthood? That's . . . something."

"Right?" Mason chuckled. "Whoever named it probably had a field day. I bet they considered names like 'Leaf It to Us' or 'Branching Out.' "

"Stop," Jill said, standing and grabbing her coat.

" 'Just Grow with It?' "

"Mason."

He held up his hands in surrender, chuckling. "Fine. So, what's the plan?"

Jill stood and grabbed her jacket. "We're going on a road trip."

"To New Hampshire?" Mason asked, following her out. "Can we stop at the Starbucks in Portland on the way? They've got this new wrap I've been dying to try. I bet it goes great with a Caramel Macchiato."

Jill glanced at him, exasperated. "How are you not three hundred pounds?"

"Good metabolism, maybe?"

The drive to Plant Parenthood was serene, the winding coastal roads flanked by evergreen trees and rocky cliffs. The late afternoon sun cast long shadows as they crossed the bridge from Kittery into New Hampshire.

The nursery was nestled at the end of a gravel driveway,

a rustic sign out front painted in cheerful green lettering: PLANT PARENTHOOD—GROWING LIFE, NATURALLY! The property was a mix of rustic charm and hippie aesthetic, with colorful wind chimes and rows of potted plants arranged in seemingly haphazard patterns. A faint smell of marijuana lingered in the air.

Keil and Madge, the nursery's owners, greeted them at the entrance. Keil was tall and lanky, with a bushy beard and a tie-dye shirt that proclaimed MAKE PLANTS, NOT WAR. Madge, shorter and rounder, wore a flowing hemp dress adorned with hand-painted flowers.

"Welcome to Plant Parenthood!" Madge said in a singsong voice, her bare feet dusted with soil.

Jill introduced herself and Mason, flashing her badge. "We're investigating a case and need to ask you a few questions."

"Of course," Keil said. "We're all about helping people."

Jill got straight to the point. "We're looking into a recent purchase of deadly nightshade."

Madge's eyes widened. "Oh, yeah, we sell that! Pretty plant, but dangerous. What's this about?"

Mason held up his phone, showing them Waldo Duggan's recent mug shot. "Do you recognize this man?"

Keil scratched his beard. "Nope. Never seen him."

Madge shook her head. "I don't think so. If he'd come in, we'd know."

Jill frowned. "So you have no other employees, it's just the two of you?"

Keil nodded. "Sorry we couldn't help. Can I interest you in a lovely Peace Lily?" He held up a plant with white spathes.

"One of my favorites," Madge cooed. "So elegant and purifying."

"No, thank you," Jill mumbled, frustrated by the lack of information after coming all the way out here.

"Well, if you change your mind, be sure to check out the online store on our website," Keil said.

"You have a mail-order business?" Jill asked, her tone sharp.

Madge beamed. "Yep! Keil set it up last year. Super-handy for customers who can't make the drive. We ship all over the world."

"Can we see a list of recent credit card purchases?" Jill asked.

Keil hesitated, glancing at Madge. "Uh, that's private information."

Jill sighed. "Fine. I'll buy something."

Mason perked up. "How about one of those marijuana plants out back?"

Jill glared at him. "How about you pick something else? Maybe a nice flower you can give to one of your many admirers."

Mason blushed. "We had a deal!"

Inside, Madge printed out a list of recent transactions.

"Two deadly nightshade plants were sold last month," the clerk explained, flipping through the invoice book. "Paid in cash—no name given. But we did ship them to a post office box not far from Halibut Cove."

"Whoever placed this order wanted to stay off the radar," Mason muttered. "Cash, no signature, just a P.O. box."

"Could be anybody hiding behind that box," Jill said, folding the receipt into her notebook. "But the plants turned up in Waldo Duggan's pantry. Let's see what he has to say about it."

By the time they arrived at Waldo Duggan's modest house, a small, weather-beaten cottage on the edge of town, its shutters askew and paint peeling from the siding, the sky was dark, and the porch light cast a weak glow over the peeling paint and cracked steps.

Jill knocked firmly, and when the door opened, she froze.

"Mom?" she blurted.

Maggie stood in the doorway, wearing an apron and holding a wooden spatula. "Jill," Maggie said evenly, stepping aside to let them in. "I wasn't expecting you."

"You're cooking for him?" Jill demanded, stepping into the house.

Waldo was sitting at the kitchen table, looking sheepish. "She insisted," he mumbled.

"Mom, are you serious?" Jill asked, incredulous.

Maggie returned to the stove, where a casserole dish bubbled enticingly. "It's chicken and broccoli with a cream sauce," she said lightly. "I figured Waldo could use a home-cooked meal."

Jill's jaw tightened. "He's a murder suspect!"

Mason, who had been silent until now, sniffed the air appreciatively. "It does smell good," he admitted.

Maggie turned, holding out a plate. "Would you like some, Mason?"

Before Mason could answer, Jill shot him a warning glare.

He cleared his throat. "Uh, no thanks, ma'am. I'm good."

Maggie sighed, setting the plate down in front of Waldo.

"Mom," Jill began, "we just came from a nursery in New Hampshire."

"Plant Parenthood!" Mason chimed in.

Maggie chuckled. "Oh, that's adorable."

Jill ignored the clatter of silverware around the table and leaned forward, eyes locked on Waldo. "We traced a shipment of deadly nightshade to a P.O. box near Halibut Cove—and then it turned up sitting in your pantry. What do you have to say about that?"

Waldo's fork froze halfway to his mouth. "I don't rent any P.O. box. Never have. And I sure as hell didn't order poison."

"Convenient," Jill said, folding her arms.

"It's the truth!" Waldo snapped. "You think I'd keep a plant in a pantry? There's no light in there. I don't even like plants—can't keep a fern alive. Somebody planted that thing in my house to frame me."

Jill's eyes narrowed. "So you expect me to believe someone went out of their way to buy a toxic plant, had it shipped under some phony claim, and then tucked it into your pantry just to make you look guilty?"

"Exactly!" Waldo's voice rose. "Why else would it be there? Somebody wants me to take the fall."

Maggie threw her napkin down. "See? That makes perfect sense. Why would Waldo go through all that trouble just to leave it sitting in plain sight?"

"Mom, please, I don't need you in my ear right now," Jill shot back.

"Well, somebody's got to talk some sense into you. You're barking up the wrong tree, and you know it."

"Don't tell me how to do my job!" Jill snapped.

There was an awkward silence.

Mason kept his eyes fixed on the floor.

Waldo continued eating as if he hadn't just been confronted with this new evidence.

Maggie gestured at Waldo with a sympathetic smile. "Does he look like a cold-blooded killer to you?"

Jill sighed, pinching the bridge of her nose. "This is unbelievable."

Waldo swallowed, wiped the corners of his mouth with a paper napkin, and leaned forward. "Chief Holbrook, I swear on my life, I didn't kill Chips. Someone planted that stuff to make me look guilty."

Mason glanced at Jill, who remained silent, her eyes fixed on Waldo.

After a long pause, she turned to Mason. "Let's go."

Mason hesitated, glancing at the untouched plate of casserole, then followed her out the door.

As they drove back to the station, Jill's mind raced. Waldo's story was flimsy at best, but Maggie's unwavering belief in his innocence planted a seed of doubt. Could there be more to this case than met the eye?

Chapter Thirteen

Cord gripped the steering wheel of his Jeep Grand Cherokee a little tighter than necessary, his knuckles turning white as the vehicle hummed along the narrow country road. In the passenger seat, Maggie glanced at her middle son, her face impassive but her thoughts churning. In the back seat, Audrey slouched, earbuds in, pretending not to notice the tension building with every mile.

"I'm not stupid, you know," Cord said, his voice tinged with annoyance. "Sandy, Oliver, and Jill could've come today if they really wanted to. They just don't like Phoebe, and they're not even pretending anymore."

Maggie kept her tone neutral. "They just need time, Cord. Change doesn't come easy for everyone."

"Sandy's always vague about his plans outside of work, he didn't even come up with a good excuse, just said he was busy," Cord huffed. "And Jill—she's the chief of police, so I guess she can use her job as an excuse to avoid anything she doesn't feel like doing. And Oliver? Don't get me started."

"To be fair," Maggie said, "Jill is in the middle of a murder investigation."

Cord rolled his eyes. "Sure, but I don't buy for one second that's the real reason. Only Katie had a legitimate excuse. Working a double at the hospital is valid. The rest of them? Gimme a break."

Maggie pressed her lips together, glancing in the rearview mirror at Audrey. The girl's eyes flicked up briefly before returning to her phone screen. It was clear she shared her grandmother's skepticism about Phoebe, but neither of them dared voice it.

"I know they don't like her," Cord continued, gripping the wheel tighter. "They think I don't notice, but I do."

"You're overthinking it," Maggie replied lightly, though her own misgivings about Phoebe made her uneasy.

Cord's frustration almost caused a fender bender when he braked too late at a stop sign. Maggie grabbed the door handle instinctively.

"Cord," she said sharply, "you need to relax. Today is going to be a great day. Let's not ruin it with a head-on collision before we even get there."

The Barker property came into view, and Maggie's first impression was one of weary charm. The large colonial house had good bones, but its weathered exterior was in desperate need of a fresh coat of paint. The shutters sagged slightly, and the roof showed signs of wear. The gardens were tidy but sparse, with bare patches where grass struggled to grow. It was clear Bert and Rhonda Barker were doing their best to keep things up, but the house's age and the family's financial limitations were evident.

Bert and Rhonda stood on the porch to greet them, waving enthusiastically. Bert's smile was broad, but his eyes held a hint of strain. Rhonda's smile was warm but didn't quite reach her eyes, as if a mountain of worry lingered just beneath the surface.

"Welcome!" Bert said as they climbed out of the Jeep.

Phoebe was conspicuously absent.

"Where's Phoebe?" Cord asked, glancing around.

"Upstairs," Rhonda said with a laugh. "She's still getting ready. Wants to look perfect for you, Cord."

Cord's irritation melted as he grinned. "She always looks perfect."

While Bert and Cord exchanged pleasantries, Maggie's attention drifted to the house next door. Chips Hogan's property was silent and forlorn, its windows dark and its once-bustling garden overgrown.

"It's so sad," Maggie murmured. "The house looks so empty now. What's going to happen to it?"

Bert shrugged. "Not sure. Chips didn't have any family left, as far as I know. His son died in that motorcycle accident years ago, and his ex-wife passed before him. If no one claims the property, it'll probably go to auction."

"Would you consider buying it?" Maggie asked.

Bert hesitated. "We've thought about it, but with the wedding costs . . . Well, money's tight. If the price is right, maybe we could scrape something together, but I'm not holding my breath."

Maggie nodded sympathetically. "I'd be happy to help with the wedding costs, Rhonda," she said softly, pulling her aside.

Rhonda's face flushed. "That's very kind of you, Maggie, but Bert wouldn't hear of it. He's proud, you know."

Before Maggie could respond, a car door slammed, and a wiry young man with unkempt hair and a sharp scowl strode toward them.

"Evan," Rhonda said, her tone cautious. "We didn't think you'd make it today."

"Why? You don't want me here?" Evan snapped, his words like a whip.

"Of course we do," Rhonda said quickly, her smile strained. "We're so happy you're here."

Bert stepped forward, clapping his son on the shoulder. "Come on, Evan, let's get you a drink."

Rhonda leaned in, her voice barely audible to Maggie. "Bert, maybe that's not a good idea."

Bert waved her off dismissively. "One drink won't hurt."

Maggie watched the interaction closely, sensing Rhonda's unease. It was clear she feared what might happen if Evan drank, but Bert seemed determined to avoid conflict.

They all headed inside the house.

As the tension ebbed, Phoebe appeared at the top of the staircase, her golden dress catching the light as she descended.

Cord beamed with pride. "You look amazing," he murmured, pulling her into a kiss when she reached him.

Maggie forced a smile, but Phoebe's polished exterior didn't reassure her. The young woman was too poised, too calculated. Something about her didn't sit right.

"I'm taking Audrey on a tour of the grounds," Evan announced suddenly, his eyes darting toward her.

Audrey hesitated, glancing at Maggie.

"Maybe we can all go after lunch?" Maggie suggested lightly.

Evan's expression darkened. "Why doesn't anyone want me to be a good host? I'm just trying to show her around!"

"Let them go," Bert said quickly, his voice placating. "We've got a bit before brunch is ready."

Audrey gave Maggie a small, reassuring nod before following Evan out.

As Evan led Audrey away, he smirked over his shoulder. "Maybe I'll trample all over the land Chips Hogan claimed was his. Not like he's around to stop me now."

The comment hung in the air, sour and heavy.

Maggie tilted her head. "Phoebe mentioned there was a disagreement with Chips about the land?"

Bert sighed, clearly reluctant to delve into the topic. "When we built the stone wall to separate the properties, Chips said part of his land was on our side. We hired a surveyor, and it turned out he was right. He wanted to tear down part of the wall to put in a fountain—said running water relaxed him—but we couldn't afford to start over. Things got heated, lawsuits were filed, but . . . well, then Chips died unexpectedly."

Phoebe crossed her arms, her voice sharp. "He was being completely unreasonable. It was so frustrating for my parents. Honestly, when I heard at your Sunday dinner that he'd died, I wasn't exactly heartbroken."

"Phoebe," Rhonda said, her tone reproachful.

"What?" Phoebe said, shrugging. "I'm not a hypocrite, Mother. I'm not going to shed fake tears over a man who made life miserable for my family." She turned to Cord with a dazzling smile. "I'd love to buy Chips's property myself, but I'm sure you wouldn't want to live next door to my parents."

Cord laughed, oblivious to the undercurrents. "I don't know . . . free babysitting might be nice someday."

Maggie's smile remained fixed, but her unease deepened. Was Phoebe angling for Chips's property? And was marrying Cord a means to acquire it? And what about Bert and Rhonda? Could the property dispute have driven them to desperate measures? But that seemed ridiculous on the surface. Would anyone really poison a man's chowder over a six-foot property line dispute? But stranger things had happened in the history of Halibut Cove.

As the group filed into the living room for pre-brunch mimosas, Maggie's unease lingered, a quiet storm brewing beneath her polite façade.

Chapter Fourteen

Audrey followed Evan across the Barker property, wishing she'd come up with a better excuse to avoid this tour. She shot a glance over her shoulder toward the house, where her grandmother, Maggie, was likely chatting with Rhonda Barker. If she called out now, maybe Maggie would swoop in and save her, but she didn't want to make a scene.

Not yet, anyway.

"So," Evan said, gesturing broadly, "this is the famous wall."

Audrey stopped, looking at the low, weathered stone wall separating the Barkers' property from Chips Hogan's. Evan stood close, his grin crooked but lacking any real charm.

"This little piece of land right here," Evan continued, pointing at a patch of grass just beyond the wall, "is what started all the drama. Chips claimed it was his, hired some surveyor to back him up, but my dad wasn't about to tear down his hard work. Lawsuits, threats, you name it. Funny how it all stopped when Chips kicked the bucket, huh?"

Audrey nodded, her gaze lingering on the wall. The dispute seemed petty, but she knew people could get heated about property lines, especially in small towns where land disputes had a way of growing roots.

Evan smirked. "You're quiet. Too quiet. Are you shy or something?"

"Just thinking," Audrey replied, keeping her tone neutral.

"Well, stop thinking so much." Evan turned and continued walking, motioning for her to follow.

They wound up at a gazebo tucked into a far corner of the property. It might have been picturesque once, but now it was falling apart, the wood warped and the paint peeling. The latticework was missing in places, and vines had claimed the steps leading up to the structure.

"Romantic, huh?" Evan said, leaning against one of the support posts with a sly grin.

"Sure," Audrey said flatly, edging away from him.

Evan reached out, brushing his fingers lightly against her arm. "You're cute, you know. You got a boyfriend?"

Audrey stiffened and stepped back. "No, I'm not dating anyone right now."

Evan chuckled, unconvinced. "Come on. Jimmy, that busboy from The Chowder House, is obsessed with you. Don't tell me you're not into him."

"Jimmy's a friend," Audrey said firmly. "That's it."

Evan's grin widened. "Then what's the problem? I'm right here."

"The problem is I'm not interested," Audrey replied, her voice cool.

Evan's eyes darkened. "You're lying." He stepped closer, too close. His hand moved to her waist, and before she could pull away, he grabbed her wrist.

"Let go," she said sharply.

"Don't act like you're too good for me," he snapped, his grip tightening.

Audrey didn't hesitate. She grabbed his hand, twisting his index finger back just enough to make him yelp in pain and release her.

"Jesus!" Evan snarled, shaking out his hand. "You're such a bitch."

Audrey glared at him, her heart pounding. "Don't touch me again."

Flushed with anger and embarrassment, Evan stalked off, muttering under his breath. Audrey stood there for a moment, catching her breath. When she was sure he wasn't coming back, she turned her attention to the stone wall.

Curiosity gnawed at her. She glanced around to make sure no one was watching, then hopped over the wall onto Chips Hogan's property.

The house was eerily quiet, its windows dark and its yard overgrown. Audrey tried the front door, but it was locked. She circled the house, testing each door and window until she found a bathroom window cracked open. After some maneuvering, she managed to climb inside, landing awkwardly on the tile floor.

The interior was just as she'd expected: empty and lifeless. Furniture was covered with dust, and the air smelled faintly of mildew and abandonment. Audrey wandered through the rooms, feeling a pang of sadness. Chips had been a regular at The Chowder House; ornery or not, he felt like family. Now, the house felt like a shell of the man he'd been.

Eventually, she found herself in a small office. A desk sat in the corner, cluttered with papers and an old computer. Audrey rifled through the documents, her curiosity piqued.

Among the papers, she found a folder labeled LAWSUIT DOCUMENTATION. Inside were plans Chips had been preparing for the lawsuit to force the Barkers to tear down the disputed section of the wall. The case was detailed, complete with surveyor reports and handwritten notes. Audrey frowned. It looked like Chips had been gearing up for a serious fight before his sudden death.

She was about to leave when something else caught her eye—a birthday card propped on the corner of the desk, half-buried under a few loose papers. Audrey slid the stack aside, tugging the card free. The papers fluttered as she did, and she caught sight of handwriting scrawled across the top sheet. Frowning, she gathered them up as well.

She opened the card first, expecting a kind note, but the message inside made her stomach drop.

Scrawled in messy handwriting were threats, detailed and graphic. The writer—Evan—had listed several violent ways to get rid of Chips once and for all. The threats were written in a stream of consciousness, as though Evan had been venting his rage onto the card.

Audrey's hands trembled as she slipped the card, along with the small stack of papers, into her pocket. Before she could process what she'd found, she heard her grandmother calling her name from outside. Heart hammering, she hurried out of the office.

Audrey climbed back out of the bathroom window, brushed herself off, and made her way back to the Barker property just in time to join everyone in the dining room for brunch. The bay windows let in the afternoon light, and the table was set with plates of scrambled eggs, bacon, home fries, and fresh fruit.

Evan was already seated, sulking. Audrey avoided his gaze, quickly sliding into the seat next to Maggie.

"Where were you?" Maggie asked softly, her eyes narrowing.

Audrey reached under the table and slipped the birthday card into her grandmother's lap. Maggie's brow furrowed as she opened it discreetly. Her eyes widened as she read the threats inside, and she gave Audrey a startled look.

Cord, seated across the table, noticed the exchange. "What are you two conspiring about? It always leads to trouble."

Maggie quickly slipped the card into her purse. "Nothing, Cord. Just sharing a little local gossip."

Rhonda entered the room with a tray of freshly baked croissants, cutting off further questioning.

"Everything looks delicious, Mrs. Barker," Audrey said, hoping to steer the conversation.

"Thank you, dear," Rhonda replied with a strained smile.

Phoebe turned to Cord, her voice light and teasing. "I'm never going to live up to my mother's cooking skills."

Cord grinned. "Doesn't matter. I'll do the cooking."

"You're a terrible cook," Audrey joked.

"Then we'll go out!" Cord declared.

Everyone laughed except a sulking Evan, who just rolled his eyes, annoyed.

As the conversation shifted to lighter topics, Audrey couldn't help but notice Evan glaring at her from across the table as he angrily chewed on a piece of bacon. His piercing gaze made her skin crawl, and she quickly looked away.

The tension in the room was palpable. Bert and Rhonda seemed nervous, their smiles forced, and Evan's sour mood loomed over the gathering like a storm cloud. Audrey's mind raced. Could Evan have carried out his threats against Chips in a fit of rage?

She considered the possibility. He could have bought the poison with cash, then planted the deadly nightshade in his pantry to frame him. Evan didn't strike her as someone who thought things through, but he was cunning enough to come up with a plan that might deflect suspicion.

When she glanced at him again, Evan gave her a wink and a chilling smile. Audrey looked away again, her stomach churning.

She'd had enough of Evan Barker for a lifetime.

Chapter Fifteen

Audrey pushed the last bite of her croissant around her plate, trying to appear engrossed in her food. She avoided looking at Evan, whose unrelenting stare had made her skin crawl since brunch began. The sunlight streaming through the bay windows of the Barker dining room felt too bright, exposing every tense line of the faces around the table.

Maggie, ever the diplomat, had offered to help Rhonda clear the dishes, but Rhonda waved her off with a tight smile. "You should relax, Maggie. Have some coffee with Phoebe. She wants to show you the wedding dresses she's been trying on."

Audrey caught the flicker of dread in her grandmother's eyes, though Maggie quickly masked it with a polite nod. "Of course," she said, rising from her chair.

As Maggie followed Phoebe to the sitting room, Audrey made her escape. She pushed back her chair, the legs scraping the floor loudly enough to draw Bert's attention.

"Where's the bathroom?" she asked.

"Upstairs," Bert said, gesturing. "Just down the hall to the right."

Audrey nodded and hurried out of the room, her heart pounding. She couldn't stand being in the same space as Evan any longer. His presence was oppressive, his dark eyes drilling into her with a mix of suspicion and something far more unsettling.

Upstairs, the hall was dimly lit, with faded wallpaper peeling slightly at the edges. Audrey found the bathroom and shut the door behind her, leaning against it with a sigh of relief. She pulled out her phone and texted her best friend, Isabella.

Stuck at this awful brunch with creepy Evan Barker. Can we hang out after your shift?

The response came almost immediately: a party emoji and a thumbs-up.

Audrey smiled faintly and slipped her phone back into her pocket. As she opened the bathroom door, she froze. Phoebe's voice echoed down the hall, her footsteps heavy on the creaking floorboards.

"I know," Phoebe said, exasperated. "It's so embarrassing. They're hosting this brunch for the Holbrooks, and the house looks like it's falling apart."

Audrey edged closer, moving silently toward the sound of Phoebe's voice.

"No, I'm not joking," Phoebe continued. "Their estate is practically a mansion. I swear, I thought about calling off the whole thing."

Phoebe's voice grew fainter as she stepped into a bedroom and shut the door. Audrey hesitated, then crept down the hall. She pressed her ear against the door, straining to hear.

"I miss you too," Phoebe said softly. There was a pause, then her tone shifted, defensive. "That's not fair. I'm not a gold digger."

Audrey's heart quickened.

"Because I love him, that's why," Phoebe snapped. "Look, marrying Cord makes sense, okay? Life will be easier. But who knows? Not all marriages last forever. Maybe one day, when I'm a wealthy divorcee, we can see if the fire's still there. But for now, I can't mess this up. My family needs that plot of land, if not the whole property. And you know we owe back taxes on this place."

Audrey's breath hitched. The Barkers were in financial trouble, and Phoebe's marriage to Cord was her way out.

Before Audrey could retreat, a voice boomed behind her.

"What are you doing sneaking around my sister's bedroom?"

Audrey spun around to see Evan standing at the end of the hall, his expression dark.

"I took a wrong turn coming out of the bathroom," Audrey said quickly, trying to sound nonchalant.

"Yeah, right," Evan said, taking a step closer.

The door to Phoebe's room flew open, and she appeared in the doorway, her phone clutched in her hand. "What's going on?"

Evan pointed at Audrey. "She was eavesdropping."

Phoebe's eyes narrowed as she ended her call. "What did you hear?"

Audrey met her gaze without flinching. "Enough."

A tense silence followed.

"I'm going back downstairs," Audrey said, her voice steady. "I think we're about ready to leave."

She started down the hall, but Evan moved to block her path.

"Excuse me," Audrey said, her tone firm. "I'd like to get by."

Evan didn't budge.

to settle down. Maybe buy a house. I'm starting to think mine's too small. Maybe I'll sign it over to Sandy."

Audrey couldn't help herself. "Are you seriously considering Chips Hogan's place?"

Cord shrugged. "I don't know. Phoebe really likes the property, but we'll see. It depends on what she wants."

Maggie shot Audrey another warning glance, silencing the retort that hovered on her lips.

When they arrived home, the atmosphere shifted. The Holbrook house, with its expansive porch and lush garden, stood in sharp contrast to the weathered Barker property. Maggie led the way inside, her stride purposeful.

"Come with me," she said to Audrey, heading straight for her office.

Audrey followed, her pulse quickening. Once inside, Maggie shut the door firmly and turned to face her.

"Let me see what you found."

Audrey pulled out the pages of legal documents she'd taken from Chips's house. Maggie's expression hardened as she took the birthday card out of her purse and reread the card, her lips pressing into a thin line.

"This is bad," she said. "If Evan wrote this, it's a smoking gun."

"It's more than bad, Nana," Audrey said. "It's evidence that Evan wanted Chips gone. Maybe enough to kill him."

Maggie sighed heavily. "I'll take this to Jill. She won't be happy—it's illegally obtained, after all—but she'll know what to do with it."

"Do you think Phoebe's involved?" Audrey asked.

Maggie hesitated. "It's hard to say. The girl's got dollar signs in her eyes, that's for certain, but whether she'd stoop to something this extreme . . ." She trailed off, her expression conflicted.

Audrey wasn't convinced. "I think they're all in on it. Evan poisoned Chips to get the land, and Phoebe's marrying Cord for the money to buy it."

Maggie nodded slowly, though she looked troubled. "I wouldn't put it past Evan. But Rhonda and Bert? I've known them for years. This doesn't feel like them."

Audrey nodded, her mind still racing. Then, she remembered something. "Hey, I better go. I'm meeting up with Isabella this afternoon." She gave her grandmother a kiss on the cheek and dashed out of the room.

Upstairs, Audrey changed out of her brunch clothes, pulling on jeans and a sweater. As she passed her bedroom window, she heard voices below. She stepped closer, peering out and saw Phoebe standing by her car, her posture casual but her expression anything but. She was talking to Sandy, who had just emerged from the toolshed with a hammer and nails in hand.

Audrey watched as Phoebe leaned toward him, her hand brushing his arm in what was unmistakably a flirtatious gesture. Sandy stiffened, taking a step back, but Phoebe persisted. Her hand moved to his waist, and she tilted her head, saying something Audrey couldn't hear.

Sandy's face twisted in revulsion. He removed Phoebe's hand with deliberate care and said something sharp, his tone cutting. Then he turned and stormed back toward the house, leaving Phoebe standing alone, her expression unreadable.

Audrey didn't wait. She ran downstairs and out the door, catching up to Sandy as he climbed a ladder to fix a sagging shutter.

"What was that about?" Audrey demanded, planting her hands on her hips.

"Nothing," Sandy muttered, hammering a nail into place.

"It didn't look like nothing," Audrey pressed. "She was all over you."

Sandy sighed, setting down the hammer. "You shouldn't have been spying."

"I wasn't spying. I saw it from my window," Audrey shot back. "Are you going to tell Cord?"

Sandy hesitated, his gaze dropping to the ground. "What good would it do? He's in love with her. He'll believe whatever she tells him."

"You don't know that," Audrey argued. "Cord trusts you."

Sandy shook his head. "I'm staying out of it, Audrey. Maybe you should too."

When Audrey returned inside, Phoebe was in the sitting room with Cord and Maggie.

"I know we just spent the whole morning together," Phoebe said, her voice strained, "but there's something I forgot to talk to Audrey about. It's urgent."

Cord and Maggie exchanged surprised looks, and Audrey felt her stomach drop.

"Sure," Audrey said cautiously. "Let's take a walk."

Outside, the air was crisp, and Phoebe's heels clicked against the stone path as they walked in silence.

"I wanted to apologize," Phoebe began, her tone soft.

"For what?" Audrey asked.

"For my brother," Phoebe said, her voice trembling. "I know he can be . . . difficult. He's always been that way, and I thought he'd grow out of it, but so far he hasn't."

Audrey stopped, turning to face her. "Do you think he's dangerous?"

Phoebe hesitated. "No. I mean, I don't think so. But I can't say for sure."

"Phoebe, I found the birthday card he gave Chips,"

Audrey said bluntly. "The threats. The violence. It's not normal."

Phoebe's eyes widened, but she quickly regained her composure. "Evan loves to cause drama. He hated Chips, sure, but he wouldn't actually hurt anyone. He just . . . likes to push buttons."

Audrey frowned. "You really expect me to believe that?"

Phoebe sighed. "Look, whatever Evan does, it has nothing to do with me. I can't control him, and it's not fair to judge me based on his actions."

"Is that why you're marrying Cord?" Audrey asked sharply.

Phoebe's face twisted with hurt. "No! I love Cord. I'm not a gold digger, Audrey. I swear."

Audrey folded her arms, unconvinced.

This was the second time in less than an hour she had heard Phoebe deny she was a gold digger.

Phoebe stepped closer, her voice pleading. "Please don't tell Cord about the card. Or my ex. Yes, we talk sometimes, but it's innocent. I swear. Audrey, I love Cord with all my heart, and I don't want to lose him."

Audrey stared at her, trying to discern the truth. Phoebe's eyes shimmered with unshed tears, and for a moment, she almost believed her.

"Will you tell him?" Phoebe asked quietly.

"I don't know," Audrey admitted.

Phoebe nodded, biting her lip. "One more thing," she said. "Will you be one of my bridesmaids?"

Audrey blinked, caught off guard.

Phoebe smiled faintly. "Think about it, okay? Tell Cord I'll call him later." Then she turned and walked to her car, leaving Audrey standing alone.

When Audrey returned to the sitting room, Cord was waiting, his expression curious.

"What did Phoebe want?" he asked.

Audrey hesitated, the words heavy on her tongue. Finally, she swallowed hard. "She, uh, she asked me to be a bridesmaid."

Cord's face lit up, and Maggie's jaw dropped, her shock evident.

Chapter Sixteen

The warm glow of The Blue Heron spilled onto the gravel parking lot as Jill parked her car. She took a moment to adjust her jacket and smooth her hair, eyeing the upscale restaurant's inviting windows. Her brother Oliver and his wife, Katie, had insisted on this dinner, and she had reluctantly agreed, though something about their eagerness had set her on edge.

Inside, the restaurant buzzed with low murmurs and the clinking of glasses. Jill spotted Oliver and Katie at a corner table. She pasted on a smile and made her way over. Her suspicion deepened when she noticed four place settings.

Katie waved enthusiastically as Jill approached. "There you are! We were beginning to think you'd changed your mind."

Jill slid into her seat, her brow furrowed. "Why are there four settings?"

"I ordered you wine," Katie said brightly, sidestepping the question. "19 Crimes Red Blend. Your favorite, right?"

Oliver chuckled. "Nineteen crimes? Is that how many cases you've solved this week?"

Jill grimaced. "No, that's probably the number of cases

I've drank. It's been a stressful week. I'm not trying to be ironic. I just like the taste."

Katie nodded in agreement. "Yes, it's perfect. As long as it's red. Nobody ever fell in love over white wine."

Jill arched an eyebrow. "Who am I falling in love with?"

Katie's answer was cut off by the arrival of a familiar voice. "Sorry to keep you waiting," Mark Haskell said, slipping into the seat across from Jill. His amusement was evident in his smile, though he kept his tone neutral. "Had to step away for a moment to take a call."

Jill's stomach sank as realization dawned.

A blind date.

Of course, they'd set her up on a blind date—with the man she was already secretly seeing.

Katie beamed. "Mark, I thought you'd be perfect for Jill. She deserves someone great."

"Very kind of you to say," Mark replied smoothly, his gaze flicking to Jill.

Jill forced a friendly smile. "What a surprise."

It wasn't going to be easy pretending they barely knew each other when they'd been hooking up for months.

It had started late one night in the DA's office—just the two of them, combing through case files and arguing over strategy. A shared takeout container balanced on a stack of depositions, a laugh that came too easily, lingering a beat too long. Then a brush of hands, a look neither of them could quite dismiss. One minute they were trading barbs about witness credibility—the next, she was perched on the edge of his desk and they weren't talking anymore.

The first course arrived—clam chowder served in delicate porcelain bowls. Jill stirred hers absently, painfully aware of Oliver and Katie's watchful eyes as she and Mark made small talk.

"So, Jill," Mark said, his tone light, "how's work been treating you?"

"Busy," Jill replied curtly.

Oliver leaned forward, grinning. "She's had her hands full with the Chips Hogan case because she never should have arrested Waldo Duggan. He didn't do it. He's an innocent man."

"Oliver . . ." Katie warned.

"What? It's just my opinion."

"You're also Duggan's lawyer." Jill sighed.

"I understand your family stands behind Duggan—" Mark started to say.

"Not all of us!" Jill interjected.

Mark smiled faintly but didn't comment further. As the county DA, he knew far more about both cases than he could say, especially in front of Oliver, one of the defense attorneys he often sparred with in court. "I can't discuss my case with you, Oliver, but you already know that. You're just fishing for information about my prosecution strategy. But I will say this. I wouldn't have filed charges if I didn't think I could get a conviction."

"Enough about Waldo Duggan, please," Katie begged.

Oliver squeezed his wife's hand. "Yes, dear. Let's discuss Clyde Peterson. His trial starts next week." He turned to Mark. "Do you honestly think you have enough evidence to sway a jury beyond a reasonable doubt?"

"I'm more confident about that case than Duggan's, to be honest with you, Oliver. Clyde Peterson has a rap sheet longer than a Maine winter, with offenses ranging from petty theft to assault and everything in between."

"Can't argue with that," Oliver admitted. "He's no Boy Scout."

Katie interjected sharply. "Stop. No more shop talk.

This dinner is about Mark and Jill getting to know each other, not hashing out cases."

Mark's eyes twinkled with suppressed laughter as he looked at Jill. "You heard her. This is about us. So tell me. Who is the real Jill Holbrook?"

She bit her lip, unsure if she wanted to strangle him or burst out laughing herself.

Jill sat up straight as Mark started to play footsies under the table.

She'd kill him later.

By the time the entrees arrived, Jill found herself relaxing slightly. Mark was good at steering the conversation into safer waters, and despite her initial annoyance, she couldn't deny he had a knack for putting people at ease.

After dessert—crème brûlée that Katie declared the best she'd ever had—Jill excused herself to the restroom.

In the bright, quiet space, Jill splashed water on her face, then dabbed it dry with a towel. She wasn't sure whether to feel irritated or touched by her family's meddling.

The door opened, and Katie stepped inside, her expression hesitant. "Did we overstep?"

Jill shook her head. "No, Katie. I know you're just trying to help. But I'm perfectly capable of finding my own boyfriend."

Katie smiled, relaxing slightly. "I just want you to be happy, Jill. After everything Sam put you through . . . leaving you to raise Audrey on your own, then starting a whole new family in Portland . . ."

Jill's jaw tightened. "Katie—"

"I know it's not my place," Katie said quickly, "but you

deserve to be happy. Mark's a great guy. And he's cute, don't you think?"

Jill chuckled despite herself. "Yeah, he's cute."

Katie smiled. "Good. Then maybe this isn't the worst idea we've ever had?"

Jill shook her head but didn't argue.

"But if it's not in the cards for you and the hot prosecutor, there's still the gorgeous new dentist in town I've been raving about. I hear he's single."

"Katie . . ."

"Never mind. We should see how this plays out first. Now come on. Let's finish this night on a high note.

Jill smoothed her blouse, took a deep breath, and followed Katie back to the table.

Outside, the night air was crisp and cool. Oliver and Katie stood by the valet station, practically glowing with self-congratulation.

"C'mon, admit it. We nailed it," Oliver said, elbowing Jill as she approached. "You and Mark hit it off, didn't you?"

Katie rolled her eyes and grabbed his arm. "Leave her alone, Oliver. Let's go before you ruin it."

"Fine, fine," Oliver said with a grin. "But I expect an update. Maybe a second date?"

Katie tugged him toward their car, waving cheerfully as they left.

Once they were gone, Mark turned to Jill, his smile playful. "Well, that was fun."

Jill crossed her arms. "You're enjoying this way too much."

"Come on," Mark teased. "It was like a first date on *The Bachelor*. Except no roses. Or cameras."

She smirked. "Or actual interest in being on a date."

Mark leaned closer, his tone softening. "Speak for yourself. I enjoyed playing my part. And we don't need roses—we can go straight to the fantasy suite. My place?"

Jill opened her mouth to respond, but her phone buzzed. She glanced at the screen and frowned. "It's the station. Another body."

Mark's smile faded. "Duty calls?"

She nodded. "Sorry."

The pier was alive with activity when Jill arrived. Red and blue lights flashed against the dark water, and the hum of voices filled the air.

Mason stood near the edge of the dock, shivering in a tank top and gym shorts.

Jill strode over, her heels clicking sharply. "Mason, what are you wearing?"

He looked sheepish. "My uniform's at the dry cleaners. I grabbed breakfast burritos to go this morning—messy ones. Got salsa all over my shirt."

She shrugged off her jacket and handed it to him. "Here. You're freezing."

He hesitated. "You're all dressed up. Was this a date?"

She fixed him with a glare. "We had an agreement. No questions about my personal life."

Mason slipped on the jacket. "Sorry."

He gestured toward the water. "Two boys were horsing around. One threw the other's cap in, and when they tried to fish it out, they saw the body."

Jill moved closer, where the CSI team had pulled the body from the water. Her breath caught as she recognized the face.

"Griffin Mead," she said softly.

Mason frowned. "Who's he?"

"Chips Hogan's old business partner," Jill said. "They had a falling-out years ago."

Before she could elaborate, a familiar voice rang out. "Jill!"

She turned to see Maggie, bundled in a thick coat, hurrying toward her.

"Mother." Jill groaned. "What are you doing here?"

"I heard it on the scanner," Maggie said, her face lined with concern. "What happened?"

Jill sighed. "This is a crime scene. You need to stay back behind the yellow tape."

Maggie glanced around. "What yellow tape?"

Jill glared at Mason. "The tape Mason is going to put up right now."

Mason blinked. "Oh. Right. On it."

As Mason scampered off, Maggie crossed her arms. "Don't dismiss this, Jill. Chips is dead, and now Griffin? That's no coincidence."

"For all we know," Jill countered, "it could be an accidental drowning. Griffin wasn't exactly known for moderation. He could've had too much to drink at the Thirsty Gull and fallen in."

Maggie shook her head. "You don't believe that any more than I do."

Jill turned back to the body, her mother's words echoing in her mind. She couldn't deny it—Griffin's death felt like more than just a tragic accident.

Chapter Seventeen

Audrey wove through The Chowder House restaurant with practiced ease, balancing trays laden with plates of pancakes and scrambled eggs while tossing out quick smiles to regulars. Isabella was at the coffee station, her ponytail bouncing as she poured refill after refill. Although relatively busy, there were half as many customers seated today as during a typical breakfast rush. Ethel's business had certainly taken a hit from the chowder scandal.

The door jingled, and Audrey glanced up to see Evan Barker stroll in, wearing that insufferable smirk that set her teeth on edge. He approached Ethel at the hostess stand with his hands in his pockets, rocking back on his heels like he owned the place.

"Good morning, Ethel," he said. "Seat me in Audrey's section, would you?"

Ethel arched an unimpressed brow. "You sure about that, honey? She's very busy, you might have to wait a bit."

Evan grinned. "That's all right. I'm a patient man."

Audrey's stomach sank as Ethel led him to a table near the window. She sighed and steeled herself, marching over to his table with her notepad in hand. "What can I get you?"

"Actually," Evan said, leaning back in his chair and drumming his fingers on the table, "I was hoping we could talk. I feel like we got off on the wrong foot the other day."

Audrey pressed her lips together. "The special is a Western omelet with hash browns and your choice of toast, bagel, or blueberry muffin. Want that, or should I give you more time?"

Evan's grin widened, and she swore he was enjoying this. "Hmm, I'm not sure. What do you recommend?"

"I recommend deciding before lunch," she snapped. "Look, I don't have time for small talk. If you want to eat, order. If you want to chat, find someone else."

"Wow," he said, holding up his hands in mock surrender. "I'm just trying to be friendly."

"I'll give you more time to decide," Audrey snapped, rolling her eyes and walking off, muttering to Isabella, "Tag, you're it. I'm taking my break."

Isabella groaned but took over the table, leaving Audrey to retreat to the break room just off the kitchen. She flopped into a chair, rubbing her temples. A few minutes later, Ethel peeked in.

"What's up, kiddo?" Ethel asked. "You're not usually this ruffled."

Audrey let out a long sigh. "It's Evan. He's . . . I don't know. He gives me the willies. The way he looks at me, toys with me, it's like he's up to something."

Ethel folded her arms. "You know we've got that sign by the door: WE RESERVE THE RIGHT TO REFUSE SERVICE TO ANYONE. Want me to toss his butt to the curb?"

Audrey shook her head. "No. It'll probably just make things worse."

After a few minutes, Audrey steeled herself and returned to the floor, determined to power through. She avoided

Evan's table, letting Isabella handle him, but her resolve wavered when Isabella stormed into the kitchen, fuming.

"That guy is impossible!" Isabella hissed. "He's complained about everything—the coffee's cold, there's a smudge on his fork, and he's run me ragged with his 'special requests.' "

Audrey sighed. "I'll deal with him."

Walking over to Evan's table, Audrey slapped the check down in front of him. "You're done."

Evan raised an eyebrow. "How do you know I'm done eating?"

"Because I said so," Audrey shot back. "I took the coffee off your bill, by the way. You're welcome."

Evan smirked, pulling a twenty from his wallet and tossing it on the table. "Keep the change."

Audrey glanced at the bill—$19.17. A wave of irritation surged through her, but she held her tongue. "Have a nice day," she said curtly, turning on her heel.

On his way out, Evan paused by Ethel. "You might want to warn your waitresses about their attitude."

Ethel's eyes narrowed. "I like my girls just the way they are. Now get lost."

The rest of the shift passed without incident, but when Audrey stepped out into the alley to take a breather, she froze. Evan was leaning against the wall, his arms crossed like he'd been waiting for her.

"What do you want?" Audrey demanded, her voice sharp.

Evan pushed off the wall and stepped closer, his expression dark. "I know you've been poking around about Chips's murder. And now you're dragging my family into it. You need to back off."

Audrey crossed her arms, standing her ground. "Why

would my questions bother you unless you had something to hide?"

Evan's face twisted in anger. "You think you're so clever, don't you? The Barkers have weathered plenty of suspicion over the years. Whatever you think you know, it's nothing. Just leave my parents out of it."

Suspicion?

Regarding what?

Audrey's mind raced.

What did he mean by that?

"Maybe it's not your parents I'm interested in," she said, narrowing her eyes. "Maybe it's you."

Evan's jaw clenched, and he took a step closer, invading her space. "You think you're smart, don't you? The Barkers have dealt with a lot worse than some nosy little waitress. You don't scare me."

"I'm not trying to scare you," Audrey shot back.

Evan's face twisted with fury, and he took another step forward, forcing her to take a step back. "You have no idea who you're messing with," he hissed.

Before Audrey could respond, the back door swung open, and Jimmy stepped out with a stuffed plastic garbage bag slung over his shoulder. He paused, taking in the tense scene, and his expression darkened.

"Hey," Jimmy said, tossing the bag into the dumpster. "Is everything okay here?"

Evan turned to Jimmy, his lip curling. "Stay out of this, kid."

Jimmy didn't flinch. "I was talking to Audrey."

Evan stepped toward him, puffing himself up. "You think you can take me? I was a college wrestler. A boxer. You're just some nobody busboy."

Audrey moved between them, placing a hand on Jimmy's chest. "Jimmy, it's fine. He's not worth it."

But Jimmy didn't back down. "If he's bothering you, it's worth it."

Evan let out a bark of laughter. "You want to have a go? Let's go."

Jimmy stepped forward, and Evan gave him a shove. Audrey grabbed Jimmy's arm, trying to pull him back, but he shook his head. "I'm fine, Audrey."

"Back off, Evan," Audrey said firmly. "Or I'm calling the cops."

For a moment, Evan looked ready to throw a punch, but something in Jimmy's steady gaze made him pause. He huffed, muttered a curse, and backed away.

"This isn't over," Evan said, pointing a finger at Audrey before stalking off.

Jimmy watched him go before turning to Audrey. "You okay?"

Audrey managed a shaky smile. "Thanks. I don't know what I would've done if you hadn't shown up."

Jimmy hesitated. "Do you, uh, maybe want to grab a coffee or something?"

Audrey gave him a grateful smile but shook her head. "Rain check? I've got somewhere I need to be."

At the library, Audrey approached the front desk, where Mrs. Whishaw was rearranging a stack of books. The librarian's booming voice filled the room. "Well, hello there, Audrey! What can I do for you?"

Audrey winced at the volume, and she responded in a whisper. "I need access to the *Halibut Cove Chronicle* archives. Digital files, if you have them."

Mrs. Whishaw clomped around the desk with all the subtlety of a marching band. "Follow me! Oh, and Betty!" She turned and hollered across the room at a woman whispering to her friend at a reading table. "This is a library! Please keep it down!"

Audrey stifled a laugh as Mrs. Whishaw led her to a computer and set her up with the database. "Happy digging!" she said, her voice echoing as she stomped away.

Once she was in the *Chronicle* files full of back issues going back decades, Audrey typed Barker into the search bar, and dozens of results popped up. Bert Barker's grandfather pulled over for a broken taillight in the Police Beat column. A great-aunt called about a prowler, which turned out to be her cat knocking over the Christmas tree. A second cousin who got a DUI while home from Bowdoin College. Nothing earth-shattering. But as Audrey continued to scroll, one headline from the 1970s caught her eye: YOUNG LOCAL, BERT BARKER, EYED IN DISAPPEARANCE OF HALIBUT COVE MAN. The byline was Lou Grady, and as Audrey read through the article, her heart raced. The story detailed the disappearance of Rhonda Barker's abusive ex-boyfriend, with suspicion falling on Bert Barker, who at the time was Rhonda's current boyfriend, after a violent confrontation. A potential witness, Griffin Mead, a teenager working for Rhonda's father at the time, was reportedly interviewed but had claimed to know nothing.

Audrey needed more. She jotted down notes and headed to the *Chronicle* office, where she found Lou Grady, still behind his desk, pecking away at his keyboard.

"Lou," she said, stepping into his cluttered office. "Got a minute?"

Lou looked up, his eyes lighting up at the sight of her. "Audrey, come on in! What's this about?"

Audrey explained what she'd found, and Lou leaned back in his chair, a nostalgic smile spreading across his face. "Ah, the Barker story. That was my first big scoop. I was fresh out of the journalism program at University of Maine Orono, eager to make my mark. The whole town was buzzing about Rhonda's ex-boyfriend vanishing into thin air."

"What do you remember about it?" Audrey asked, leaning forward.

Lou stroked his chin. "I remember interviewing Griffin Mead. He was just a kid, working odd jobs for Rhonda's father. Said he didn't know anything, but I always had my doubts. The cops never found a body, so the case went cold. But there were always whispers about what might've happened."

Audrey's mind spun. If Griffin had known something back then, could that knowledge have put him in danger now? And what about Chips? What had he stumbled onto that suddenly made him a target?

Lou leaned forward, his eyes gleaming. "You think this ties back to Chips's murder?"

"I don't know," Audrey admitted. "But I'm starting to think the Barkers have more skeletons in their closet than a reality star's deleted Twitter history."

Lou grinned. "Sounds like you've got yourself a story. Keep me posted, will you?"

Audrey nodded, her thoughts racing as she left. She didn't have all the pieces yet, but one thing was clear: she was getting closer to the truth—and the Barkers weren't going to like it.

Chapter Eighteen

The bridal shop in Halibut Cove was the epitome of small-town charm, with lace curtains, shelves of delicate tiaras, and soft classical music playing in the background. Maggie and Audrey stepped through the door, the little bell above jingling to announce their arrival. Phoebe Barker, standing on a raised platform in a sea of ivory satin, caught sight of them in the mirror and gasped.

"You came!" she exclaimed, turning toward them with an excited smile. She turned and whispered loudly to her mother, everyone in the shop overhearing, "I didn't think they liked me!"

Rhonda looked equally relieved. "It's so nice to see you both here. Phoebe's been a wreck over this dress. We finally chose one, but—"

"It's a disaster!" Phoebe interrupted, tugging at the too-tight bodice with a dramatic groan.

Lesley, the shop's owner, bustled over, tape measure slung over her shoulder and a pin cushion strapped to her wrist. "Phoebe, stop pulling at it! You'll stretch the fabric. Let me take a look." She crouched and began examining the dress, pinning a section of the dress with expert hands.

"A few alterations, and this dress will be perfect. Trust me, you'll be the picture of elegance."

Phoebe sighed, but a flicker of hope crossed her face. "You really think so?"

"I know so," Lesley said confidently, patting her on the arm.

"You look so gorgeous already!" Audrey chimed in, knowing she was laying it on a bit too thick.

Phoebe didn't seem to care. "Oh, thank you!"

The bell jingled again, and all eyes turned as Dr. Bradley Comstock, the town's handsome new dentist, stepped into the shop. His athletic build and easy smile were enough to make half the women in Halibut Cove swoon, even without the perfectly coiffed brown hair and friendly, boyish smile. Phoebe immediately perked up at the sight of him.

Lesley brightened. "Dr. Comstock! What brings you here today?"

Bradley looked slightly sheepish. "I need a birthday gift for my receptionist, Melanie, and I'm a bit lost. I'm not great at picking out clothes."

Lesley nodded knowingly. "Melanie Blaisdell? Not to worry, I've got just the thing. She tried on a blouse last week and loved it, but she's been waiting for her next paycheck to pick it up. I'll go grab it from the back." She disappeared into the stockroom.

Phoebe wasted no time sidling up to the dentist, extending her hand. "Hi, I'm Phoebe Barker. I don't think we've met yet."

Audrey leaned closer to Maggie, whispering, "Is it just me, or is it hilarious that she's flirting with another man while wearing a wedding dress?"

"Peak Phoebe," Maggie replied with a smirk.

Phoebe dragged Dr. Comstock over to Rhonda. "This is my mother, Rhonda Barker."

Dr. Comstock smiled and shook her hand. "Pleasure to meet you, Mrs. Barker."

When he saw Maggie, recognition dawned on his face.

"Mrs. Holbrook! I've been meaning to find you and introduce myself ever since I moved to town. I hear you're the one to know in Halibut Cove."

Maggie waved a dismissive hand. "My reputation is grossly exaggerated."

Audrey chimed in, "I have an appointment with you tomorrow, Dr. Comstock."

Bradley flashed a perfect smile. "Yes, I know. Your sister-in-law, Katie, recommended me. She's been my greatest promoter. But honestly I think it's because of the Starbucks gift card I hand out for referrals."

They all laughed.

"Well, Audrey, I'm looking forward to it. And what about you, Mrs. Holbrook? Can I count on seeing you in my office anytime soon?"

Maggie sighed theatrically. "I'm afraid I'm going to have to stay loyal to my dentist of over fifty years, Dr. Lawry."

"I hear he's retiring and running off to Florida," Phoebe interjected. "Can't compete with the new blood."

Maggie frowned. "I didn't hear that." She turned to Bradley. "Then I suppose I'll be in touch—eventually."

Lesley returned with a neatly wrapped package. Bradley paid and waved goodbye, promising to see Audrey the next day.

Phoebe eventually flounced off to the dressing room to peel out of the gown. When she emerged, fully dressed again, she thrust the crumpled dress at Lesley with a huff.

"Work your magic, Lesley," she pleaded. "I need this to be perfect."

With Phoebe out of earshot, Maggie turned to Rhonda, steering the conversation carefully. "Did you hear about poor Griffin Mead?"

Rhonda nodded solemnly. "Yes, such a tragedy. Poor man. I remember him from when I was young. Always polite, always kept to himself."

Maggie leaned in just a touch. "He worked for your father back then, didn't he?"

A flicker crossed Rhonda's face. "Yes. For a time. I wouldn't say we were close." She smoothed an invisible wrinkle from her skirt. "Best to leave the past where it belongs."

Before Maggie could press further, Phoebe returned to earshot and jumped right in. "If you're asking whether Mom and Griffin were ever a thing—no way. She only had eyes for Billy what's-his-name back then. From what I've heard, he was awful—always belittling her and calling her stupid. Then she started seeing Dad, and that's when the gossip started. When Billy disappeared in the seventies, people whispered that Dad had something to do with it. My mom never talks about any of it, but I've heard the stories."

Rhonda's shoulders stiffened, her gaze dropping to the floor as if Phoebe had spoken out of turn. "Bert was just a scared kid—he couldn't have done anything like that. The truth was, Billy left Halibut Cove to start over. He'd already been in jail for his temper. Me, Bert, my father, we were all like, 'Good riddance!' "

Maggie felt a chill run through her. Old rumors had a way of lingering in small towns, twisting with each retelling, but she couldn't ignore the detail—Bert Barker's name tied to a disappearance decades earlier. Whether there was truth to it or not, it was another shadow hanging over the Barker family.

* * *

Later that day, Maggie and Audrey parked outside the mail center in the next town, ready for a stakeout. Armed with snacks and thermoses of coffee, they kept their eyes peeled for anyone approaching the PO box linked to the nightshade shipment.

Hours passed with little action. Maggie amused herself by pointing out pedestrians.

"Look, it's Dorothy from bridge night," she said, nudging Audrey. "Bet she's sneaking chocolate again. And with her diabetes . . ."

Audrey groaned. "Focus, Nana."

Their patience was rewarded when finally, after two and a half hours, a teenager on a shiny new motorcycle pulled up and went straight to the box in question. Neither Maggie nor Audrey recognized him, but he clearly had a purpose. They followed him as he roared off, Maggie's lead foot turning the quiet stakeout into a hair-raising chase.

"Nana, slow down!" Audrey yelled, gripping the dashboard.

"This car has more get-up-and-go than you think," Maggie replied, a gleam in her eye as she took a sharp turn.

"You're going to kill us before we figure out who he is!"

"Relax, I've got this," Maggie said, narrowly avoiding a parked car.

They finally followed the teen to a ramshackle house on the outskirts of town. A burly man stepped out onto the porch as the boy parked his motorcycle in the driveway.

"Troy, move that bike into the garage!" the man barked.

Maggie squinted. "That's Kurt Foley. Trouble, with a capital *T*."

She got out of the car, plastering on her most charming smile. "Kurt! Long time no see."

Kurt gave her a wary look. "Maggie Holbrook. What brings you all the way out here?"

"Staying out of trouble, Kurt?"

Kurt smirked. "That wouldn't be any fun now, would it?"

Maggie chuckled. "Fair enough. I couldn't help but notice your son picking up mail at a PO box over in Hadley Point. There's been talk about nightshade being shipped to that address."

Kurt's expression darkened, his posture stiffening. "So?"

Audrey jumped in. "You've got a perfectly lovely mailbox at the end of your driveway. Why do you need the PO box?"

"That's my business," Kurt said gruffly. "I don't always want people knowing where I live."

Troy came out of the garage, wiping his hands on a rag.

Maggie gestured to the shiny motorcycle. "That's a nice bike. Did your dad buy it for you?"

Troy shook his head. "No, I earned it by mowing lawns over the summer. And working for my uncle, running errands."

"Your uncle?" Audrey asked.

Before Troy could answer, Kurt cut him off. "Enough, Troy. Go inside."

Troy hesitated but obeyed, leaving Maggie and Audrey alone with Kurt.

"If the cops have questions, let them come out here," Kurt said, his tone defensive.

At that moment, a woman appeared in the doorway. "Supper's ready!" she called. Then, seeing Maggie, her face lit up. "Oh my word, Maggie! What a surprise."

"Midge!" Maggie said warmly. "It's been ages."

"How is everyone?"

"Fine, fine."

"I hear Cord's getting married."

"Surprised us all."

Audrey's brow furrowed. "You're Clyde Peterson's sister, aren't you?"

Maggie's eyes narrowed as realization struck. She turned back to Kurt. "Your son mentioned his uncle. Uncle Clyde, perhaps?"

Kurt's expression hardened. "You're barking up the wrong tree, Maggie."

But Maggie wasn't so sure.

Chapter Nineteen

Audrey stepped into Dr. Bradley Comstock's dental office. The walls were painted a soft coastal blue, with framed photos of lighthouses and boats lining them. It was warm, inviting—almost enough to distract from the fact that she was about to willingly sit in a chair and have someone prod around in her mouth. She tried to push aside the memory of Katie gushing about how "sexy" the new dentist was—Katie had gone as far as claiming he could make a root canal enjoyable. Audrey rolled her eyes at the thought, but as Melanie, the receptionist, called her name with a cheerful wave, she was struck by how everyone in the office seemed downright delighted to be there.

Melanie greeted her at the counter. "Audrey! So good to see you! How's your grandmother doing?"

"She's great," Audrey said, handing over the clipboard of completed forms. "Settling in here okay?"

Melanie's face lit up. "Absolutely. Dr. Comstock is a dream to work for. Kind, patient, and—well, let's just say there's never a dull moment with someone so . . . I was going to say charming, but why not just say it, so hot!"

Audrey laughed softly, thinking Katie wasn't the only one who'd been captivated. "Sounds like you love it here."

"I do," Melanie said, lowering her voice conspiratorially. "And you'll love him, too. Trust me."

Audrey followed Melanie back to the treatment room, where Dr. Comstock was waiting. When he turned and flashed her that dazzling smile, Audrey mentally cursed Katie for putting the idea in her head.

He *was* handsome.

Annoyingly so.

"Ah, Audrey," he said, extending a hand. "Maggie Holbrook's granddaughter, right? We met at the bridal shop."

"That's right," Audrey said, shaking his hand before settling into the chair. "You have a good memory."

He chuckled, snapping on a pair of gloves. "Hard to forget the Holbrooks. Your family seems to be the heart of Halibut Cove—connected to just about everyone."

Audrey smiled, but her thoughts were already turning over. "Well, small-town life, you know. Everyone knows everyone else's business."

"True enough," he said, adjusting the overhead light. "I have to admit, I was a little apprehensive about moving here. I thought Halibut Cove would be sleepy, quiet—a safe place to settle down. I didn't expect to walk straight into a murder investigation."

Audrey tilted her head. "I know. I can't believe someone around here deliberately poisoned Chips Hogan. It's got everyone on edge. Anymore suspicious deaths and they could rename this town Cabot Cove."

Dr. Comstock looked puzzled. "Cabot Cove?"

"*Murder, She Wrote*? Jessica Fletcher? Never mind."

Dr. Comstock nodded and smiled, leaning forward to begin his work. "Open wide for me."

As he scraped at her teeth with precision, Audrey tried not to squirm. He was thorough but surprisingly gentle, the sharp tools clicking against her teeth with expert rhythm. When he picked up a small mirror to inspect his work, he glanced at her. "Does that feel all right?"

Audrey mumbled a response, and he set the tools down to rinse her mouth with the water tube, holding the suction close so it wouldn't overflow. "Spit into the cup for me."

She obeyed, wiping her mouth with a tissue. "So, do you usually handle cleanings yourself? Or do you have a dental hygienist?"

He grinned as he picked up the polishing tool. "I like to do the first cleaning for new patients. Helps me get to know their teeth."

Audrey gave him a skeptical look. "That's a bit unusual."

"Maybe," he said, the whir of the polisher filling the room for a moment. "But I figure, if you're going to trust me with your smile, I should at least take a good look myself."

Audrey wasn't sure how to respond to that. Instead, she let him finish polishing before he rinsed her mouth again, his movements careful and efficient. He leaned back, setting the tools aside, and said, "All done. Your teeth look great. You do have a loose filling that should be fixed at some point, but it's not an immediate concern."

"Thanks," Audrey said, sitting up in the chair.

"So, speaking of suspicious deaths, how much do you know about the old man who drowned recently?" Dr. Comstock said, his tone casual as he pulled off his gloves. "There's a lot of buzz that his death might not have been an accident."

Audrey frowned. "Griffin? I thought the police ruled it a drunken accident."

"Maybe," he said, tossing the gloves into the trash. "But I've heard a few of my patients talking. You know how rumors spread."

Audrey narrowed her eyes slightly but said nothing.

Then he added, "Your grandfather—Wes Holbrook. Is he still around?"

Audrey blinked, caught off guard. "No, he passed away a few years ago. Why do you ask?"

"I'd heard of him," Dr. Comstock said, almost too casually. "He was well-regarded, wasn't he?"

"He was a great man," Audrey said. "But I didn't think anyone outside Halibut Cove would know about him."

He shrugged, giving her that charming smile again. "I've heard his name mentioned a few times since I got here. I guess small towns have long memories. Funny thing, though—my family spent some time up this way years back. Maybe that's why the name stuck with me."

Before Audrey could reply, her phone buzzed. She pulled it from her pocket and saw a text from Maggie.

Courthouse. Clyde's trial. You'll want to see this.

The courthouse was already bustling with activity when Audrey arrived, finding Maggie waiting on the steps. Maggie grabbed her arm and hustled her inside.

"Hurry up," Maggie said. "Oliver's in there putting on quite a show."

Inside the courtroom, they slipped into the gallery. Clyde Peterson sat at the defense table, arms crossed and scowling, while Oliver stood in front of a witness, his tone confident and his movements animated.

"So, Mr. Harper," Oliver said, addressing the wiry man on the stand. "You're saying Clyde Peterson wasn't the aggressor?"

"That's right," Harper said, nodding emphatically. "Clyde was minding his own business, and the other guy came at him."

Mark Haskell, seated at the prosecution table, stood abruptly. "Objection, Your Honor. Speculation."

Judge Baxley, seated behind the bench, gave Oliver a pointed look. "Mr. Holbrook, rephrase your question."

"Of course, Your Honor," Oliver said smoothly. "Mr. Harper, did you see Clyde Peterson throw the first punch?"

"No, I didn't," Harper replied.

"And what did you see him do?" Oliver asked.

"He tried to back off," Harper said. "But the other guy kept coming at him . . ."

"So Clyde had no choice but to defend himself," Oliver suggested.

Mark stood again. "Objection. Leading the witness."

"Sustained," Judge Baxley said, her tone sharp. "Mr. Holbrook, stick to the facts."

Oliver raised his hands in mock surrender. "I'll do my best, Your Honor."

The questioning continued, with Oliver poking holes in the prosecution's case while Mark Haskell objected when necessary.

Finally, Judge Baxley banged her gavel. "We'll adjourn for lunch. Court will reconvene at one."

As the courtroom emptied, Maggie nudged Audrey. "Let's grab some sandwiches and crash Oliver's meeting with Clyde."

They found Oliver in a private meeting room, going over notes with Clyde. Maggie strode in with a bag of deli sandwiches, earning an exasperated look from her son.

"Mom, this is a private meeting," Oliver said.

"Nonsense," Maggie replied, setting the sandwiches down. "You need to eat, don't you?"

Audrey stifled a laugh as Clyde scowled, eyeing the sandwiches suspiciously. "What do you want, Mrs. Holbrook?"

"I want answers," Maggie said, sitting down. "Did you hire your nephew Troy to pick up a package of deadly nightshade in Hadley Point?"

Clyde leaned back, crossing his arms. "What are you talking about?"

"We know a package of nightshade was shipped to a PO box connected to your family," Maggie said. "And now Chips Hogan is dead from ingesting it."

Clyde smirked. "You've got nothing."

"If not you, who was Troy working for? Who did he deliver that package to?"

"How the hell am I supposed to know?"

Audrey could tell he was lying.

He knew way more than he was letting on.

"Look, Mrs. Holbrook, I'm a jack-of-all-trades. I've done odd jobs for just about everyone in this town. If someone's willing to pay, I'll provide a service. Whatever that may be."

Maggie's eyes narrowed. "Even murder?"

"Now you're out of line," Clyde seethed.

Oliver frowned. "Mom, we're in the middle of a trial here. Now is not the time for this."

Maggie was undeterred. "I think someone hired you to order that nightshade, and you had your nephew pick it up for you and deliver it to the person who later used it to poison Chips's clam chowder. Who was it?"

Clyde shrugged. "I have no idea what you're babbling about. Go on. Prove I had anything to do with Chips's murder—or Griffin Mead's."

Audrey's ears perked up. "Griffin?"

Clyde shrugged. "Everyone thinks he was drunk and fell off the dock. But what if he didn't? What if someone wanted him out of the way too? What if there's some kind of serial killer running around loose in Halibut Cove?"

Maggie's eyes narrowed. "Where are you getting this from, Clyde?"

Clyde's smirk deepened. "You're asking me? You should ask your son."

Oliver groaned. "Clyde, eavesdropping isn't a good look. Yes, I got a call from Jill earlier. The autopsy results are in. Griffin Mead didn't drown accidentally. Someone drugged him and pushed him into the water."

Maggie gasped. "What?"

"The coroner found Clonidine in his system," Oliver clarified. "It's an incapacitating agent which can be absorbed into the mouth or swallowed. Causes drowsiness, low blood pressure, sedation, possible unconsciousness. Griffin wouldn't have taken something like that willingly."

Clyde leaned forward, his tone mocking. "So, what's next, Mrs. Holbrook? You gonna pin that one on me too?"

Audrey watched her grandmother's face carefully, noting the determination that flashed in her eyes. Maggie wasn't done—not by a long shot.

Chapter Twenty

Maggie and Audrey hurried into the Halibut Cove Police Department, brushed past the officer at the reception desk and headed down the hall to the chief's office. Jill, seated behind her desk with a phone pressed to her ear, gave them a look that was equal parts exasperation and resignation. She sighed audibly as she ended her call.

"I should've known you two would show up the minute you heard about the autopsy results," Jill said, leaning back in her chair.

Maggie didn't miss a beat. "Two murders in Halibut Cove, Jill. Something strange is going on, and you know it."

Jill raised her hand. "Mom, don't start. I already told you. I'll get to the bottom of it. You don't need to interfere in my investigation."

Maggie ignored the warning and plopped into the chair across from Jill's desk. "I think Clyde Peterson knows who killed Chips. That package of nightshade delivered to the PO box? Whoever hired Clyde and Troy probably killed Chips and tried to frame Waldo Duggan."

Audrey nodded. "You have to admit, it's too coincidental to ignore, Mom. You should at least bring Clyde and Troy in for questioning."

Jill pinched the bridge of her nose. "I already plan to. But whether or not Clyde knows who killed Chips doesn't mean he's going to tell me."

Maggie leaned forward, her voice quieter but insistent. "What about Griffin? Do you think his murder is connected to Chips's?"

Jill hesitated. "I don't know. I'd like to say no, but . . ." She trailed off, shaking her head. "Two murders in one town, this close together? Audrey's right. It's not something I can just chalk up to coincidence."

Maggie sat back, satisfied for the moment. "Well, I trust you'll figure it out."

"I will," Jill said firmly. She grabbed her jacket. "Right now, though, I've got to pick Katie up for lunch. Mason!"

Mason popped his head into the room, looking slightly nervous. "Yes, Chief?"

"Hold down the fort while I'm gone," Jill instructed.

Mason nodded quickly, though he looked anything but confident. "Will do."

Jill turned back to Maggie and Audrey. "Why don't you two join us for lunch? I know Katie would love to hear about your latest adventures as Miss Marple and Veronica Mars."

Unlike The Chowder House, the Seaview Diner was buzzing with its usual lunchtime energy when Maggie, Audrey, and Jill walked in. Katie spotted them immediately from her corner booth, waving them over. Dressed in her blue nurse's uniform, her stethoscope dangling around her neck, Katie looked every bit the exhausted health-care worker taking a well-earned break. She grinned as they approached.

"There you are! I was beginning to think you'd gotten yourselves arrested for meddling," Katie teased, sliding over to make room.

"Not yet," Maggie said dryly, sliding into the booth next to her. Audrey took the seat across from them with Jill.

The waitress, Katty, appeared almost instantly, notepad in hand. "Well, if it isn't the Holbrook clan. What can I get you troublemakers?"

"Coffee, to start," Maggie said.

"Same here," Jill added, while Audrey scanned the menu.

"I'll do a tuna melt," Katie said, handing Katty her menu. "Extra pickles. Thanks, hon."

Audrey glanced up. "Turkey club, no mayo, please."

Katty nodded, jotting it down. "And for you, Maggie?"

"Soup of the day, and whatever sandwich you've got that'll fill me up. I'm starving."

"Coming right up," Katty said, vanishing toward the kitchen.

Katie turned to Audrey with a mischievous glint in her eye. "All right, spill. How was your appointment with the hottest dentist in Halibut Cove? Is he as dreamy as I promised?"

Audrey sighed, already regretting mentioning it. "He's good-looking, I'll give you that. But there's something about him that feels . . . off."

"Off?" Katie echoed, raising a skeptical eyebrow. "What's off about being devastatingly handsome and ridiculously charming?"

Audrey rolled her eyes. "You sound like you're writing his dating profile for Tinder."

"Maybe I should," Katie quipped. "He's a catch, Audrey. Do you know how rare it is to find someone that good-looking, single, and employed in Halibut Cove? You'd better lock that down before the rest of the town figures it out."

Audrey snorted. "He's a little old for me, Katie."

Maggie, listening with a bemused expression, finally chimed in. "Handsome or not, I hate going to the dentist."

Katty reappeared, expertly balancing a tray with their drinks. "Coffee for the two in charge," she said, sliding mugs to Jill and Maggie, "and a cola for the nurse who looks like she's running on fumes."

"Bless you," Katie said, taking the soda.

"Food's coming right up," Katty said before heading to another table.

Jill shook her head. "How do I always end up with you two stirring up trouble? It's a full-time job just keeping tabs on you."

"Well, it's not every day Halibut Cove has a murder," Audrey said.

"Let alone two!" Maggie exclaimed.

"By the way," Audrey said quietly, "Dr. Comstock mentioned his family had spent some time in Halibut Cove years ago. At least, that's what he told me. Do you know anything about that, Nana?"

Maggie tilted her head, thinking. "What's his last name again?"

"Comstock," Katie chimed in, clearly still on Team Bradley.

Maggie's expression shifted as the name sparked something in her memory. "Comstock . . . That rings a bell. Back when Wes and I were just starting out, there was a young couple—Ed and Lily Comstock. We didn't really socialize, but I remember running into them at parties occasionally."

Audrey leaned forward. "Do you think they're related to Dr. Comstock?"

"Maybe," Maggie said, her voice trailing off. "Bradley would've been too young to remember, if he was even born yet. But Wes did mention Ed's name once or twice. Something about a business deal. It was so long ago. I was pregnant and so preoccupied getting ready for Oliver's arrival, I can barely remember."

"Do you think there's anything lying around from that time?" Audrey asked.

Maggie hesitated. "I'm not sure if Wes kept it, but if he did, it would be in his office. That man never threw anything away."

Katty returned with their food, expertly distributing plates around the table. "Soup, tuna melt, turkey club, and a chicken salad sandwich," she announced.

"Thanks, Katty," Maggie said, already reaching for her spoon.

"Need anything else?"

"We're good," Jill said.

As they ate, the conversation drifted to lighter topics, though Audrey's mind was racing. By the time the check arrived, she was already calculating how quickly they could get home to start searching.

Maggie pulled out her wallet, ignoring Jill's protests. "Lunch is on me."

Jill smirked as Maggie handed the bill back to Katty. "There's no stopping you, is there?"

"Never has been," Maggie replied, standing. "Come on, Audrey. Let's see what we can dig up."

Back at the house, Maggie led Audrey into what used to be Wes's office. The room was a time capsule of old files, faded photos, and shelves of books that hadn't been touched in years. Papers were stacked precariously on every surface, a monument to Wes's decades of meticulous recordkeeping.

"Welcome to the chaos," Maggie said, gesturing to the clutter. "If it's here, it's somewhere in this mess."

Audrey surveyed the room, feeling both overwhelmed and determined. "What year are we looking for?"

"It would've been in the 1980s," Maggie said, already pulling open a filing cabinet. "Oliver was born in 1985, so it had to be right around then."

They worked in companionable silence, sifting through folders and stacks of papers. After nearly an hour, Maggie pulled out a yellowing file labeled COMSTOCK REAL ESTATE DEAL.

"Found it," she said, her voice tinged with triumph. She opened the folder and quickly scanned the contents. "Look at this—Wes was considering a deal with Ed Comstock, Chips Hogan, and Griffin Mead."

"What? Are you serious? The two murder victims?"

"I know," Maggie gasped, shaking her head. "That can't just be a wild coincidence, can it?"

Audrey's brow furrowed. "Most likely not. What kind of deal was it?"

Maggie handed her the file. "A real estate development. There was some waterfront property for sale that they planned on revitalizing—fifteen boat slips, a public market, plaza, and a significant amount of open space, aiming to blend commercial and recreational spaces. But it looks like it fell apart."

Audrey flipped through the documents, stopping when she found a folded piece of paper. "There's a letter in here." She opened it and began to read aloud.

Dear Ed,

I've given your proposal a great deal of thought. Unfortunately, I must decline further involvement. While I was initially interested in your project, the way this deal has unfolded has left me uneasy.

Maggie leaned in. "Keep going."

You failed to disclose to Chips and Griffin that the other was involved in the deal. You referred to them only as "silent partners." Once they discovered the truth, their past history and unresolved resentments surfaced, making it impossible for them to move forward together.

Maggie nodded slowly. "That tracks. Chips and Griffin have always butted heads ever since the failed hardware store project."

Audrey kept reading.

Griffin, who is struggling financially, was especially angry. He gambled what little he had on this deal, believing it to be a sure thing. But he refused to take the risk once he realized Chips was involved, having already been burned by him once.

Maggie frowned. "So Ed kept them both in the dark on purpose."

"It gets worse," Audrey said.

I initially considered investing more to keep the project afloat, but after reviewing the financials, I dis-

covered discrepancies in your accounting. I cannot in good conscience proceed with this venture. My family's financial stability must come first.

Maggie sat back, stunned. "Wes must've seen through Ed's mismanagement. That's why he backed out."

Audrey folded the letter carefully. "Do you think this is connected to Dr. Comstock?"

Maggie's expression hardened. "It's too much of a coincidence not to be. We need to find out what Bradley knows—and if Ed Comstock's past is catching up to his family."

Chapter Twenty-one

The aroma of Maggie's famous seafood casserole filled her cozy kitchen as she pulled the bubbling dish out of the oven. Layers of shrimp, scallops, cod, and creamy sauce were topped with a golden breadcrumb crust, the ultimate comfort food for a cold Halibut Cove evening. Audrey leaned against the counter, arms crossed, watching her grandmother work.

"Are you sure Waldo's going to eat this?" Audrey asked. "The man has made it pretty clear he's not our biggest fan."

"He'll eat it," Maggie said firmly, grabbing a tea towel to wrap the hot dish. "Waldo Duggan may hold a grudge, but he's not going to turn down free food—especially not something this good. Besides, this is the third time I've cooked him dinner since his arrest."

Audrey smirked. "You're really trying to win him over, aren't you?"

Maggie sighed, straightening up and brushing her hands on her apron. "He's been through enough. Being accused of murder, having someone plant that nightshade in his pantry—it's taking a toll on him, and I'm not about to stand by and let him waste away. Besides, it's high time we had a civil conversation about this whole 'Holbrooks stole the chowder recipe' nonsense."

"Good luck with that," Audrey muttered, grabbing her coat as Maggie picked up the casserole.

Waldo Duggan's small, weathered house was tucked at the end of a narrow dirt road. It had a crooked charm, with smoke puffing lazily from the chimney and a porch cluttered with fishing gear. Waldo himself answered the door, his face lined with weariness but softening at the sight of Maggie and Audrey.

"Well, well," he said, stepping aside to let them in. "If it isn't the Holbrooks. What brings you out here tonight?"

Maggie held up the casserole. "I made this for you. Thought you could use a good meal."

Waldo blinked in surprise, then grunted. "That's mighty kind of you, Maggie. I'm starting to get used to you cooking for me while I'm out on bail. Come on in."

The warmth of the house was a stark contrast to the chilly evening. Audrey's nose immediately picked up the savory scent of something simmering on the stove.

"Smells good in here," Maggie said, setting the casserole on the counter.

"Clam chowder," Waldo replied, stirring the pot on the stove. "I usually just whip up a batch every week when I'm cooking at the Seaview, but now that I'm on leave due to all this murder nonsense, I decided why not make it at home?"

Audrey raised an eyebrow at Maggie, who hesitated before saying, "Well, it certainly smells delicious. You can freeze my casserole and eat it any time. It's the perfect night for a steaming bowl of chowder. You wouldn't mind if we stayed for a helping, would you?"

Waldo looked startled but then waved a hand. "Sure, why not? Pull up a chair. Bowls are in the cupboard."

Maggie and Audrey settled at the kitchen table while Waldo ladled generous servings of chowder into bowls and placed them in front of them. Maggie took a tentative sip, her practiced palate immediately picking out the subtle notes of thyme and a faint smokiness.

"This is good, Waldo," Maggie said genuinely.

Waldo sat down with his own bowl, eyeing her suspiciously. "I suppose it's close to your recipe, huh?"

Maggie set her spoon down with a sigh. "Waldo, we've been over this. Your chowder and ours aren't identical. They're different recipes, even if they end up tasting pretty similar. I can still tell them apart."

He shrugged, his expression guarded. "My grandfather swore that the Holbrooks stole the recipe. And considering how successful your family's brand has been, it's hard not to hold a little resentment."

Maggie resisted the urge to argue further. "I can promise you, Waldo, our recipe came from my grandmother. It's a Holbrook original."

Waldo gave a noncommittal grunt, and they ate in silence for a moment before Maggie shifted the conversation. "How are you holding up, Waldo? With everything that's been going on?"

He snorted. "How do you think? I've never been accused of murder before. Hard to get a good night's sleep when you're constantly thinking about how someone's trying to frame you."

Audrey glanced at Maggie, who gave her a small nod. "Do you have any idea who might've put the nightshade in your pantry?" Audrey asked.

"Like I told the cops, I don't have a clue," Waldo said

bitterly. "But I wouldn't put it past Jill to be working me over just to make herself look good."

Maggie's eyes narrowed. "That's my daughter you're talking about. Jill is doing her job, Waldo. And she doesn't believe for a second that you're guilty. She's trying to clear your name."

Maggie flicked her eyes toward Audrey, who knew that was a lie. Jill was ready to close the case.

Waldo huffed but didn't argue further. "I'm more upset about Griffin Mead, to be honest. He was a good drinking buddy. Can't believe he's gone."

Audrey leaned forward, sensing an opening. "Did you ever meet Ed and Lily Comstock when they lived here in town?"

Waldo blinked, his brow furrowing as he tried to remember. "Sure, I knew Ed. We used to go ice fishing together back in the day. He'd bring a bottle of bourbon to my shack on the lake, and we'd spend hours catching fish and talking about life."

"What about the business deal involving my husband Wes, Chips Hogan, and Griffin Mead?" Maggie asked.

Waldo shook his head. "Ed never mentioned anything like that to me. But I do remember Lily being upset at a potluck supper once. She said Ed was in a pickle over something, and it was going to ruin them. Next thing I knew, they packed up and left Halibut Cove."

"Did you ever find out where they went?" Audrey asked.

"I heard they moved to New Hampshire. Somewhere near Manchester, I think," Waldo said, scratching his chin. "I tried to keep in touch, but they didn't seem interested in hearing from anyone back here."

Maggie tilted her head. "What happened to them?"

Waldo's face darkened. "Word through the grapevine was that Ed killed himself."

Maggie and Audrey froze, their spoons halfway to their mouths.

"*What*?" Maggie whispered.

Waldo nodded grimly. "Yup. Shotgun, I heard. Shame too. Lily had just given birth to a baby boy. Don't know why poor Ed would go to such extremes, especially with a child to take care of."

Audrey's mind raced. "The baby . . . He'd be grown now. That has to be Dr. Comstock."

Maggie looked equally shaken. "Ed must've been desperate if he took his own life. Something must have pushed him over the edge."

"He was a good guy," Waldo said, shaking his head. "I can't imagine what would've driven him to do something like that."

Audrey exchanged a glance with Maggie. They didn't need to say it out loud to know they were thinking the same thing: what if Bradley had grown up harboring a grudge against the men who'd been involved in his father's downfall? And now, all these years later, was he seeking revenge?

As Waldo continued talking about the Comstocks, Maggie's mind churned with questions. She had a sinking feeling they were only scratching the surface of a much deeper mystery.

Chapter Twenty-two

Audrey took a deep breath before stepping into Dr. Bradley Comstock's office. The reception area was as pristine as ever. Melanie, perched behind the front desk, looked up with a bright, hopeful smile.

"Audrey! What brings you here? Are you switching your follow-up appointment?"

Audrey shook her head. "Nope. I'm actually here because Dr. Comstock and I are going out."

Melanie's smile faltered. "Oh . . . you mean . . . like on a date?"

Audrey gave an easy shrug. "I'm just taking him on an evening tour of Halibut Cove. He's still new here, and I figured he should learn a little about the town's history, its landmarks, that sort of thing."

Melanie's face crumbled like a soufflé in a thunderstorm. "Oh. That's . . . nice of you."

Before the conversation could get any more awkward, the man himself emerged from his office. "Ready to go?" Bradley asked, flashing his signature charming smile.

"Yep," Audrey said cheerfully.

Bradley turned to Melanie. "Have a good evening, Melanie."

Melanie nodded stiffly. "You too, Dr. Comstock."

As they walked out together, Audrey cast a glance back at Melanie, who looked like she was about to cry.

Maggie had not been thrilled when Audrey told her about her plan.

"You're putting yourself in a vulnerable position," Maggie had warned. "This is a man we suspect of not one but possibly two murders, Audrey."

Audrey had waved off her concerns. "I can handle this, Nana. Besides, if we want to know what he's really up to, I need to get close. He's not going to just confess over coffee at the diner."

And now, as she walked beside Bradley through the cool Halibut Cove evening, she was starting to wonder if Maggie perhaps had a point.

They strolled through the quiet downtown area, the glow of street lamps casting long shadows. Audrey played the perfect tour guide, pointing out the town's historical landmarks, the old cobblestone streets that had been laid back in the 1800s, the inns that had once been Gilded Age mansions for the robber barons who summered here.

Bradley listened attentively, nodding at all the right moments, but he seemed more interested in her than the history of the town.

"You're so passionate about this place," he said.

"It's my home," Audrey said simply.

"It's nice," he admitted. "I never really had a place that felt like home."

Audrey seized the opportunity. "But your family spent time in Halibut Cove, didn't they? You mentioned that before."

Bradley's expression didn't change, but something about

his posture stiffened. “A long time ago, yeah. But my family’s all gone now. Either relocated or . . . well, gone.”

“Your father?” Audrey pressed carefully.

Bradley hesitated, then sighed. “He took his own life when I was just a baby. I never really knew him. My mother raised me.”

“I’m sorry,” Audrey said, studying his face. “That must have been hard.”

He gave a half-smile, but it didn’t reach his eyes. “It was a long time ago.”

Audrey felt a cold prickle at the back of her neck. He was so smooth, so carefully measured in his words.

But was there pain there?

Or just calculation?

Before she could probe further, as they walked past a row of shops, a familiar voice called out.

“Audrey?”

Audrey turned to see Isabella walking toward them, her purse slung over one shoulder, a light jacket pulled tightly around her. She was clearly on her way home from work at The Chowder House, but the expression on her face was somewhere between shocked and suspicious. Her gaze flickered between Audrey and Bradley, eyebrows raised.

“Hey, Isabella,” Audrey said, forcing a casual smile.

Isabella’s eyes widened. “Uh . . . what’s going on here?”

Bradley glanced at his watch. “I’ll give you two a moment,” he said smoothly. “I need to make a quick call. I’ll be right back.”

As he walked a short distance away, Isabella stepped in close, lowering her voice. “Audrey, is this a date?”

“No,” Audrey whispered back. “I’m just showing him around town.”

Isabella crossed her arms. "You do realize he looks old enough to be your dad, right? And he's a dentist, Audrey. A dentist. That alone gives me the creeps."

Audrey sighed. "Look, this is just part of our investigation."

Isabella's frown deepened. "And what would your grandmother say about this?"

"She already gave me the lecture," Audrey admitted. "She thinks I'm out of my depth. But I know what I'm doing."

"Do you?" Isabella asked, looking unconvinced. "Because I gotta say, this seems very dangerous. What if he catches on?"

Audrey forced a reassuring smile. "I'm being careful. I promise."

Isabella exhaled sharply, shaking her head. "I don't like this, Audrey. You're playing with fire."

Before Audrey could respond, Bradley returned, slipping his phone back into his pocket. "Shall we continue?"

Audrey hesitated, giving Isabella one last reassuring look before turning back to him. "Yeah. Let's keep going."

Isabella gave her a look that clearly said *this is a bad idea*, but she didn't argue further.

As they strolled down the street, Bradley turned toward Audrey. "You've spent the evening showing me the town," he said, "but I'd like to return the favor. At the risk of sounding immodest, I'm a pretty decent cook. Come back to my place and let me prove it."

Audrey hesitated. Every instinct screamed that this was a bad idea. But getting a look inside his house might give her more insight into who he really was.

"That depends," she said. "What's on the menu?"

Bradley grinned. "It's a surprise. Which means I haven't really figured it out yet. Let's see what's in the fridge."

* * *

Bradley's home was as neat and polished as his office. Everything was in its place, from the modern furniture to the gleaming stainless-steel kitchen appliances. It didn't feel lived in—more like a showroom.

Dinner, however, was as impressive as promised. He whipped up a perfectly seared salmon with a citrus glaze, served alongside a risotto so creamy that Audrey briefly forgot she was sitting across from someone she suspected of murder.

But then, the conversation turned back to his family.

"You were close to your mother?" Audrey asked.

Bradley nodded. "She was everything to me. She passed away when I was in high school. Cancer."

"I'm sorry."

"She did her best to make sure I had a good life," Bradley said, sipping his wine. "I don't think she ever really got over what happened to my father. But she kept going. That's what you do, right? You just . . . keep going."

"So it was just the two of you, you and your Mom?"

There was a long pause.

Bradley shook his head. "I had a stepfather for a while, but we sort of lost touch after my mother died."

"Is he still alive?"

He shrugged. "As far as I know. I'm not sure. Like I said, we haven't spoken in years."

Audrey studied him carefully.

Was there bitterness there?

A grudge held against the people who had driven his father to ruin?

Before she could ask more, there was a knock at the door.

Bradley sighed, setting down his glass. "Excuse me."

Audrey listened as he opened the door, and a familiar voice floated in.

"Dr. Comstock, I know it's late, but I wanted to show you these X-rays before tomorrow's appointments."

It was Melanie.

Audrey peeked around the corner, watching as Bradley folded his arms. "Melanie, this could have waited until the morning. You know I don't like business being done outside of office hours."

Melanie's face fell. "I just thought . . . I mean, I wanted to make sure you saw them before—"

Bradley sighed. "Melanie, I appreciate your dedication, but you need to draw some boundaries."

Melanie looked mortified. "I . . . I'm sorry. I didn't mean to intrude."

Bradley softened. "It's okay. But go home. Get some rest."

Melanie nodded quickly and left, closing the door behind her.

Audrey hid her smirk.

"That happens often?" she asked when Bradley returned.

Bradley groaned. "She's got a bit of a . . . fixation. I try to be nice about it, but she's overly devoted."

"Poor girl's in love with you," Audrey teased.

Bradley shook his head. "That's unfortunate for her."

Audrey excused herself to the bathroom and used the opportunity to snoop. She opened the medicine cabinet, scanning the shelves. Toothpaste, ibuprofen, aftershave . . . nothing suspicious. No sign of Clonidine.

Maybe they were wrong about him.

But then again, what kind of killer would leave poison in plain sight for anyone to see?

Like a deadly nightshade plant in the pantry.

There was no way she was going to get the opportunity to search the entire house. She instinctively reached up and flipped the latch on the small bathroom window, unlocking it. If she came back later when Bradley wasn't home and managed to squeeze through that window, then she'd have more time to conduct a more thorough search.

She returned to the dining room, forcing a smile. "It's getting late. I should go."

Bradley looked disappointed. "Already?"

"I have an early shift at the diner."

He nodded, walking her to the door. "Audrey . . . what's your real goal?"

She blinked. "What do you mean?"

He leaned against the doorframe. "You're smart. You could do anything. What do you really want?"

She hesitated before answering honestly. "I want to run my own restaurant someday. Create my own dishes. Make something people remember."

Bradley smiled. "You will."

Audrey nodded. "Thanks again. Dinner was delicious."

"Anytime," Bradley said, smiling.

"Good night!"

Then she quickly turned and left before she had to deal with any kind of goodbye kiss.

As soon as she was outside, she heard hurried footsteps behind her. She turned to see Melanie.

"You should be ashamed of yourself," Melanie hissed.

Audrey frowned. "Excuse me?"

"The man is twice your age. He could be your father."

Audrey crossed her arms. "There's nothing going on between us."

Melanie scoffed. "Sure. Just keep your hands off him, or you'll regret it."

Audrey stared at her, agog. "Is that a threat? Did you just threaten me, Melanie?"

Melanie opened her mouth but no words came out. She stood there, frozen, unable to speak, her whole body shaking. Then, finally, she screamed, "What would your grandmother say?"

Audrey watched as Melanie stormed off, unsettled.

That was the second person in one evening to ask that question.

Maybe it was just a coincidence.

Or maybe she needed to start listening.

But something weird was going on with Dr. Bradley Comstock.

And she was going to find out what.

As she walked away, her mind spun with new possibilities.

Had Bradley been planning his revenge for years? Was he carefully calculating each move? Her mind raced about who the real Bradley Comstock might be.

Chapter Twenty-three

Jill stretched, savoring the quiet morning light filtering through her bedroom window. It had been a long time since she'd woken up next to someone she actually liked, and she wasn't eager for the moment to end. Lying next to her, tangled in the sheets, was Mark Haskell, the town prosecutor and, apparently, her secret boyfriend.

She hadn't meant for this to happen. At least, not like this. But Mark was charming, funny, and had a way of making her forget, at least temporarily, that her last serious relationship, namely her first and only marriage to Sam, had ended in disaster. She turned her head to look at Mark, still half-asleep, hair mussed in a way that would make every juror in town swoon.

"Morning, Counselor," she murmured.

Mark cracked an eye open, grinning. "Morning, Chief."

Jill smirked and leaned in, intending to steal another kiss before the day rudely interrupted them, but Mark groaned and sat up, scrubbing a hand over his face.

"As much as I'd rather stay here all day, I have to get to court. I have an appointment to make your brother look bad."

Jill snorted. "Good luck with that. Oliver's been making prosecutors like you look bad since law school."

Mark stood and stretched before heading toward the bathroom. "Then I guess I'd better bring my A-game." He winked. "Give me ten minutes."

Jill smiled as he disappeared into the shower. She lounged in bed a few minutes, debating whether she should join him in the shower, but they both had to get to work, so she decided to leave him be. Suddenly her moment of peace was shattered by the sound of the front door downstairs opening and closing.

"Mom?"

Jill's stomach dropped.

Audrey.

She launched out of bed, grabbed her robe, and raced toward the door. "Be right down!"

She flew down the stairs to intercept her daughter before she could go any further.

Audrey frowned at her. "What's with the panicked expression?"

Jill forced a casual smile. "What? I'm not panicked. I'm just surprised to see you. What's up?"

"I need to talk to you about something important," Audrey said, brushing past her and heading toward the kitchen. "I hope you have coffee."

Jill winced. "Actually, I was just about to leave for the station—"

Audrey rolled her eyes. "This has directly to do with one of your cases. Sit down, Mom."

Jill sighed, reluctantly following Audrey into the kitchen, silently praying Mark would take forever in the shower.

Audrey poured herself coffee and leaned against the counter. "I think you need to take a hard look at Dr. Comstock."

"The new dentist?"

"Yes, the one everyone's swooning over. He's too good to be true."

Jill exhaled, rubbing her temples. "Audrey, I already have a man awaiting trial for Chips Hogan's murder."

Audrey set down her mug with a clunk. "Mom, don't be one of *those* cops."

Jill narrowed her eyes. "Excuse me?"

"You know," Audrey pressed. "The ones that decide this guy is guilty and ignore any evidence that might prove someone else did it. Don't you watch any Netflix documentaries?"

Jill crossed her arms. "You think I don't do my job thoroughly?"

"I think you have a whole town looking at Waldo Duggan like he's a murderer, and you owe it to him—and to Griffin Mead—to make sure you have the right guy."

Jill considered her daughter for a long moment. "Why Comstock?"

Audrey hesitated. "It's a feeling."

Jill raised an eyebrow. "A *feeling*?"

"Mom, I spent the night having dinner at his house," Audrey said.

Jill nearly spit out her coffee. "You *what*?"

Audrey held up her hands. "Relax! It's not what you think. Nothing happened! I offered to show him the town, and he invited me over for a quick meal when we were done. Totally innocent."

"And since when are you Halibut Cove's official ambassador and tour guide?"

"I was just trying to get a read on him. And something about him doesn't sit right with me."

Jill exhaled, drumming her fingers on the table. "I don't make arrests based on gut feelings, Audrey."

"I'm not asking you to arrest him," Audrey said. "I'm asking you to take a second look."

Jill sighed. "Fine. I'll take a second look."

Before Audrey could say more, the unmistakable sound of someone coming down the stairs echoed through the house.

Both women turned just in time to see Mark Haskell walk into the kitchen.

Bare-chested.

Wrapped in a towel.

Still damp from the shower.

Mark froze. "Oh. Morning."

Audrey stared at him.

Then turned to Jill.

Then back to Mark.

"Oh, come on." Audrey groaned.

Jill sighed. "Audrey, you remember Mark Haskell, right? The prosecutor?"

Mark was doing his best to look respectable despite the fact that he was half-naked in the police chief's kitchen. "Uh. Nice to meet you. Again."

Audrey stared at him. "So . . . this is what you've been hiding?"

Jill sighed. "It's . . . complicated."

Audrey scoffed. "Unbelievable."

Mark, sensing the need for an exit, grabbed a cup of coffee and pointed toward the stairs. "I'm gonna, uh, get dressed. Nice seeing you." He quickly retreated.

Audrey watched him scurry off, her eyes landing on his firm butt. "Same here." She turned to her mother, crossing her arms. "So, this is why you've been so busy lately?"

Jill groaned. "It's not what you think."

Audrey rolled her eyes. "Mom, why couldn't you just tell me?"

Jill hesitated. How could she explain that she wasn't sure if she even knew what this was? That a part of her still didn't trust relationships after Audrey's father left, started a whole new life, and acted like they were nothing more than a footnote in his story?

Instead, she just shook her head. "Because I didn't know what it was yet. Don't be mad."

"I'm not mad. I'm frustrated. I don't care that you're dating someone. I care that you felt you couldn't tell me."

"You're right. I should have said something. I'm sorry."

"He's really cute, though," Audrey noted.

"Yes, I know."

Mark reappeared, now fully dressed and carrying his briefcase. He attempted a casual exit, but not before awkwardly attempting to kiss Jill goodbye. She turned her head at the last second, and his lips brushed her cheek instead.

"Right," Mark said, adjusting his tie. "Well. Bye, Audrey."

Audrey gave him the once-over. "Bye, Mark."

Mark nodded awkwardly. "Jill, I'll talk to you later."

He deposited his coffee cup in the sink and practically sprinted out the door.

Audrey watched him go before turning back to Jill with a smirk. "Smooth."

Jill groaned. "Shut up."

The waiting room at Dr. Bradley Comstock's dental office was busy, with three patients already seated and flipping through old copies of *Coastal Living* and *Maine Life*. A thin, elderly woman in a fleece jacket sat closest to the counter, peering over her reading glasses at Jill and Mason as they walked in. Across from her, a middle-aged man in work boots and a plaid jacket glanced up from his magazine, curiosity flickering across his face. A teenage boy, slumped in his chair and scrolling on his phone, barely acknowledged them.

The second Jill flashed her badge, the room shifted. The elderly woman sucked in a sharp breath, setting her magazine down with great interest. The man in plaid leaned forward slightly, clearly invested. Even the teenager looked up, pulling out an earbud.

Melanie, the ever-peppy receptionist, started to stand but hesitated. "Uh, Chief Holbrook, Officer Dooley! What a surprise."

Jill smiled tightly. "Is Dr. Comstock in?"

Melanie's gaze darted to the full waiting room. "He's with a patient right now."

"We'll wait," Jill said, her voice light but firm.

Melanie's fingers fluttered nervously over the keyboard. "It's just that he's really busy today. He has back-to-back appointments."

Jill folded her arms. "We won't take much of his time."

By now, all three waiting patients were openly listening. The man in plaid gave a low whistle under his breath. The teenager muttered, "Damn," under his breath.

The exam room door opened, and Dr. Comstock emerged with an elderly woman, helping her to the counter. "Mrs. Parker," he said in his warm, professional tone, "I recommend you come back for a deep cleaning to keep your teeth and gums in great shape."

As soon as he turned toward the waiting room and spotted Jill and Mason standing by the front desk, his smile faltered.

Melanie's voice rose an octave. "I told them you were busy, Doctor—"

Bradley glanced at her sharply, then immediately smoothed his expression. "It's fine, Melanie," he said, but there was a stiffness to his voice. "Chief Holbrook. Officer Dooley. To what do I owe the pleasure?"

Jill didn't miss the slight tension in his shoulders. She smiled politely. "If we could have a moment of your time, Doctor?"

Bradley hesitated. His gaze flicked toward the patients, all of whom were now blatantly staring. Even the elderly woman with the fleece jacket was staring over her glasses like she was watching the climax of a courtroom drama.

"Of course," he said smoothly. "Come into my office."

As soon as the door shut behind them, the tension in the air thickened. Comstock moved behind his desk, adjusting a stack of files like he needed something to do with his hands.

Jill got straight to the point. "Where were you the night Chips Hogan died?"

Comstock raised an eyebrow. "Am I a suspect now?" He gave a small, breathy laugh. "I thought you already had someone in custody."

"We're covering all our bases," Jill said evenly.

Comstock hesitated, then sat down. "To be honest, I don't know where this is coming from, why I'm suddenly on your radar, but I was at a dental convention in Portland. Didn't get back until late that night. What time was the body discovered?"

"Before you returned," Jill admitted.

Comstock exhaled, looking relieved. "Well, then."

Jill didn't let the moment pass. "And where were you the night Griffin Mead died?"

There it was—a flicker of something.

Not shock.

Not confusion.

Just a pause.

Before Comstock could answer, the door burst open, and Melanie nearly stumbled inside. "We were working late that night!" she blurted out.

Jill's head snapped toward her.

Melanie's face was flushed. "He—he was with me. We worked very late that night. And then he walked me home. After 10 p.m."

Jill studied the two of them.

Comstock wasn't looking at Melanie.

Melanie, however, was watching him closely, as if waiting for him to agree.

Something unspoken passed between them.

Comstock's jaw clenched. "That's correct."

Jill turned back to Bradley. "You remember that exact night?"

Melanie nodded too quickly. "Of course!"

Mason finally spoke up, breaking the tense moment. "Hey, while I'm here—can you take a look at my teeth?"

Comstock blinked at him. "Excuse me?"

Mason opened his mouth dramatically, pointing to his molars. "I think my wisdom teeth need to come out. My gums feel weird. What do you think?"

Jill sighed. "Mason."

"What? While we're here."

Comstock stared at him for a long moment, then managed a small, forced chuckle. "Well, at first glance, I'd say you have a few older fillings that might need to be checked."

Mason grinned. "Knew it."

Comstock gestured toward the door. "Make an appointment with Melanie on your way out."

Mason turned to Jill. "Should I?"

Jill shot him a look. "Not the time."

As they walked out of the office, Mason muttered, "My Spidey sense is tingling, Chief. I really don't like him."

Jill nodded. "Me neither. But we need evidence."

Mason straightened. "What do you want me to do?"

"Find out if that convention was real," Jill ordered. "And get security footage from every hotel in Portland."

Back at her desk at the station, Jill exhaled, running a hand through her hair.

Something wasn't sitting right.

She pulled up the autopsy report for Griffin Mead on her computer, scanning through the findings.

Then she stopped.

Her heart skipped.

In addition to the poison . . .

There was residue of novocaine in Griffin's mouth.

Jill's breath came slow and steady as she leaned back in her chair.

Novocaine.

Had Griffin Mead seen Dr. Comstock on the day he was murdered?

And if so . . .

Why hadn't Comstock mentioned it?

Chapter Twenty-four

Audrey looked up from her coffee as she spotted her mother's car rolling up the long driveway. A slow smile spread across her face. This was perfect.

She pushed away from the kitchen table and darted outside, determined to intercept her mother before she could escape. Jill barely had time to put the car in park before Audrey yanked open the passenger door and leaned in.

"You have exactly thirty seconds before Nana finds out about your relationship."

Jill groaned. "Can we not do this now?"

"Oh, we're doing this," Audrey said, practically bouncing with excitement. "I'm not keeping this to myself another second."

Before Jill could protest, Audrey turned and marched back toward the house.

Inside, Maggie was at the stove, flipping bacon in a cast-iron skillet. A pot of coffee brewed beside her, and a plate of scrambled eggs and toast already sat on the table.

"Well, look who finally decided to show up," Maggie said without turning around.

Jill sighed as she stepped inside. "Great. A breakfast ambush."

"This is going to be fun," Audrey said, plopping into a chair. "Go ahead, Mom. Tell her."

Maggie turned, raising an eyebrow. "Tell me what?"

Jill shot Audrey a glare before muttering, "I'm . . . I can't believe I have to say this . . . I'm seeing Mark Haskell."

Maggie gasped and nearly dropped the spatula. "*The* Mark Haskell? Oh, Jillian, finally!"

Audrey grinned as her mother visibly shrank into herself.

Maggie clutched her chest dramatically. "That man could prosecute me, and I'd still thank him afterward."

"Nana!" Audrey burst out laughing.

Jill groaned. "This is exactly why I didn't say anything."

Maggie ignored her. "When were you going to tell me? Oh, let me guess—you weren't."

Jill sighed. "It's not a thing. It's casual."

Maggie smirked. "Mm-hmm. Sure."

"Can we move on?" Jill said desperately. "I have actual news."

Maggie relented, though she looked far too pleased with herself as she turned back to the stove. "Go on, then."

Jill exhaled. "Mason secured the hotel security footage from Portland. It shows Bradley Comstock leaving his hotel with his overnight bag around 7 p.m. that Sunday—the same time Chips was poisoned."

Audrey sat up straighter. "So he's in the clear for that murder."

"Rock-solid alibi," Jill confirmed. "He wouldn't have gotten back to Halibut Cove until 8:30, maybe 9:00 at the earliest. Chips was already dead."

Maggie pursed her lips. "That's one murder he didn't commit. But what about Griffin Mead?"

Jill hesitated. "That's the big question. According to his receptionist, they worked late. But I have a feeling she's smitten enough to say just about anything to protect him."

She leaned closer. "And there's something else I just confirmed. The autopsy report found clonidine in Griffin's system—enough to sedate him so someone could push him into the water. That's what killed him. But there were also traces of novocaine in his mouth, which proves he was in Comstock's dental chair the day he died."

Audrey's eyes widened. "So he was drugged at the office and then drowned afterward?"

Jill nodded grimly. "Exactly."

Maggie and Audrey exchanged a look, their wheels already turning.

Jill sighed. "I hate that look."

Maggie smiled innocently. "What look?"

"The one that means you two are about to do something reckless," Jill muttered.

"I don't do anything reckless, dear," Maggie assured her.

Jill folded her arms, skeptical. "Uh huh."

The next day, Audrey and Maggie entered Dr. Comstock's dental office. Maggie grumbled the entire way inside.

"Listen, I don't need the whole cleaning and scraping nonsense," Maggie announced as they stepped up to the reception desk. "Just one tooth. One lousy tooth. Cracked it eating lobster, and now it's giving me grief. In and out. Five minutes. That's it. That's all I have time for."

Melanie beamed. "Mrs. Holbrook, I promise Dr. Comstock will take great care of you. Just fill out this quick form—"

Maggie shot her a glare. "Do I have to?"

Melanie giggled. "Standard procedure."

Before Maggie could argue further, the exam-room door opened and Bradley Comstock stepped out, flashing his signature smile.

"Maggie Holbrook! What a pleasure," he said, shaking her hand. "I have to say, I never thought I'd see you in my chair."

"To be honest, I never thought I'd be in your chair," Maggie grumbled. "As I told you, I liked my old dentist, Dr. Lawry, before he needed to fly south for his arthritis, apparently."

Bradley chuckled. "Well, I'll do my best to live up to Dr. Lawry's legacy." He gestured for her to follow him. "Come on, let's take a look at that tooth."

Maggie sighed dramatically and shot Audrey a look. "If I don't make it out of here alive, tell Oliver he still owes me money from Christmas. That's part of your inheritance."

Audrey smirked as Maggie disappeared into the exam room.

Now was her chance.

Audrey leaned against the counter. "Hey, Melanie, I think I left a scarf here at my last cleaning. Nana knitted it for me last Christmas, so it has sentimental value. Can you check your lost and found?"

"Oh! Sure," Melanie said. "Hold on. Let me take a quick look."

The second Melanie disappeared into the back, Audrey slipped behind the desk and pulled up the patient records. She quickly typed Griffin Mead into the search bar.

Appointment date: Thursday, October 25th.

Audrey's stomach clenched.

The day he died.

That confirmed it.

Before she could read further, a shadow loomed over her.

"What are you doing?"

Audrey's breath caught.

Melanie stood there, arms crossed, eyes sharp.

Audrey quickly clicked out of the screen. "Oh! I got a call from my insurance company—there was an issue with my coverage, and I just wanted to make sure you had the right information."

Melanie narrowed her eyes. "I handle all insurance issues. Why didn't you just ask me?"

"I didn't want to bother you," Audrey said with a sheepish smile. "Did you find my scarf?"

"No. Shockingly, it wasn't there."

Melanie obviously sensed that she had been sent on a wild goose chase.

Suddenly the exam room door opened, and Dr. Comstock stepped out. "Everything all right?"

Melanie pointed at Audrey. "She was on my computer."

Comstock's gaze flicked to Audrey, his expression unreadable.

Audrey feigned an embarrassed smile. "Totally my fault. Just checking on that insurance thing. Didn't mean to cause a fuss."

Bradley studied her for a beat too long, then finally nodded. "No harm done." But his eyes were suspicious.

At that moment, Maggie emerged, rubbing her jaw. "Tell me good news, Doc."

Bradley smiled. "Unfortunately, you need a root canal."

Maggie groaned. "I knew I should've just let the damn tooth break."

Bradley chuckled. "Make sure you schedule an appointment with Melanie before you leave." He flashed a too-white smile as he handed Maggie a small plastic bag. "A parting gift for you, Maggie. A little something to keep that smile in tip-top shape—travel-size toothpaste, floss, mouthwash, the works."

Maggie took the bag without looking inside. "How nice. Thanks," she muttered, barely suppressing a grimace.

"Before you go," he added, his voice dipping into something more serious, "you really need to come back and deal with that tooth."

Maggie exhaled sharply through her nose. "I'll call," she said, already inching toward the door.

Dr. Comstock tilted his head, studying her like an uncooperative patient in one of his textbooks. "Don't put it off. I'd hate to have to fit you with dentures."

Maggie turned back just long enough to smirk. "I came into the world with these teeth, I'm going out with them . . . same with my hips the doctors keep wanting to replace."

Dr. Comstock chuckled as she walked out and Audrey followed.

The moment they left the office, Audrey called Jill.

"You were right," she said as soon as her mother picked up. "Griffin definitely had a dental appointment with Comstock on the day he died."

"He did?"

"Yep. His appointment was on October 25th—the same day he was found floating in the harbor."

"That's . . . interesting."

Audrey could hear the gears turning in her mother's head.

Jill exhaled. "What I find curious is that Comstock didn't mention that Griffin was a patient when Mason and I questioned him the other day."

Audrey hesitated.

Jill's voice sharpened. "And how exactly did you find this information?"

Audrey cleared her throat. "Um. Well—"

Jill sighed, already knowing the answer. "You promised me you'd stay out of it."

"I promised I wouldn't interfere," Audrey corrected. "This was just . . . strategic information gathering."

She could picture her mother gritting her teeth. "I mean it, Audrey. No more snooping."

Audrey crossed her fingers behind her back. "Fine. No more snooping."

"Promise?"

"Yes, I promise," Audrey sighed.

Maggie leaned in and whispered in her ear. "Don't make promises you can't keep, dear."

Jill exhaled on the other end of the line. "Okay, I'll look into it."

Audrey ended the call, her mind racing.

Why would Comstock omit such an important detail?

And more importantly . . . what else was he hiding?

Chapter Twenty-five

Maggie and Audrey had barely stepped through the front door when the shouting hit them like a tidal wave.

"I trusted you!" Cord's voice boomed through the house. "And this is what you do? With *him*?"

Maggie and Audrey exchanged wary glances before stepping quickly toward the living room, where Cord stood, face red with fury, pointing a shaking finger at his younger brother. Sandy, seated on the arm of the couch, looked more exasperated than guilty.

"Cord, would you calm down?" Sandy said, arms crossed.

"You were kissing my fiancée!" Cord roared.

Sandy scoffed, shaking his head. "You're being ridiculous right now, Cord."

"I saw you!"

Phoebe, standing off to the side, looked frazzled, her eyes darting between the two brothers. "Guys, please, let's just—"

"No!" Cord snapped. "You don't get to smooth this over, Phoebe! I walked in, and it sure as hell looked like my brother was kissing you."

"I wasn't kissing her!" Sandy shot back.

"You expect me to believe that?"

Sandy let out a dry, humorless laugh. "You know what? Yeah, actually. Because this whole situation is stupid. And you know why?" He stood up, meeting Cord's glare head-on. "Because everyone in this damn room knows I'm gay."

A stunned silence fell over the room.

Maggie felt her breath catch slightly, though not in surprise. She had always suspected. She wasn't a fool—Sandy had always been different from his headstrong, bull-in-a-china-shop brother. Cord had always stormed through life, unafraid of confrontation, diving headfirst into whatever situation he found himself in. But Sandy was quieter, more sensitive. Thoughtful. More careful about what parts of himself he chose to share with the world.

Maggie had long wondered when—or if—he'd feel comfortable enough to tell her. She never wanted to pry, never wanted to make him feel pressured, but a part of her had always hoped that when the time came, he'd come to her.

And now, standing in their living room, with anger and tension thick in the air, her son was finally saying it out loud.

She exhaled slowly, keeping her voice steady. "Sandy, honey, you've never formally come out to me. So I've never assumed."

Sandy huffed. "Well, *I* assumed you assumed."

Cord looked shell-shocked. "Wait. What?"

Audrey rolled her eyes. "Come on, Cord. I've known for years." She smirked at Sandy. "Remember that cute guy who used to work at the bait shop? What was his name—Jackson? We both had a crush on him at one point."

Sandy chuckled. "Yeah. And I let you have him."

"You did not," Audrey shot back. "He turned me down and moved to Portland to join a folk rock band."

Maggie sighed. "So that's what happened."

Cord shook his head, still looking dazed. "I—I had no idea."

Sandy shrugged. "You didn't want to have an idea, Cord. You never asked, and I didn't feel like making it a big announcement."

Cord exhaled, raking a hand through his hair. "Sandy, I don't give a whit that you're gay."

"Great," Sandy said dryly. "Then maybe we can move on from this idiotic accusation."

Cord turned sharply toward Phoebe. "We're not done. Not by a long shot."

Phoebe's face paled slightly. "Cord—"

"You did throw yourself at him," Cord accused. "Did you think I wouldn't walk in? Or were you hoping I would?"

Phoebe let out a nervous laugh, plastering on a charming smile. "It was nothing, Cord. Sandy and I just have a natural rapport. It was just playful teasing—"

"That wasn't playful," Sandy cut in, his voice hard. "That was months of you flirting with me, touching me when I made it clear I wasn't interested, and now suddenly I'm the bad guy?"

Phoebe's expression hardened. "Oh, don't act like you hated the attention."

Maggie stepped forward, voice calm but firm. "Enough."

Phoebe's face twisted. "You never wanted me in this family, did you?"

Maggie raised an eyebrow. "I beg your pardon?"

Phoebe's voice rose. "You don't approve of our marriage. You never have. You've been influencing Cord—"

Maggie's eyes narrowed. "Cord is a grown man who makes his own decisions. If he has doubts about this marriage, that has nothing to do with me."

Cord exhaled slowly, as if willing himself to stay calm. "Phoebe, I've been trying so hard to ignore the doubts I've been having. To not let all the half-truths and secrets eat away at me. But I can't anymore."

Phoebe's face tensed. "What half-truths?"

Cord's expression darkened. "Your family's legal problems with Chips Hogan, for one. Every time I bring it up, you either dodge the question or tell me I don't need to worry about it. And that's not how a partnership works, Phoebe. If I marry you, I inherit everything—your baggage, your mess, your family's shady dealings. And I'm not walking into something blind."

Tears welled up in Phoebe's eyes. "Shady dealings? Is that what you think of me and my family?"

Cord held up a hand. "No, I'm sorry, poor choice of words. What I'm trying to say is . . ." His voice trailed off.

Phoebe's face went slack for a moment before she scoffed, crossing her arms. "You don't trust me."

Cord hesitated, and that was answer enough.

Phoebe's mouth tightened, her face filled with hurt and something else—something less like heartbreak and more like panic.

Sandy scoffed. "Wow. Guess this is where I exit." He turned to Maggie and shrugged. "Well. That was not how I was expecting this afternoon to go."

Maggie's expression softened. "I would have liked for you to be honest with me sooner."

Sandy smirked, brushing it off. "Yeah, yeah. I know. We'll talk later, Ma."

Sandy seized his opportunity and scooted out of the room.

Cord turned back to Phoebe and let out a deep sigh. "I think we need to put the wedding on hold."

Phoebe's eyes widened. "Cord, no—"

"I need to figure out if I can trust you," he said firmly. "And right now, I don't."

Phoebe clenched her fists, face darkening. "Fine. If you don't trust me, then maybe we should just call the whole thing off."

Cord, looking exhausted, shook his head and walked out of the room.

Phoebe let out a sharp breath, then turned toward Maggie and Audrey. "I hope you're both happy!"

With that, she stormed out.

The house fell silent.

Audrey flopped onto the couch. "Man, that was so much worse than I thought it was going to be."

Maggie sighed, rubbing her temples. "Come on. We need a debriefing."

Maggie and Audrey headed into the kitchen and settled at the breakfast table, both deep in thought.

Maggie sipped her coffee, eyes focused on the swirling steam. "We might have been looking in the wrong direction."

Audrey nodded. "Phoebe."

Maggie exhaled. "Every time someone mentions her family's legal dispute with Chips Hogan, she loses it."

"Like she's guilty," Audrey said.

"Or scared she's going to get caught," Maggie added.

"Or scared she's going to lose Cord," Audrey said thoughtfully.

Maggie tapped her fingers on the table. "If Chips had plans for that land—maybe building something, maybe digging something up—who would that have hurt?"

"The Barkers," Audrey said immediately.

Maggie nodded. "And if someone was willing to kill to keep their secrets buried . . ."

Audrey's smirk faded. "Then maybe Phoebe's not just desperate for a wedding."

Maggie's lips pressed into a firm line. "Maybe she's desperate to cover her tracks."

A long silence stretched between them.

Then Audrey stretched her arms. "Well. Guess we better start digging."

Maggie smirked. "Metaphorically. For now."

Chapter Twenty-six

The bell over the door jingled as the last customer of the night left The Chowder House. Audrey stretched her arms behind her back, rolling out the tension from a long shift. It had been a relatively uneventful night—just how she liked it.

Behind the counter, Isabella was wiping down the espresso machine, but her eyes flicked toward Audrey with poorly contained curiosity. "Okay, so spill. What really happened between you and Dr. Comstock?"

Audrey groaned, rolling her eyes. "We had dinner at his place. That's it. And trust me, he is *not* my type."

Jimmy was clearing the last table and suddenly perked up. "What is your type?" he asked, setting down a stack of plates with careful precision.

Audrey smirked. "Hmm. Smart, funny, sensitive—most importantly, kind. Not some jerk with a mean streak like Evan Barker."

Jimmy's hopeful expression faltered slightly at the mention of Evan, but before he could press further, Ethel's sharp voice rang out from the kitchen. "Jimmy! Get that mop on the kitchen floor before you punch out!"

Jimmy sighed, giving Audrey a regretful look before slinking off toward the back, mop in hand.

Isabella grinned. "Poor guy's got it so bad for you."

Audrey shook her head. "He's sweet, but *no*."

Before Isabella could tease her more, the door jingled again, and Melanie, Dr. Comstock's receptionist, strode in with stiff posture and an air of barely contained irritation.

"Pickup for Melanie," she said curtly, not even glancing at Audrey.

Ethel handed her a neatly packed to-go bag. "Here you go, sweetheart."

Melanie took it with a tight-lipped nod and turned on her heel without so much as a goodbye.

As the door slammed shut behind her, Isabella raised an eyebrow. "Wow. I thought she might turn to ice and shatter on her way out."

Audrey sighed. "Yeah, she's not exactly my biggest fan."

"Why?"

"She's in love with her boss," Audrey said with a shrug. "And she thinks I'm some kind of competition."

Isabella scoffed. "That woman is one 'Dr. Comstock doesn't notice me' away from boiling a bunny."

Audrey snorted, shaking her head.

"You wanna head out? I can finish up here," Isabella offered.

Audrey glanced at the kitchen. "Nah, I was thinking of staying and baking some muffins for breakfast service."

Ethel wiped her hands on her apron and turned to her with a knowing look. "Audrey, you work hard enough. I can handle the muffins. Go home, get some rest."

Audrey hesitated, but Ethel gave her a firm nod.

"You wanna run your own place someday, cook all

your favorites for the locals, but that doesn't mean running yourself into the ground before you even get the chance."

That, at least, was true. Audrey smiled, touched by the gesture. "Thanks, Ethel. I am kind of tired."

"Go on, kid."

Audrey grabbed her coat and waved goodbye before stepping out into the crisp night air.

Halibut Cove was eerily quiet this late in the evening. The streetlights cast long shadows on the cobbled sidewalks, and the smell of salt and fish drifted in from the docks.

Audrey took a deep breath, letting the cool air wash over her. She loved these quiet nighttime walks—usually. But tonight, something felt off.

Footsteps suddenly echoed behind her, quick and hurried.

Audrey tensed, glancing over her shoulder.

Jimmy.

She exhaled, her shoulders relaxing.

"Hey!" he called out, jogging up to her, slightly out of breath.

Audrey stopped, forcing a smile. "Jimmy, what are you doing?"

"I, uh . . ." He ran a hand through his hair, suddenly looking nervous. "I just—I was wondering if maybe you'd want to—go out sometime? Like . . . a date?"

Oh, Jimmy.

She gave him a gentle smile. "That's really sweet, but I don't think so."

Jimmy's face fell, but he nodded quickly. "Yeah. Yeah, no worries. Just thought I'd take a shot and ask."

Before she could say anything more, he turned and hurried off in the opposite direction, shoulders hunched.

Audrey sighed. She hated turning people down, especially someone as sweet as Jimmy, but she couldn't pretend she felt something she didn't.

She started walking again, but the uneasiness hadn't left.

A cold prickle ran down her spine.

She turned her head slightly, trying to be subtle.

A shadow.

At first, she thought it could still be Jimmy. Maybe he'd taken a different route, maybe he was heading home—

But then she saw another figure—tall, broad-shouldered, moving with purpose.

Her stomach twisted.

He was across the street, just far enough away to make it look casual, but he was matching her pace.

Audrey forced herself to keep walking, her pulse starting to race. Maybe she was being paranoid. Maybe it was just another person heading home.

But then she picked up her pace.

And so did he.

Her breath quickened.

She turned a corner. So did he.

The prickle of fear turned to ice in her veins.

She crossed the street. He did too.

Audrey's heartbeat pounded in her ears.

Okay.

This is not normal.

She sped up, walking fast now, her steps quick and clipped.

The man wasn't running, but he didn't have to. He was closing the distance, walking with purpose, his stride longer than hers, deliberate.

A few more seconds and he'd be right on top of her.

Her breath caught.

Oh, hell no.

She bolted.

The man chased her.

Her heart slammed against her ribs as she sprinted down the empty streets, feet pounding against the pavement. She cut down a narrow alley, trying to shake him, but he was right behind her.

Panic clawed at her chest. She pushed herself faster, tearing toward the docks, where the boats bobbed gently in the dark water.

She had to lose him.

Her eyes darted wildly. There—a fishing boat, tied to the dock, its deck just low enough to climb over.

She lunged, scrambling over the side, dropping down into the shadows.

Seconds later, footsteps.

Stopping inches from the boat.

Audrey held her breath, pressing herself against the deck, heart hammering.

The man was right there.

She could hear his breathing.

A long, excruciating pause.

Then, retreating footsteps.

Audrey waited until the silence felt real.

Then, cautiously, she peeked over the boat's edge.

No one.

She ran.

Maggie looked up from her book when Audrey burst through the front door, face pale, breath coming in short gasps.

Maggie immediately set her book down. "What happened?"

Audrey swallowed hard, trying to steady herself. "Someone—someone chased me."

Maggie's eyes hardened. "Who?"

"I don't know," Audrey admitted, pacing the living room. "I was walking home, and I could feel someone following me. I thought it was just nerves, but then I saw him—a man, tall, broad—and he started chasing me. I barely lost him."

Maggie's jaw tightened. "Did you recognize him?"

Audrey shook her head. "No. It was dark. But I don't think this was some random guy lurking around town. This felt personal."

Maggie exhaled slowly, folding her arms. "Someone's sending a message."

Audrey nodded. "Yeah. And the only question is, Who?"

Silence hung between them for a moment.

"Bradley?" Maggie suggested.

"Maybe," Audrey said. "Or Evan Barker. He's been creepy since day one."

Maggie tapped her fingers against the armrest. "Whoever it was . . . they wanted to scare you."

"Well, mission accomplished," Audrey muttered.

There was something fierce in Maggie's eyes.

"Nobody threatens my granddaughter," she said, voice low, dangerous.

Audrey swallowed.

If someone thought they could intimidate the Holbrooks into backing off . . .

They'd just made a very big mistake.

Chapter Twenty-seven

Maggie sat across from Cord at the kitchen table, hands wrapped around her coffee mug, watching her son wrestle with his thoughts. He looked exhausted, his broad shoulders slumped, his face lined with frustration.

"I just don't know if I jumped to conclusions," Cord finally admitted, rubbing a hand over his face. "Maybe I was too hard on Phoebe. Maybe I let my temper get the best of me."

Maggie took a slow sip of coffee, carefully measuring her response. She wanted desperately to tell him what she thought—that Phoebe was an opportunist through and through. That she was playing him. But Cord needed to figure this out on his own. He wasn't the type to be told things. He had to see them for himself.

"If you're feeling this unsettled," Maggie said, "maybe it means something. Maybe it's your gut trying to tell you what your head doesn't want to admit."

Cord exhaled sharply. "Or maybe I'm overthinking everything. Her parents won't even speak to me now. They believe I humiliated her."

Maggie tapped her fingers against the mug. "Do you want my help, or am I overstepping?"

Cord met her eyes. "No. I want your help."

Maggie nodded and reached for her phone. "Then let's clear the air."

Maggie and Cord walked up the stone steps of the Barker house, the air between them heavy with tension. Maggie glanced at her son, who looked uncertain, his brow furrowed in deep thought. She gave him a reassuring pat on the arm before knocking on the door.

Rhonda Barker answered, her lips pressed into a thin line, her posture stiff. "Maggie. Cord."

Maggie offered a polite smile. "Rhonda, thank you for agreeing to see us. I hate how we left things with Phoebe. I thought it might be good for us to talk. To figure this out properly."

Rhonda hesitated, then nodded and stepped aside, allowing them in. The house smelled faintly of cinnamon—an attempt, Maggie thought, to make things feel warm and inviting. But there was a tension in the air that no amount of homey scents could mask.

Phoebe sat curled up on the couch, eyes red and puffy. She sniffled as Cord took a seat across from her.

"I'm sorry," she murmured, voice barely above a whisper. "I know I made mistakes, but I love you, Cord. I never meant to hurt you."

Cord hesitated. He looked at his hands, exhaled, then finally met Phoebe's gaze.

"I need to know the truth," he said, his voice quieter than he intended. He glanced at his mother, then back at Phoebe. "About everything."

Phoebe's expression wavered between hopeful and wary. "Just say it, Cord. Whatever's on your mind."

Cord swallowed.

Did she really want him to say it?

Maybe she thought if she kept playing the wounded, heartbroken fiancée, he'd fold.

He didn't.

"This marriage," he said, his voice firmer now, "it wasn't about the land dispute, was it?"

Phoebe gasped, shaking her head. "Cord! How can you even think that?"

"I don't know," he admitted. "I want to believe you. But I can't shake the feeling that I'm being played here. That I was part of a bigger plan to hold on to this property."

Maggie noticed Bert taking a step forward, ready to defend his daughter's reputation, but Rhonda placed a firm hand on his arm, holding him back.

Tears welled up in Phoebe's eyes, and she covered her face with her hands. But Maggie noticed something—Phoebe's fingers were slightly splayed, allowing her to peek through them, watching everyone's reactions.

Interesting.

"I love you," Phoebe sobbed, peeking again through her fingers. "Yes, my family is desperate to keep our land. But I never used you. I wanted to marry you because I love you. I still do."

The room fell into a thick silence, broken only by Bert clearing his throat.

"You know," he said, "when Rhonda and I first got together, it wasn't an easy road for us either. Lots of drama, lots of difficulties. But we stuck it out, and we got through it."

Maggie tilted her head. "Drama?"

Bert hesitated. "Yeah, well, you know how it is when people first get together. Things can get . . . messy."

Something in his tone sent a flicker of recognition through Maggie's mind.

"Bert, I believe you were already dating Rhonda when I first met you," Maggie said. "But wasn't she engaged to Billy Sawyer around that time, before he suddenly left town?"

Rhonda went ghostly pale.

She gripped the armrest of her chair as though the room had tilted.

Maggie noticed immediately. "Is everything all right, Rhonda? You look as if you might faint."

Rhonda waved her off. "I'm fine, fine."

Bert immediately jumped in. "This whole land dispute has taken a huge toll on Rhonda. It's been stressful for all of us."

Rhonda forced a tight smile, nodding rapidly. "Yes. Yes, it's just been . . . overwhelming."

Maggie's eyes narrowed slightly.

That reaction was not normal.

Before she could press further, Evan Barker stormed into the room, stopping short when he saw Maggie and Cord.

His eyes darted between them, suspicion flickering across his face. "What's going on here?"

Maggie turned to him, offering a warm, disarming smile. "Evan, you know how it is. Family matters. Just trying to sort things out."

Evan gave a noncommittal grunt, clearly not buying her act.

Maggie leaned in slightly. "You look tired, dear. Long night?"

Evan blinked at her, thrown off by her sudden interest in him. "I was home last night," he said stiffly.

Maggie's expression remained pleasant. "Oh? The *whole* night?"

Evan's jaw tightened. "Yeah. Why?"

Phoebe furrowed her brow. "No, you weren't. You went out for a walk earlier, remember?"

Evan whipped his head toward her, his face twisting with anger. "*Phoebe*."

Her eyes widened. "I—I just meant, you did go out, I saw you . . ."

"What I do is *my* business, nobody else's," he seethed.

Evan looked like he was about to explode. His hands clenched into fists at his sides, and for a moment, Maggie thought he might actually lunge at his sister.

Bert quickly stepped in, placing a firm hand on Evan's shoulder. "Now, now, let's not make a big deal out of this." He turned to Maggie, his voice calm, placating. "Evan was upset over something stupid—we lost our internet service for a few minutes, and he was right in the middle of—"

"I was doing something important! It wasn't stupid!"

"You're right, son, of course," Bert quickly replied, hoping to calm him down. He turned back to Maggie with a benevolent smile. "He just needed to blow off steam. He was only gone for ten, fifteen minutes at most."

Maggie nodded. "So in that time, did you happen to see Audrey?"

Evan's face darkened. "Audrey? No, why?"

"She was out walking around the same time last night and thought she might have seen you skulking around in the dark?"

"Skulking? Did she say I was skulking? I don't skulk! How am I supposed to respond to that?"

"I just want to know if you saw her, that's all."

"No," he snapped. "Stop interrogating me."

Maggie held up her hands, giving him a small, understanding nod. "All right. No need to get all worked up."

Evan huffed, crossing his arms, but didn't say anything else.

But Maggie wasn't fooled.

She'd gotten exactly what she needed.

Cord drove in silence for a long stretch, the truck rumbling along the quiet roads back toward the Holbrook house. Maggie sat beside him, staring out the window, her mind racing with the day's revelations.

Evan's reaction had been disturbing. The anger, the defiance. The way he'd practically snapped when she questioned him. She had no doubt in her mind now—he was hiding something.

Finally, Cord broke the silence. "So . . . what do you think?"

Maggie pulled herself from her thoughts and turned to her son. "I think you handled that about as well as anyone could. You were honest. Direct. That's what the situation needed."

Cord exhaled through his nose, gripping the wheel a little tighter. "I still don't know what to think about Phoebe."

Maggie nodded. "That's fair. She's saying all the right things. But do you believe her?"

Cord hesitated. "I don't know," he admitted. "She seemed . . . desperate. And I get it, her family's under a lot of stress. But something still feels off."

Maggie studied him. "Trust is funny like that. Once it cracks, it's hard to put back together."

Cord tapped his fingers against the steering wheel. "I

just keep thinking—if there was nothing to hide, why did she react like that? Why did her parents get so weird when you brought up Billy Sawyer?"

Maggie turned her gaze back to the road ahead. "I think there are a lot of things that family doesn't want us looking into."

Cord swallowed hard. "You think they had something to do with Chips?"

Maggie took a long, measured breath. "I don't know. But I do think they're hiding something. And I think you were right to question everything."

Cord nodded, his jaw tightening. "I'm not ready to marry her. Not yet."

Maggie gave him a small, approving nod.

Good.

At least her hot-headed son was starting to see things clearly.

Chapter Twenty-eight

Audrey sat at the Holbrook dining room table, hunched over her laptop, fingers drumming impatiently against the wood as she scrolled through search results. Dr. Bradley Comstock was proving to be a ghost.

"Dentists usually have a digital footprint," she muttered. "Online reviews, conference bios, something."

Maggie, across from her with her morning tea, smirked. "The less you find, the more interesting it gets."

There was little to go on, but one detail stuck out—a mention of a small New Hampshire town called Woodhaven, where Bradley's parents had moved just before he was born.

"Ever heard of it?" Audrey asked.

Maggie sipped her tea and shook her head. "Nope. But there's only one way to find out more."

Audrey shut her laptop and sighed. "We're going to New Hampshire, aren't we?"

Maggie stood, stretching. "Pack a bag, sweetheart. It's time for a Thelma and Louise road trip."

"Let's just not drive over any cliffs, okay?"

* * *

Maggie, to Audrey's horror, selected one of her late husband Wes's classic roadsters for the trip—an emerald green 1958 MG MGA. It looked more suited for a museum than the highway.

Audrey hesitated before climbing into the passenger seat. "Are you sure this thing is safe?"

Maggie scoffed. "Wes kept all his cars in pristine condition. This baby could outrun anything on the road today."

Audrey buckled in, muttering, "Yeah, but can you drive it safely?"

Maggie shot her a look. "Audrey, the younger generation needs a stronger backbone and a sense of adventure."

Audrey deadpanned. "You drive like Mrs. Magoo."

Maggie grinned. "And yet, I've never had an accident. Hold on tight."

With that, she threw the car into gear and gunned it out of the driveway.

By the time they hit the highway, Audrey had white-knuckled the door handle into submission.

"This isn't NASCAR, Nana!" Audrey yelped as Maggie took a turn far too sharply.

"Relax," Maggie said, completely unbothered. "We're making excellent time."

By some miracle, they arrived in Woodhaven, New Hampshire, in one piece. It was the kind of town where time had stalled sometime in the 1950s, with a single main street featuring a post office, a hardware store, and a diner with a neon sign missing a few letters.

Before they started knocking on doors, Audrey suggested they visit the local cemetery, knowing that Bradley's parents had both passed away.

It didn't take long to find the Comstock family plot—it was a small cluster of gravestones near an old maple tree.

Ed Comstock
1953–1988
A Man Who Tried His Best

Lily Comstock-Harrington
1957–2016
A Mother First

Maggie exhaled. "She remarried."

Audrey crouched down, running her fingers over the Harrington inscription. "If she took another last name, maybe she had other kids?"

Maggie pointed at the engraving below Lily's name.

Beloved Mother to Bradley

Audrey's brows furrowed. "No mention of any other children."

At the foot of the grave was a space left empty, as if meant for someone else's name one day.

"Bradley's stepfather must still be alive," Maggie mused.

Audrey chewed her lip. "And nowhere to be found."

"Give me time. We just got here," Maggie said with a wink.

Back in town, they pulled into The Griddle & Grit, the kind of diner where the coffee was strong and the waitresses didn't tolerate nonsense. Not unlike The Chowder House.

Inside, the place was pure small-town nostalgia—red

vinyl booths, checkered floors, and an old man in a faded flannel perched at the counter, nursing a cup of coffee.

Maggie took a seat next to him, flashing a dazzling smile. "Mind if we join you?"

The old man nearly dropped his spoon. "Well, now! You can sit anywhere you like, darlin'. How about my lap?"

"I can already tell you're going to be trouble." Maggie chuckled.

"That's what they call me. Trouble. With a capital *T*!"

Audrey stifled a laugh as the waitress, a battle-ax of a woman with a pencil shoved behind her ear, appeared. "What'll it be?"

"Coffee. And a tuna melt," Maggie said sweetly.

Audrey ordered a club sandwich and then leaned toward the old man. "You from around here?"

"Born and raised," he said proudly. "Name's Roy Baxter."

Maggie turned on her charm. "Roy, we're trying to find Lily Comstock's family. Did you know her?"

Roy's smile faded slightly. "Oh, yeah. I knew Lily. Nice girl. She married that poor fella Ed. Didn't end well."

Audrey glanced at Maggie.

Bingo.

Roy scratched his chin. "Lily's sister, Eloise Hastings, still lives here. Out near Deer Hollow Road."

The waitress huffed. "Eloise doesn't get many visitors. Good luck with that."

Maggie beamed. "I can be very persuasive."

Roy leaned on the counter, eyeing Maggie with an approving grin. "Persuasive, huh? Well now, that sounds like a challenge."

Maggie gave him her most dazzling smile. "Roy, you wouldn't stand a chance."

* * *

Eloise Hastings's quaint blue house was tucked between two sprawling maple trees, her yard meticulously kept. When Maggie knocked, there was a long pause before a curtain twitched, and the door cracked open.

"If you're selling something, I already have a vacuum and a decent set of knives."

Maggie chuckled. "No selling. We're from Halibut Cove, and we're looking into Bradley Comstock's past."

Eloise narrowed her eyes. "Why?"

"We think he might be hiding things," Audrey said bluntly.

Eloise hesitated. Then, after a sigh, she swung the door open. "Might as well come in."

Inside, over cups of black coffee, Eloise filled in the gaps.

"When Ed and Lily came back, Ed was a broken man. Couldn't get his footing in business, failed at everything. Lily thought having Bradley would help heal him. It didn't. And one day . . ."

She trailed off.

They all knew how that sentence ended.

Audrey exhaled. "And Bradley?"

Eloise shook her head. "Bradley was trouble from the start. After Lily remarried, her new husband didn't take to Bradley. Didn't want him around. Sent him to a private school."

"His name was Harrington?" Audrey asked.

"Yes, Gil Harrington."

Maggie took a sip of her coffee. "Does he still live around here?"

"No, Gil left shortly after Lily passed away. I'd be surprised if he was still in contact with Bradley. Those two never got along."

Audrey and Maggie exchanged a look.

Maggie set her cup down. "Who else might know about Bradley?"

Eloise considered. "Penny Woodworth. She runs a bookstore in town. She dated Bradley once—briefly, as I recall."

The Book Nook & Cranny was small, cozy, and packed with books. Penny Woodworth, a petite woman in her mid-thirties with cropped auburn hair, was behind the counter.

At the sight of them, she froze. "Eloise called and said to be on the lookout for you two."

Maggie raised an eyebrow. "Word travels fast in this town."

Audrey smiled. "So you must already know we're looking into Bradley Comstock."

Penny immediately turned her back and started rearranging a shelf. "I don't really—" Before she could brush them off completely, Maggie let out a dramatic sigh and began perusing the shelves with keen interest.

"What a lovely shop," she said, running her fingers along the spines. "It's been ages since I let myself indulge." She pulled a book from the nearest display. "Ooh, *The Paris Library*! Audrey, did you read this one?"

Audrey blinked. "Uh, no?"

"You'd love it," Penny piped up before she could stop herself. "It's based on the true story of the American Library in Paris during World War II. A great mix of historical fiction and espionage."

Maggie beamed. "Perfect. I'll take it." She plucked another off the shelf. "And this one?"

Penny hesitated. "That's *Lessons in Chemistry* by Bonnie Garmus. It's been out a while but is still really popular."

Maggie nodded approvingly and added it to her growing pile. "And this?" She grabbed *Demon Copperhead* by Barbara Kingsolver.

"That's a modern reimagining of *David Copperfield*. Won the Pulitzer," Penny said, momentarily forgetting she had no intention of talking to them.

Maggie gasped dramatically. "A Pulitzer Prize winner? Sold!"

Within five minutes, Penny had recommended no fewer than twelve books, and Maggie had gathered them all on the checkout counter.

Audrey crossed her arms, barely hiding her smirk.

Now let's see her ignore us.

Penny sighed, resigned, and walked to the register. "All right, let's ring these up."

Maggie whispered to Audrey, "See? I told you I was persuasive."

Penny huffed but couldn't help a small smirk as she scanned the first book. "All right. What do you want to know about Bradley?"

Audrey leaned in. "Anything you can tell us. What was he like?"

Penny hesitated, then lowered her voice. "I dated Bradley. For a split second."

"And?" Audrey pressed.

Penny hesitated again, shifting uncomfortably. "He was . . . off. Possessive. Angry. Mean streak a mile wide. My parents hated him. Warned me to stay away."

"But you didn't?" Maggie guessed.

Penny shook her head. "I was young. Defiant. Thought my parents just didn't understand." She let out a humorless laugh. "Until I saw it up close for myself. The way he'd snap over small things. The cruelty. His erratic behavior. It was scary."

Audrey's stomach churned. "Did anything happen?"

Penny nodded grimly. "Not with me. I broke it off with a text and then blocked his number. Never heard from him again. But I did hear something bad happened at his prep school. Police got involved."

Audrey and Maggie exchanged a glance.

"Where's the school?" Maggie asked.

"Conner Prep. Fifteen minutes outside town."

Audrey exhaled. "Then I guess that's our next stop."

Penny finished bagging up Maggie's massive book haul and sighed. "You're gonna find out some things you won't like."

Maggie took her bag and gave Penny a knowing smile. "That's usually how these things go."

As they stepped outside, Audrey nudged her grandmother. "So, you're really gonna read all those?"

Maggie patted the bag as they crossed the street where her MG was parked. "Probably not. But I do like supporting small businesses."

When they reached Maggie's car, Audrey planted herself in front of the driver's side door.

Maggie arched an eyebrow. "What are you doing?"

Audrey folded her arms. "I'm driving. For my own mental health."

Maggie sighed, tossing her the keys.

As they sped off toward the prep school, one thing was certain—Bradley Comstock had a dark past. And they were about to find out just how deep it went.

Chapter Twenty-nine

The Conner Prep Academy campus looked like something out of a New England postcard—red-brick buildings, perfectly manicured lawns, and looming oak trees that had probably stood there since before the Revolution. It was the kind of place that screamed privilege, discipline, and old money.

Audrey pulled the MG MGA into the visitors' lot, cutting the engine. She still wasn't convinced the car wouldn't explode, but at least it had gotten them this far without breaking down.

Maggie stretched in the passenger seat. "See? No reason to doubt this beauty."

Audrey shot her a look. "You mean the car, or me as the driver?"

Maggie smirked. "Both."

Rolling her eyes, Audrey climbed out and surveyed the imposing main building. A gold-embossed sign beside the doors read: CONNER PREP ACADEMY—EST. 1892.

Audrey whistled. "Fancy."

Inside, the air smelled like leather-bound books, expensive furniture polish, and years of repressed rebellion.

An older receptionist in a tweed blazer sat behind a grand mahogany desk, typing on an ancient-looking desktop computer. She looked up, adjusting her cat-eye glasses, and eyed them with well-practiced skepticism.

"May I help you?" she asked, voice clipped and exquisitely unimpressed.

Maggie flashed her most disarming smile. "We're looking for information on a former student, Bradley Comstock. We were told someone here might remember him."

The woman's face immediately soured. "Comstock."

She removed her glasses and set them down. "Yes. That name rings a bell."

Audrey exchanged a glance with Maggie.

Pay dirt.

The receptionist sighed heavily. "Bradley was a . . . challenging student. Always in trouble. There were incidents, several disciplinary actions, and let's just say, the administration was relieved when his stepfather withdrew him before we had to formally expel him."

Maggie tilted her head. "What kind of incidents?"

The woman's lips pressed together. "I can't disclose specifics. However . . ." She seemed to consider them for a moment before continuing. "If you want more insight, Robbie Cavendish, one of our English teachers, was a student at the time and knew Bradley well."

She checked her watch. "His class should be finishing shortly. You can wait for him outside his classroom. The Madison Building."

Following the receptionist's directions, Maggie and Audrey made their way across the quad to a large academic building.

Through the open window of Lecture Hall 204, they spotted Robbie Cavendish, mid-lecture, pacing in front of a whiteboard covered in notes. A lively discussion was unfolding, and the name George Orwell was scrawled across the board.

"Now, class," Robbie said, perching on the edge of his desk, "why is *1984* still relevant today?"

A girl in the front row raised her hand. "Because governments still try to control people's thoughts?"

Robbie nodded approvingly. "Exactly. Orwell wasn't just writing about the dangers of a dystopian future. He was warning us about how easily we surrender our freedom without even realizing it."

A boy in the second row muttered, "Kinda feels like my parents when they check my phone."

The class laughed, and Robbie grinned. "See? Orwell knew what he was talking about."

Audrey leaned over to Maggie as they entered the lecture hall and whispered, "I like this guy."

Maggie nodded. "He's got flair."

When class dismissed, Robbie spotted them lingering at the back and approached, tilting his head curiously.

"Ladies, I assume you're not here for the Orwell lecture."

Maggie smiled. "As riveting as it was, no. We're hoping you can tell us about Bradley Comstock."

Robbie's expression darkened. "Bradley . . ." He exhaled. "Now there's a name I haven't heard in a long time."

He gestured for them to follow him. "Come on. Let's talk in my office."

As they crossed the sun-dappled quad, Robbie fell into a thoughtful silence.

"I haven't thought about Bradley in years," he admitted. "I knew he ended up becoming a dentist, but I didn't realize he was living in Halibut Cove. Back in school he used to mention his folks had spent time there before he was born—but Bradley himself? He was always a tough one to figure out."

"He is," Maggie said. "And we're trying to get a better sense of who he really is."

Robbie let out a dry laugh. "Then you've got your work cut out for you."

The campus bustled around them—students rushing to class, professors engaged in deep discussions. But Robbie's face was tight, like he was digging through memories he'd rather leave buried.

By the time they reached his modestly cluttered office, he gestured for them to sit in the two guest chairs while he took a seat behind his desk.

"So," he said, folding his hands. "What exactly do you want to know?"

Maggie leaned forward. "We heard there were a few behavioral problems here at Conner when it came to Bradley."

"That's a mild understatement. There were a lot of incidents," Robbie admitted, rubbing his chin. "Fights, anger issues, destroyed school property—even suspected arson."

Audrey's eyebrows shot up. "*Arson*?"

Robbie leaned forward. "One of our teachers—Mr. Faraday—flunked Bradley in chemistry. Not long after, his house burned down."

Maggie sucked in a breath. "Was there proof he did it?"

Robbie shook his head. "Never any concrete evidence, but the timing was too suspicious. Plus, the school's security footage mysteriously disappeared that week. Bradley's stepfather, Gil Harrington, made a generous donation—

fixed up the teacher's house and threw in a tennis court just to smooth things over."

Audrey's stomach turned. "So his stepfather just . . . paid his way out of trouble?"

Robbie nodded. "That was the pattern. Gil didn't want Bradley moving back home and disrupting his life with Lily. So, whenever Bradley did something terrible, Gil just threw money at the problem to make it go away."

Maggie crossed her arms. "And he paid for his dental school, too, I assume?"

"Absolutely," Robbie said. "Anything to keep him away." He let out a humorless chuckle. "Then when Lily died, Gil cut him off completely. Blamed him for her death, said he drove her to an early grave."

Audrey leaned back in her chair, letting that sink in.

"So when Gil stopped protecting him," she said slowly, "Bradley was on his own."

Robbie nodded. "For the first time in his life."

The room was silent for a beat.

Maggie tapped her fingers against the armrest, thinking.

"Bradley lost everything," she murmured. "His father, his mother, his financial safety net."

Audrey's stomach churned. "And now, suddenly, he shows up in Halibut Cove?"

Maggie's eyes narrowed. "Maybe he's looking for someone besides his stepfather to blame."

Maggie and Audrey walked back to the roadster, the weight of the conversation hanging heavy between them.

Audrey exhaled sharply. "That's one hell of a backstory."

Maggie nodded, lost in thought. "Bradley doesn't have anyone left. No family, no safety net. He's been cut loose, and now he's in Halibut Cove where his father's whole life took a terrible turn."

Audrey slid into the driver's seat, gripping the wheel. "And if he blames Halibut Cove for what happened to his father . . ."

Maggie finished the thought. "Then Chips Hogan, Griffin Mead, and even your grandfather Wes—the men involved in Ed Comstock's downfall—might have been his revenge targets."

Audrey felt a cold shiver run down her spine.

Maggie's voice was quiet but firm. "We need to find out what he's planning next."

Chapter Thirty

Jill hated the morgue.

It wasn't the dead bodies—she had seen enough of those in her years as police chief. It wasn't even the eerie quiet or the scent of antiseptic trying (and failing) to mask the underlying smell of decay.

No. It was Iggy.

The county coroner, Ignatius "Iggy" Demers, had the hygiene standards of a middle-school boy and the eating habits of a gremlin.

Jill sighed as she and Officer Mason Dooley pushed open the door to the forensic lab, immediately hit with the unmistakable aroma of pastrami, mustard, and fries.

Iggy was mid-bite into an obscenely overstuffed sandwich, a smear of mustard on his lip and a blob of ketchup decorating his cheek. Beside him, on one of the exam tables, was an order of fries in a grease-stained takeout box, with ketchup smeared on the metal surface dangerously close to an autopsy file.

He was hovering over an open body, chewing enthusiastically.

"For God's sake, Iggy!" Jill snapped. "Can you not eat directly over the corpses?"

Iggy looked up, completely unfazed, licking ketchup off his cheek from the fries. "What? They're not gonna complain."

Mason made a strangled sound and immediately turned five shades paler.

Jill groaned. "You're getting condiments all over the place!"

Iggy glanced down at his autopsy files, where a generous dollop of ketchup had landed.

"Whoops." He wiped it with his sleeve, which somehow made it worse.

Mason audibly gagged.

Jill shot him a look. "Do not throw up in here."

Mason gulped, doing his best to look anywhere but at the corpse lying on the table, which had an exposed chest cavity.

"Jesus, Iggy," Mason muttered. "Have you ever heard of the word *sanitation*?"

Iggy took another big bite, waving him off. "Germs can't live in here long. Too cold."

Jill shook her head, exasperated. "Remind me to talk to the county about replacing you."

Iggy winked. "Come on, Chief. You'd miss me."

Jill let out a long suffering sigh. "Doubtful. Let's talk about Griffin Mead."

Iggy licked mustard off his thumb before flipping through a greasy file.

"Right," he mumbled, scanning the autopsy notes. "So we know Griffin Mead had Clonidine in his system, which explains why he was incapacitated before he drowned."

Jill crossed her arms. "And no other drugs? Nothing else that could have knocked him out?"

Iggy shook his head. "Nope. Just Clonidine. Enough to seriously impair motor function. He would have been disoriented, weak, and unable to swim if he ended up in the water."

Jill tapped her fingers on the stainless steel exam table. "So, could the Clonidine have been delivered through something like . . . novocaine?"

Iggy perked up, intrigued. "Oh, yeah, definitely. If someone dosed him earlier in the day, it would take about thirty to sixty minutes to really kick in. If he was given Clonidine at the dentist's office, he would've started feeling disoriented shortly after."

Mason grimaced. "So . . . Griffin goes about his day, starts feeling weird, and by the time he's near the docks, he's so out of it that someone who followed him could have . . . pushed him in?"

Jill nodded. "And if the Clonidine had already weakened him, he wouldn't have been able to fight back."

Iggy picked up a clear evidence bag and waggled it at them. "Or he could have gotten it another way."

Mason glanced at it warily. "What is that?"

Iggy grinned. "Stomach contents."

Mason's face turned green. "Nope. No, I do not want to know."

Jill ignored him. "What was in his stomach?"

Iggy flipped through the report, smearing a bit of mustard on the paper. "Let's see . . . we found beer, half a ham sandwich, some kind of seafood chowder, a few ibuprofen, and what looked like potato chips. Any of those could have been laced with Clonidine."

Mason turned to Jill. "Seafood chowder? That's how Chips ingested the deadly nightshade! Someone could have put it in his chowder."

Jill considered that, but then shook her head. "I'm still leaning toward novocaine. It's the easiest way to administer something like Clonidine without the victim realizing it."

Iggy nodded. "It's a solid theory."

Jill leaned against the exam table, deep in thought.

"So if Griffin was dosed with Clonidine at the dentist's office earlier in the day," she said, "then that means Bradley Comstock was most likely the one who drugged him."

Mason nodded slowly. "That fits. But . . . Bradley couldn't have been the one to push Mason into the water. He has an alibi."

"Melanie." Jill muttered. "She swears they were working together the whole night."

Mason scratched his chin. "You think she's lying?"

Jill frowned. "I don't know."

Mason hesitated. "But . . . what if someone else did it for him?"

Jill's head snapped up. "An accomplice."

Mason nodded. "What if Bradley drugged Griffin during the dental appointment, but he had someone else finish the job later that night? The whole town knows Griffin turns up at the Thirsty Gull every night of the week for a few beers. They could have been lying in wait for him to leave for home, knowing he'd be nearly incapacitated by that point, and followed him to the docks."

Jill's stomach twisted. It made sense. Bradley had a pretty firm alibi for both murders—he had been in Portland the night Chips Hogan was poisoned and at his dental office the night Griffin supposedly fell into the water and drowned.

And yet . . .

They kept circling back to him.

Mason frowned. "So if Bradley had help . . . who the hell is his mystery accomplice?"

Jill sighed, staring down at the autopsy report, her brain working overtime.

That was the million-dollar question.

Who was helping Bradley cover his tracks?

And how much danger were they all in?

Jill closed the file, ignoring the mustard stains, and turned to Mason. "All right, we're done here."

Mason shot up so fast he nearly knocked over a stool.

"Thank God," he muttered, practically speed-walking to the door.

Iggy grinned, taking another massive bite of his sandwich. "Come back anytime, guys."

Mason muttered something under his breath that sounded suspiciously like, "Over my dead body."

Jill followed him out into the hallway, inhaling fresh air like it was her first breath in an hour.

Mason shuddered. "How does that man still have a job?"

Jill smirked. "No one else wants it."

Mason groaned. "I need a shower."

Jill clapped him on the back. "Buck up, Dooley. We've got a killer to catch."

As they stepped into the cold evening air, Jill's mind kept turning over the puzzle.

Bradley wasn't working alone.

And whoever was helping him?

They weren't done yet.

Chapter Thirty-one

Audrey wasn't easily rattled, but the ugly rumors creeping through town were starting to feel like a slow poison.

She and Maggie had gone to Bayside Pharmacy to pick up Maggie's blood pressure medication, and while waiting at the counter, Maggie had overheard two women whispering in one of the aisles.

"I'm telling you, Norma," one of them muttered, "I won't eat their chowder again. Not after two deaths."

The other hummed in agreement. "I mean, what are the chances? First Chips Hogan, now Griffin Mead? Makes you think, doesn't it?"

Audrey tensed, but Maggie's expression remained neutral—a lifetime of high-stakes family debates over recipes and restaurant deals had made her an expert at keeping her cool under pressure.

Maggie took her time, then, with surgical precision, drifted into their line of sight, plucking a bottle of antacid off the shelf.

"Heartburn?" she said sweetly. "Funny thing—I get that sometimes when I hear people spreading nonsense."

The two women froze.

"Maggie, I—I wasn't sayin'—"

Maggie smiled, but there was steel behind it. "You *were*. And let me remind you, the Holbrook chowder recipe has been around for generations. It's been enjoyed by fishermen, lobstermen, tourists, and presidents." She tilted her head. "Not a single one has dropped dead after eating a bowl."

Norma gripped a bottle of Metamucil like it was a lifeline.

The other woman cleared her throat. "Of course, I'd never suggest—"

Maggie held up a hand. "Don't worry, dear. It's not your fault if you don't know the difference between gossip and fact."

The women shuffled away, defeated, while Audrey tried not to laugh.

At the counter, Doug, the pharmacist, handed Maggie her prescription bag with an amused grin.

"Don't let the town chatter get to you," he said. "My wife and I still order your chowder every Sunday night at Ethel's place. Not gonna stop now."

Maggie patted his hand. "Doug, you and your wife have impeccable taste."

As Doug rang up the total, Audrey's eyes drifted to the newspaper rack beside the counter.

And then her stomach dropped.

There, bold as day, was the front-page headline of the *Halibut Cove Chronicle*:

CHIPS HOGAN'S DEATH LINKED TO LONG-LOST MISSING PERSON?

She snatched up the paper and scanned the article.

A missing persons case from decades ago.

A man named Billy Sawyer—Rhonda Barker's ex-boyfriend.

Connections between Chips Hogan and the missing man.

And rumors swirling about whether the Barkers knew what happened to him.

Was the land dispute somehow connected to Sawyer's disappearance?

How a source identified Griffin Mead as someone who had knowledge of what really happened to Billy Sawyer.

A direct mention of Audrey visiting Lou's office, inquiring about Billy Sawyer and the Barkers, which "sparked" Lou's interest in reinvestigating the case.

Audrey exhaled sharply.

She had started this.

She looked at Maggie, who was still chatting with Doug, then steeled herself.

"I have to get to the diner. I'm filling in for a couple of hours for Isabella," she told her grandmother. "I'll be home for dinner."

Before Maggie could question her, Audrey was already heading for her car, her mind racing, worried how Lou's article would turn the case on its head.

The bell above the diner door clattered violently as Phoebe Barker burst inside, her face flushed, hair disheveled, and a look of frantic desperation in her eyes.

A few diners startled, forks clinking against plates, conversation halting mid-sentence.

Audrey barely had time to react before Phoebe stormed toward her, gripping the newspaper like a weapon.

"You did this," Phoebe hissed, shoving the crumpled copy of the *Chronicle* at Audrey.

Audrey took a step back, eyes flicking to the damning paragraph with her name.

Lou had spelled it out—her visit to his office had sent him digging, ultimately leading to this explosive article.

Phoebe's hands shook. "You handed this to him! You put my family in the spotlight—now everyone thinks we're murderers!"

Audrey exhaled, keeping her voice calm. "Phoebe, I never meant for him to publish anything."

"Cord already thinks all of us Barkers are monsters," Phoebe whispered harshly. "Now the whole town will, too. Lou Grady basically claimed my parents killed Billy Sawyer and buried him on our land! I need to prove my parents are innocent."

Audrey folded her arms. "And how exactly do you plan on doing that?"

Phoebe's breath hitched. "We dig up the land."

"*We?*"

"Yes, come with me now."

Audrey blinked. "Oh, hell no."

"I'm begging you!"

"I'm working, Phoebe!"

Phoebe's eyes burned with desperation. "We have to fix this, Audrey. You got us into this mess. Help me get us out."

Audrey wavered.

Then, from behind the counter, Ethel sighed. "Audrey, go clock out. I'll finish closing up."

Audrey and Phoebe crept into the Barker garage, grabbing two shovels. As they headed out toward the property line near Chips's house, they heard an upstairs window creak open at the Barkers and froze. They had assumed no one was home. Phoebe was under the impression Evan had gone to dinner with her parents.

Audrey barely had time to duck back inside the garage and hide behind a stack of storage bins before Evan's voice boomed down from above.

"What the hell are you doing?" Evan barked.

Phoebe hesitated. "Just . . . grabbing a screwdriver from Dad's toolbox."

Evan squinted. "For what?"

Phoebe swallowed hard. "I have a loose drawer handle in my room. It's driving me crazy. Thought I'd try fixing it."

Audrey had to bite her tongue. Phoebe had never fixed anything in her life.

Evan narrowed his eyes. "Since when do you do handyman work?"

Phoebe forced a laugh. "Since I got tired of waiting for Dad to do it."

A long pause. Then Evan sighed, rubbing his face.

"Whatever. Don't mess up the tools," he muttered, slamming the window shut.

Audrey let out a slow breath and emerged from her hiding place behind the storage boxes. "That was way too close."

They hurried to the disputed patch of land, keeping their voices low, shovels slicing through the damp soil. The earth was heavy, each movement making Phoebe's breathing more erratic.

After twenty minutes of digging, they found nothing.

Just plenty of dirt.

Audrey was about to call it quits when suddenly Phoebe's shovel hit something solid.

Audrey froze.

Phoebe tossed her shovel aside and dropped to her knees, scraping at the dirt with her bare hands until bones surfaced.

She let out a choked scream.

Before Audrey could shush her, Phoebe's eyes fell on what looked like a skull. She let out a bloodcurdling wail.

Loud enough for Audrey to see a neighbor looking out his window, his phone to his ear.

Then, without warning, a car pulled up, the headlights momentarily blinding them.

The car shut off, the lights went out, and Phoebe's parents got out.

Bert and Rhonda had come home early.

Rhonda clutched her stomach, looking on the verge of collapse.

Phoebe stood up quickly and with a guilty look on her face, squeaked, "Why are you home so early?"

"Your mother's got an upset stomach," Bert said as his eyes fell to the hole in the ground.

Rhonda let out a horrified gasp.

Bert roared. "What is this?! What have you done?!"

A dog barked in the distance. A porch light flicked on across the street.

"Please, Bert, keep your voice down. We don't need one of the neighbors calling the police!"

Bert's eyes locked onto the hole—and the bones.

His face went white.

"Omigod!"

Before anyone could react, red and blue lights flashed.

Jill and Mason stepped out of the squad car.

Jill's gaze swept over the scene. "Would someone mind telling me what's going on here?"

Bert cleared his throat, trying for calm. "Nothing, Chief. Just a misunderstanding."

Mason's eyes scanned the property. "We got a noise complaint."

"Just a family squabble, nothing serious," Bert assured her.

Jill noticed Audrey hovering in the background behind Phoebe. "What are you doing here?"

Before Audrey could answer, Evan stormed out of the house, shotgun in hand.

"Get the hell off our property! You're trespassing!" Evan cried.

Jill raised her hand. "Evan, put the gun down! Now!"

Bert's shoulders sank. "Son, please, no. You don't need to get in the middle of all this—"

Mason's hand flew to his gun.

Evan whipped his gun in Mason's direction. "Don't do it."

Mason kept his hand hovering over the gun in his holster.

Evan cocked the shotgun, chest heaving.

Jill's voice was like steel. "I don't ask twice, Evan. Pointing a gun at a police officer can land you in jail for a long time, so I suggest you stand down."

A long, agonizing pause.

Then, Bert pleaded, his voice hoarse with desperation. "Evan, please. Go back inside. Don't make this worse."

Evan's jaw tightened.

Then, finally, he turned and bolted back inside.

They all let out a breath.

Jill's tone was sharp. "Does he even have a license for that thing?"

Then her eyes fell on the bones sticking out of the ground.

And a skull next to Phoebe's feet.

Her expression hardened.

"Somebody better start talking."

Chapter Thirty-two

The weight of thirty years of buried secrets hung thick in the air as Jill stared at the shallow grave in the Barker backyard. The old bones—long hidden beneath dirt and tangled roots—were finally exposed, along with the truth.

Jill exhaled sharply, then turned to Bert and Rhonda Barker, their ashen faces lined with fear.

"Inside. Now."

Bert hesitated. "Jill—"

"I said inside."

His shoulders slumped. Rhonda let out a weak whimper, clutching her stomach, and Bert wrapped an arm around her protectively. They trudged toward the house, their heads bowed under the crushing weight of old sins.

Mason followed closely behind them, keeping a sharp eye on Evan, who stood, fists clenched at his sides, just inside the door. He appeared ready to swing at the next person who looked at him the wrong way.

Audrey and Phoebe trailed behind, the latter shaking so hard Jill thought she might collapse right there on the porch.

Inside, the kitchen was eerily silent.

Jill walked in last and shut the door. "Sit," she ordered.

Bert and Rhonda sank into the chairs at the scarred oak kitchen table, their expressions a mix of guilt, exhaustion, and something else—relief, maybe? The kind that comes when a terrible secret can no longer be contained.

Jill crossed her arms. "Start talking."

Rhonda let out a shaky breath. "It was self-defense," she whispered.

Jill waited, giving them space to unravel the story they had clearly kept bottled up for decades.

Rhonda's hands gripped the table so hard her knuckles turned white. "I was young, scared . . . pregnant. Billy Sawyer—" Her voice caught, and she turned to Bert for strength.

Bert cleared his throat, his voice gruff but steady. "Billy was a violent son of a bitch. Beat the hell out of her. Everyone in town knew it." His eyes met Jill's. "He wasn't the father of Phoebe. I was."

Phoebe let out a soft sob, covering her mouth.

Rhonda continued, her voice trembling. "I didn't tell Billy I was pregnant, not at first. But when he found out . . . he just went into a blind rage. He said if the baby wasn't his, I had no right to have it."

Jill's stomach clenched.

Bert's hands curled into fists on the table. "He came at her. Would've killed her if I hadn't stepped in."

A long, heavy silence.

Jill caught a quick worried glance between husband and wife.

Audrey noticed it too.

Jill finally asked, "And that's when you killed him?"

Bert nodded once. "Didn't mean to. We fought, and I—

I shoved him. Hard. He hit his head. That was it. He was gone."

Rhonda wiped at her eyes. "We wanted to go to the police. We really did. It was self-defense, but . . ."

Bert swallowed hard. "But Arthur—he wouldn't let us."

Jill's brow furrowed. "Arthur? Your father, Rhonda?"

Rhonda nodded mutely, eyes wide with tears.

Bert rubbed a hand over his face. "Arthur . . . took control. He made us bury Billy in the yard."

Jill's stomach turned. "He covered it up?"

Bert nodded grimly. "Forged a letter from Billy. Made it seem like he ran off with his motorcycle gang, said he'd never come back."

Jill could hardly wrap her head around it.

Arthur passed around 2010.

He wasn't here anymore to corroborate their story.

Rhonda's voice cracked. "We thought we could move on. Billy had no one . . . or so we thought. Billy had told me once that his parents had disowned him after he got arrested too many times. They had been out of the picture for years. But it turned out his parents did care what happened to him. They filed a missing persons report. And when a detective came sniffing around Halibut Cove . . ."

Bert let out a harsh laugh. "Arthur sent us on a honeymoon to Bermuda until it all blew over. When we got back, the detective was gone."

"We figured Daddy showed him the forged letter and the detective bought it," Rhonda confirmed.

Jill exhaled slowly, the pieces snapping into place.

A forged letter. A hushed investigation. A body buried under their feet for decades.

And now? Everything was finally out in the open.

Jill pushed back from the counter. "Bert Barker, you're under arrest for the murder of Billy Sawyer."

Phoebe let out a wail. "No, you can't!"

Evan shot out of his chair, rage flashing in his eyes. "Sawyer was a violent thug! He deserved what he got!"

Jill stood firm. "That's not for you to decide."

"Son, sit down and keep quiet, please, for your mother's sake!" Bert shouted.

Evan did what he was told but didn't look happy about it.

Mason moved toward Bert, pulling out his cuffs.

Bert held up his hands in surrender. "I knew this day would come." He turned to Rhonda. "It's okay, honey."

Jill looked at Rhonda. "You knew about this. You helped cover it up."

Rhonda stiffened, her expression filled with resignation.

Jill sighed. "I'm arresting you as an accessory to the crime."

"No, please, you can't! I was the one who killed Billy! Don't punish Rhonda for what I did!"

"I'm sorry, Bert, I'm just following the law. You can make your case in court," Jill said softly.

Mason moved to cuff Rhonda as well, but before he could, Evan lunged forward, his face twisted in fury.

"This is all your fault!" he roared, his glare burning into Audrey. "You dug this up! You ruined everything!"

Audrey barely had time to flinch before Jill stepped between them, a protective wall.

"You want to go after someone?" Jill's voice was low and dangerous. "You go through me first."

Evan hesitated, his whole body shaking with rage, before he let out a frustrated snarl and stormed out of the kitchen and out of the house, slamming the front door behind him.

Phoebe collapsed into a chair, sobbing into her hands as Mason led Bert and Rhonda out the door.

Audrey stood there, stunned, arms wrapped around herself.

Finally, she whispered, "Something's not right about this."

Jill turned to her. "Audrey—"

"No." Audrey shook her head. "They're not telling us everything."

They had both seen the look between Bert and Rhonda. There was definitely more to this story.

Jill sighed. "And let me guess. You're planning on digging further?"

Audrey lifted her chin. "You know I am."

Jill let out a heavy breath, knowing there was nothing she could do to stop her.

"Just . . . be careful."

Chapter Thirty-three

Audrey was halfway down the stairs when the doorbell rang, the sharp sound echoing through the house. She hesitated for a moment, wondering whether to answer it or let Cord handle it. Before she could make up her mind, she heard Cord's voice from the entryway.

"Phoebe," he said, his tone warmer than she'd expected.

Audrey paused, her feet still on the stairs, trying to catch the words.

"Hey, I just want to say, I'm really sorry about what's happening with your family," Cord continued.

Phoebe's reply was cool and distant. "I appreciate that, Cord. Thank you."

Audrey frowned, feeling the tension in the air. She wasn't sure what she'd expected from the conversation, but it seemed clear that Phoebe was still hurt by the accusations Cord had made about her being a gold digger. She could hear the frustration in Phoebe's voice, the sting still fresh. Audrey couldn't believe she had gone from one of Phoebe's main detractors to now her staunchest cheerleader in the span of a few days.

"I was wrong, Phoebe," Cord said, sounding almost

apologetic. "I'm sorry. I was too quick to judge. I—I shouldn't have assumed what I did about you."

Audrey stepped down a few more steps, still out of sight but close enough to hear the exchange clearly.

"I'm not here to talk to you, Cord," Phoebe said sharply. "I'm here to see Audrey."

Audrey could hear Cord's breath catch, a slight tension in his voice as he said, "Fine. I understand." He sighed before adding, "Just know that I do regret how things went between us, Phoebe. I really do."

Phoebe nodded, keeping her emotions in check.

Cord turned toward the staircase and called up. "Audrey! Someone's here to see you!" He turned back to Phoebe. "I better go. Ma's waiting for me to pick her up at the hairdresser's. See you later?"

Phoebe just shrugged, refusing eye contact.

There was a moment of silence before Cord turned to leave, his footsteps growing fainter as he headed out the door.

As the door clicked shut behind him, Audrey took a breath and descended the last few steps, smoothing her shirt as she came into view. Phoebe was standing by the door, her arms folded tightly across her chest. There was a wariness in her eyes but also a tiredness, like someone who had been holding it all together for too long.

"Hey," Audrey greeted her gently.

Phoebe didn't smile, but her eyes softened. "Hey. I—Uh, I need you to come with me to the arraignment. I don't want to go alone, and I don't feel comfortable going with Evan. He's . . . unpredictable . . . and volatile . . . Sometimes I'm scared of how he reacts. You seem to be the only one who can keep me calm."

Audrey nodded. "Of course I'll go with you. You're not alone in this."

Phoebe's posture seemed to relax slightly, the tension lifting just enough for Audrey to see the strain in her face. "Thanks. I can't do this without someone I trust."

As they stepped outside, they were met with the rumbling sound of a truck engine approaching. Audrey glanced toward the driveway just in time to see Sandy's truck pulling to a stop, his truck bed bouncing slightly as it came to a halt.

Sandy rolled down his window and waved. "Cord still inside?"

"He went to pick up Maggie from the hairdresser," Phoebe replied, offering a polite smile. "He'll be back soon."

There was an awkward pause. Sandy shifted in his seat, glancing from Audrey to Phoebe, his brow furrowing slightly.

Phoebe cleared her throat, then turned to him. "Sandy, I—Uh, I owe you an apology. I was out of line before. I wasn't thinking straight. I've always gotten positive attention from men, and when it hit me that I was settling down, the weight of all that, my whole life changing, well, I just panicked. I needed validation, and I went about it in the wrong way. I chose the completely wrong person to flirt with. It was stupid and thoughtless, and I really hope you can someday forgive me."

Sandy let out a slow sigh, his gaze flickering to the ground before meeting Phoebe's eyes again. "I accept your apology, but I'd be lying if I said I wasn't still rattled by it, Phoebe. It was . . . a lot."

Phoebe nodded, her face filled with regret. "I get that. I'm sorry for making things so . . . complicated."

After a long, uncomfortable moment, Sandy muttered something about needing to find Cord so they could head out for lobstering, his voice still a bit tight. "I'll be around when Cord gets back. See ya, ladies."

With that, Sandy started the truck and drove off, leaving a tense silence behind him. Phoebe let out a breath, her shoulders drooping as if she were trying to shake off the weight of everything.

"You okay?" Audrey asked, giving Phoebe a concerned glance.

Phoebe nodded slowly, her eyes distant. "I will be. Just . . . everything's falling apart, and I don't know how to fix it."

They got into Audrey's car and drove to the courthouse in silence. It wasn't a long drive, but every mile seemed to carry more weight. When they arrived, the place was alive with activity. The usual courthouse hustle and bustle was heightened today, with whispers floating around about the latest high-profile case.

First Clyde Peterson.

Then Waldo Duggan.

Now Bert and Rhonda Barker.

The usually sleepy town of Halibut Cove was reeling from all the drama.

Audrey's stomach tightened as they entered the building. As they walked through the crowded hall, Audrey's eyes scanned the crowd for familiar faces. That's when she spotted her uncle Oliver, standing near the entrance to the courtroom, his voice low as he spoke with Bert and Rhonda.

Phoebe stopped dead in her tracks, her face pale as she whispered, "Is that your uncle . . . is he . . . ?"

Audrey nodded, just as surprised as Phoebe. "I guess he's your lawyer."

Phoebe swallowed hard, her voice barely above a whisper. "I don't know if that's a good thing or not."

Inside the courtroom, the tension was palpable. The judge sat at the bench, his eyes scanning through the papers in front of him. On one side, the prosecutor, Mark Haskell, looked every bit the part of a seasoned litigator.

Across from him, Oliver was calm, confident, his posture relaxed despite the gravity of the situation.

"Your Honor, we ask for the highest possible bail, given the severity of the crime," Prosecutor Haskell said, his voice firm. "The defendant, Mr. Bert Barker, is accused of the murder of Billy Sawyer, and the evidence against him is overwhelming."

Oliver stood, his hand resting lightly on the table as he spoke. "Your Honor, we're requesting a reasonable bail, considering that Mr. Barker and his wife, Mrs. Rhonda Barker, are law-abiding citizens with no criminal history. This was a clear case of self-defense. The allegations that have been made against them are rooted in misunderstandings from over thirty years ago."

The judge nodded slowly, tapping his gavel lightly. "I've heard the arguments. Given the nature of the charges, I will set bail at $250,000 for each defendant."

Bert and Rhonda exchanged a tense look, but they nodded in acceptance. Rhonda reached over and squeezed Bert's hand, her fingers trembling.

"Bert, we'll need to post bail as soon as possible," she whispered. "It will wipe out our life savings, but we can't afford to stay here any longer than necessary."

Bert's face tightened, and he turned to his scowling son who was seated directly behind them in the gallery. "Evan, go to the bank. Get a cashier's check. Hopefully we'll be home in time for supper."

Evan narrowed his eyes and leaned forward. "I don't trust Holbrook defending you. What if he tries to talk you into taking a plea deal?"

"Just go," Bert said, his voice sharp. "Oliver's the best lawyer in the county, if not the entire state. He knows what he's doing."

"Dad . . ." Evan mumbled.

Bert snapped. "You'll go get the damn check, Evan. *Now.*"

Evan grumbled but didn't argue. He stormed out of the courtroom, his footsteps heavy with frustration.

Audrey sat two rows back in the gallery, watching the exchange with growing concern. Beside her, Phoebe shifted anxiously in her seat, her hand twitching toward her purse. Neither of them spoke, but their eyes followed every movement like hawks. When the judge adjourned, Audrey stood and gently nudged Phoebe forward.

Oliver turned to Bert and Rhonda. "We'll meet in the conference room to discuss strategy. You two need to be prepared for what comes next."

As they walked into the hallway, Audrey and Phoebe fell into step behind them, silent shadows as the group moved toward the conference room. Phoebe glanced nervously at Audrey, but Audrey kept her focus locked on Oliver's back.

The group passed Clyde Peterson, who seemed unusually nervous. He was standing by a pillar, his arms crossed tightly across his chest. "Oliver," Clyde said, his voice strained. "Are you sure about taking on *another* case? You've already got a lot on your plate with Waldo Duggan's case. You're not spreading yourself too thin, are you?"

Oliver gave him a patient smile. "Clyde, I've been doing this long enough to know how to balance my cases. Don't worry about me. I can handle it."

But Clyde wasn't convinced. "I'm just saying, if you don't focus, you're going to miss something important, and that could cost us both."

"I'm handling it, Clyde," Oliver said firmly, brushing past him. "Go home and get some rest. I'll call you later."

Clyde grabbed him by the coat sleeve, stopping him. "You're distracted, and that's making me very nervous."

Oliver glared at Clyde. "I said I'm handling it. If you don't like it, get another lawyer."

It was a standoff, the two men staring each other down. Clyde blinked first, threw his hands in the air, and stalked off.

As Oliver led Bert and Rhonda into the conference room, Audrey and Phoebe followed close behind. Once everyone was inside, Oliver closed the door, and the mood shifted. There was no more small talk.

"Now," Oliver began, sitting at the head of the table. "We need to discuss the self-defense strategy. First, we need to establish that there were no witnesses that night. Were there?"

Bert and Rhonda exchanged a tense glance before Bert answered. "No. There was no one else there."

Oliver quickly picked up on it. "What? What are you not telling me?"

"No one else was there," Bert assured him.

Audrey, unable to help herself, spoke up. "What about Griffin Mead?"

Bert stiffened. "What about him?"

Oliver turned to look at Audrey, then back to Bert. "Was Griffin there?"

Bert shook his head.

Rhonda just looked down at her lap.

Bert's eyes flickered nervously. "No, he wasn't."

Audrey piped in again. "But Lou Grady said in his article about the case—"

Bert abruptly cut her off. "Lou Grady got it wrong. Griffin wasn't there."

Rhonda's face was drained of color. She let out a shaky breath, her hands wringing in her lap.

"Rhonda?" Oliver pressed gently.

With a sob, Rhonda finally spoke. "Griffin was there that night. He worked for Daddy. He might have seen something, but he never came forward. Daddy—he either paid him off or threatened to fire him in order to keep him quiet."

Oliver's face darkened as he processed this new information. "This is bad," he muttered. "Griffin Mead was a key witness. And now he's dead. Murdered. If the prosecutor gets ahold of this, it's going to look like you silenced the one person who could have testified against you."

Rhonda gasped, her hands trembling. "No. No, we didn't . . ."

Oliver placed a steadying hand on her shoulder. "We'll do everything we can. But we need to prepare ourselves for what comes next."

Phoebe's face crumpled as she turned to Audrey, eyes filled with panic. "What do we do now?"

Audrey didn't have an answer, but she squeezed Phoebe's hand gently. "We fight. Oliver will do everything he can to protect you."

But even Audrey couldn't shake the feeling that things were slipping away faster than they could catch them.

Chapter Thirty-four

Audrey sat at her laptop, staring at the screen. She had spent the last twenty minutes doing a Google search on Billy Sawyer, hoping to dig up anything useful—an old mug shot, a newspaper clipping, anything that might give her a clearer picture of the man buried in the Barker backyard.

But nothing came up.

No images, no photographs, no social media remnants—just scattered mentions of a missing persons report and some vague references in old crime logs.

Audrey frowned. Billy was arrested a few times—probably right here in Halibut Cove. There had to be a mug shot on file somewhere. If the police had booked him, his photo should exist in some dusty archive or digital record.

And if it did, Audrey was determined to find it.

Audrey texted Maggie, who was at the grocery store, that she was going out and would be back soon.

Half an hour later, Audrey pushed open the heavy wooden doors of the Halibut Cove Public Library and immediately heard the unmistakable clomp, clomp, clomp of Mrs. Whishaw's sensible orthopedic shoes against the hardwood floor.

"Audrey Holbrook! No running! This is a library, dear!" Her voice boomed, shattering the peaceful silence.

Audrey, who hadn't even been moving that fast, sighed. "I know, Mrs. Whishaw."

The elderly librarian clomped closer, hands on her hips, as if ready to lecture Audrey on proper library etiquette, but instead, she squinted at her.

"What brings you here? Let me guess, you're trying to dig up dirt on someone again!" Mrs. Whishaw cackled as if she'd just cracked the case of the century.

Audrey forced a smile. "Just looking for an old newspaper article from about thirty years ago. Arrest records."

"Police beat section?" Mrs. Whishaw's eyes twinkled with nosy enthusiasm as she waved a dismissive hand. "I'll get the microfilm."

The librarian clomped off, leaving Audrey standing in front of the desk. She took a breath, glancing around at the handful of patrons in the library—one of whom was a sweet-looking old woman whispering to a friend at a nearby table.

Mrs. Whishaw returned, dragging a heavy file drawer behind her. She set it down with a dramatic thud before glaring at the old woman.

"Betty! I must have told you a hundred times! This is a library! Keep your voice down!"

The woman flushed and muttered a quick apology.

Audrey bit her lip, suppressing a laugh. Mrs. Whishaw was the only librarian she knew who seemed to be the loudest person in the building.

Together, they went through decades-old newspapers that had yet to be digitized, scanning the police beat section. Finally, Audrey found an article mentioning Billy's arrest for disorderly conduct outside a bar.

But there was no photo.

Audrey groaned. "There has to be a mug shot somewhere."

Mrs. Whishaw shrugged. "If he was arrested, it's probably in the police files."

Which meant one thing.

Audrey was going to have to get her mother involved.

Audrey strolled into the Halibut Cove Police Department, mentally preparing for battle. She found Jill sitting at her desk, typing away, her expression focused.

Audrey cleared her throat. "Mom, I need a favor."

Jill didn't look up. "No."

Audrey blinked. "I didn't even tell you what it is yet."

Jill paused her typing, finally meeting Audrey's gaze. "You want me to pull a mug shot from the police database. I'm saying no before you even ask. Mrs. Whishaw already called to tell me you were on your way."

Audrey sighed.

What a gossip.

Audrey exhaled. "Mom, Billy Sawyer was arrested in this very town. There has to be a mug shot in the system."

Jill leaned back in her chair. "And? You're not a cop, Audrey."

Audrey gritted her teeth. "This could help your case."

"From my vantage point, the case is already solved. Bert and Rhonda Barker have been arrested."

"I just have a hunch there is more to the story. Don't you want to know if there's something bigger going on?"

Jill crossed her arms. "What I want is for you to stay out of my investigation. Correction. *Investigations.*"

Audrey knew there was no point arguing. Instead, she turned on her heel, heading straight for Mason's desk.

Mason looked up warily as Audrey plopped into the chair opposite him.

"Hey, Mason. I need a favor."

Mason, ever-gullible, glanced toward Jill's office, then back at Audrey. "Uh, what kind of favor?"

Audrey grinned. "I need you to look up a name in the database. Mom said it was okay."

Mason's brows furrowed. "She did?"

Audrey nodded enthusiastically. "Yep. She totally gave me permission."

Mason, clearly not wanting to risk angering Jill, hesitated. But after a long pause, he turned to his computer and began typing.

"Who are we looking up?"

"Billy Sawyer," Audrey said, leaning in.

After a few clicks, Mason whistled. "Whoa. Here we go. Multiple arrests, mostly for bar fights and disorderly conduct."

Then the mug shot appeared.

Audrey's breath caught.

There, staring back at her, was Billy Sawyer's face.

And there was no denying it.

Phoebe was his daughter.

The resemblance was uncanny—same nose, same sharp cheekbones, same fiery eyes.

Mason glanced at her. "You okay? You look like you saw a ghost."

Audrey nodded slowly. "Print that out for me."

Just as Mason clicked the print button, Jill walked in.

"What are you two doing?"

Mason froze.

Audrey shot him a warning glance.

Mason fumbled for an excuse. "Uh, we were just, um . . . looking up my favorite band."

"What band?"

"Car Seat Headrest," Mason blurted out.

"Never heard of 'em," Jill said.

"Uh, well, they're an alternative band, more popular with the Gen Z crowd."

Jill narrowed her eyes. "Mason, I swear if you and Audrey are up to something . . ."

Audrey grinned. "Relax, Mom. Mason's just expanding my music taste beyond Billie Eilish."

Jill shook her head. "Okay, fine. But just please tell me nothing's going on between you two. I couldn't handle my deputy dating my daughter."

Audrey snorted. "Trust me, Mason is not my type."

Mason, pretending not to be offended, turned to Audrey. "Wait, what is your type, then?"

Audrey grabbed the printed mug shot and bolted for the door. "Thanks, Mason. Can't wait to check 'em out!"

Audrey arrived at the Barker home, where Rhonda was home alone.

Rhonda let her in, offering tea or coffee, but Audrey was too focused.

After a few pleasantries, Audrey placed the mug shot on the table in front of Rhonda.

"Notice anything peculiar?"

Rhonda's eyes flicked to the image. At first, she shook her head, feigning indifference.

"No," she said, but her hands trembled.

Audrey leaned forward. "Phoebe looks exactly like him."

Rhonda sat frozen.

"Come on, Mrs. Barker, you can't tell me you don't see it."

Rhonda's expression cracked. She let out a shaky breath, tears forming in her eyes.

"Yes," she whispered. "It's true. Billy was Phoebe's real father."

Audrey sat back, absorbing the weight of the revelation. "Does Mr. Barker know?"

Rhonda nodded slightly. "I always suspected Bert knew. But he loved her so much, it never mattered." Rhonda's voice trembled as she spoke of that fateful night. "Poor Bert. He was only trying to protect me, and now he may spend the rest of his life in prison."

Audrey remembered something in Lou Grady's article.

"There was a source close to Griffin Mead," she murmured. "Lou Grady mentioned something about it in his article."

"I don't understand."

"It's hearsay, but there's a chance that maybe Griffin Mead recently, like before he drowned, confided to this person what he actually saw that night."

Rhonda looked up sharply. "*What*?"

"Maybe if we find this person, we can help prove it was self-defense."

Rhonda flinched.

Audrey noticed a trace of panic in her expression.

"What is it, Rhonda?"

"N-nothing, I just don't see what good it will do at this point to keep digging into this—"

"It could help get the charges against you and Bert dismissed!"

Rhonda couldn't argue.

And Audrey suddenly wanted to know why she was hesitant to find someone who could corroborate their story.

Audrey picked up Maggie and filled her in. Together, they tracked down Lou Grady at the *Halibut Cove Chronicle*.

Lou leaned back in his chair, arms crossed. "Can't reveal sources. Journalistic ethics."

Maggie snorted. "Lou, don't act like you've ever in your life had a whiff of ethics."

Lou grinned. "Fair point."

Maggie thought for a moment. "Who's the source? A friend? A girlfriend?"

Lou hesitated.

Maggie's eyes twinkled. "I know this town, Lou."

Audrey watched as realization dawned on Maggie's face.

"Adelaide Hutchins," Maggie said triumphantly.

Audrey blinked. "Who?"

"I saw her around town a few times with Griffin after his wife died. Also they sat in the same pew at Sunday services. They appeared close but didn't seem to want to go public with whatever was going on between them." Maggie turned sharply to Lou. "Am I right, Lou?"

He shrugged, but the slight grin on his face told her she had just nailed it.

"What did she tell you?" Maggie pressed.

Lou sighed. "Just that Griffin had a story to tell about the night Billy Sawyer was killed, but when I asked her for details, she refused to say anything more out of respect for his wishes."

Audrey sat up, excited. "How do we find her?"

"She goes to the pancake breakfast at the firehouse. Every third Sunday of the month," Maggie said.

"She won't talk. I tried everything. Pressure, charm, bribery. Nothing worked."

"I have one advantage that you don't, Lou," Maggie said.

Lou looked at her curiously. "What's that?"

"I'm not you."

Chapter Thirty-five

The Halibut Cove Fire Department pancake breakfast was in full swing by the time Maggie and Audrey arrived. The firehouse had been transformed into a bustling community gathering, with long communal tables set up beneath banners announcing FIREFIGHTERS' COMMUNITY OUTREACH FUNDRAISER.

Maggie, as expected, was in her element.

"Morning, Bob!" she called out, waving at Bob Pickens, the owner of the bike rental shop in the summer.

"Lookin' sharp, Maggie," Bob grinned, patting his considerable stomach. "Came for the pancakes or the gossip?"

"Both," Maggie quipped, making Bob chuckle.

Audrey, meanwhile, had her eyes peeled for Adelaide Hutchins.

They had to be strategic—Adelaide wasn't just a chatty local, she was their one lead. Griffin Mead's friend, occasional companion, and potentially the one person who knew what he knew.

Audrey spotted her at the far end of the firehouse, sitting at a table near the coffee station, stacking her pancakes with a frankly concerning amount of whipped cream.

Maggie nudged Audrey. "There's our girl."

Audrey grabbed two plates, piled high with pancakes, and led the way to Adelaide's table.

"Mind if we join you?" Maggie asked with her usual effortless charm.

Adelaide glanced up, her lips dusted with powdered sugar. "Well, if it isn't the Holbrook ladies. Take a seat—long as you don't try to steal my whipped cream."

Audrey smiled as she and Maggie sat. They made small talk first, chatting about the weather, the fundraiser turnout, and whose kids had gotten engaged.

Finally, Maggie steered the conversation where they needed it to go.

"So, Adelaide," Maggie said lightly, cutting into her pancake, "I heard you and Griffin used to keep each other company every now and then before . . . he so tragically passed."

Adelaide hesitated, her fork pausing mid-air. "Why do you want to know?"

Audrey exchanged a quick glance with Maggie. "We're just trying to understand what happened to him."

"Well, we did spend time together, but I was always the second choice. It was no secret Griffin had his eye on Ethel Primrose, so I knew I was going to be forever a lady in waiting."

"That must have been hard," Maggie whispered.

Adelaide shrugged, resigned. "Was what it was. He wasn't without his charm. And life as a widow in this town can get mighty lonely, so I enjoyed his company when I could get it."

She sighed wistfully. "That man could drink." She shook her head. "Whenever he had a few, he'd want to talk about everything—our spouses, our regrets, the past. He carried a lot of ghosts. But now that he's gone . . . well, I don't see the harm."

Audrey leaned in. "Did he ever talk about the Barker family?"

Adelaide frowned slightly, then shrugged. "Few times. One night, he got really drunk, started rambling on about something that happened when he was young, back when he worked for Rhonda's father, Arthur."

Audrey's pulse quickened.

"What did he say?" Maggie asked, her voice casual.

Adelaide glanced around and lowered her voice. "He said he saw everything."

Audrey and Maggie exchanged a glance.

Adelaide leaned in, spearing a piece of pancake with her fork. "Griffin told me that Billy Sawyer was stalking Rhonda. He was convinced the baby was his and not Bert's, and he was pressuring her for a paternity test. But Rhonda refused, which only made Billy more paranoid."

Audrey frowned. "And that night?"

Adelaide took a long sip of coffee before answering. "Billy got into the house. Confronted Rhonda. From what Griffin saw, it wasn't self-defense. He wasn't attacking her. She just wanted him gone so she could be with Bert."

A chill ran down Audrey's spine.

"Griffin was definitely there?" Maggie pressed.

Adelaide nodded. "He was outside, working late for Arthur. Saw the whole thing from the window."

Audrey exhaled. "And Arthur covered it up."

Adelaide nodded again. "Paid Griffin a nice sum of money to keep his mouth shut. And he did. Kept his promise. But once he got into the sauce, he had loose lips."

Maggie swirled her coffee in thought. "And Bert?"

Adelaide shook her head. "Bert wasn't even there that night. But he's taking the fall for it now."

Maggie pushed her plate away, her expression serious. That was new information. "That's one hell of a secret to keep. Why didn't you tell this to Lou Grady?"

"Because Lou would exploit it for his own gain, splash it all over the front page of the paper, and most importantly, I don't like Lou Grady. But I like you, Maggie."

Audrey felt her stomach twist. "So Bert is willing to go to prison for a crime he didn't commit, all for Rhonda."

Adelaide shrugged. "Love makes people do stupid things."

After leaving Adelaide, Audrey and Maggie continued mingling. Maggie was deep in conversation with the fire chief, who looked positively smitten, while Audrey wandered toward the coffee station.

That's when she saw him.

Dr. Bradley Comstock.

He was standing near the exit, engaged in what looked like an intense conversation with a man Audrey didn't recognize—tall, broad-shouldered, with a sleek business casual look.

Audrey, feeling bold, approached. "Bradley," she said smoothly.

Bradley turned sharply, and Audrey caught the flicker of alarm in his eyes before he smoothed his expression.

"Audrey," he greeted, flashing his trademark charming smile. "Enjoying the pancakes?"

Audrey glanced at the man beside him. He muttered something to Bradley and hurried off.

Bradley adjusted his cuffs. "What can I do for you?"

Audrey raised a brow. "Who was that?"

Bradley's smile didn't falter, but Audrey noticed the tension in his jaw.

"No one important."

Audrey crossed her arms. "Interesting. He looked important enough for you to stop talking the moment I showed up."

Bradley chuckled. "I didn't realize I was under investigation."

Audrey gave him a tight smile. "I don't know, Bradley. Seems like you have a lot of secrets. Like your family's history with mine."

Bradley's expression didn't change, but she saw the flicker in his eyes.

"I did a little digging," Audrey continued, folding her arms. "Turns out my grandfather Wes, Chips Hogan, and Griffin Mead were all involved in a real estate deal with your father, Ed. That is, until they all backed out."

Bradley's jaw twitched. "Is that so?"

Audrey tilted her head. "Your father was left high and dry after that deal fell apart. Then he left town. And not long after, he . . . well." She hesitated, watching his reaction carefully. "I imagine that must have been hard on your family."

Bradley's pleasant expression cooled.

"Digging up old business deals?" he said lightly. "That doesn't seem like your area of expertise."

Audrey's smile was sharp. "Neither does murder, but someone in town seems to be getting creative."

Bradley let out a slow breath, then suddenly flashed another grin, flipping the switch back to charm mode.

"You really should stay out of things that don't concern you, Audrey." His voice was smooth, but there was an edge to it now.

Audrey refused to flinch. "Halibut Cove concerns me. Especially when people start dying left and right."

Bradley exhaled slowly, then suddenly stepped back with an easy smile. "Enjoy your day."

Audrey watched him go, her pulse steady but her instincts screaming.

She'd just hit a nerve.

As Audrey turned away, she suddenly felt something cold and sticky drip down her shoulder.

"Oh no!"

She looked up to see Melanie, Dr. Comstock's receptionist, standing there with an upturned syrup container.

Melanie gasped dramatically. "I'm so sorry, Audrey! My hands just slipped!"

Audrey narrowed her eyes. "Right."

Melanie dabbed at Audrey's sleeve with a ridiculous amount of napkins.

"I just hate seeing women throw themselves at men, don't you?" Melanie murmured, voice dripping with false sympathy. "It's just . . . so desperate."

Audrey smiled. "You seem awfully invested in Bradley's love life."

Melanie flushed. "I just care about him, that's all. And you—you're wasting your time."

Audrey wiped syrup off her hand. "Don't worry, Melanie. I have no romantic interest in your boss."

Melanie sniffed. "Well, good. Because he deserves someone . . . more sophisticated. And let's face it, you're way too young for him. He needs a more experienced woman."

Audrey laughed. "If you think I'm competition, you've got bigger problems than syrup."

Melanie huffed and stormed off.

Audrey found Maggie chatting animatedly with the fire chief, who looked practically ready to offer her free fire safety inspections for life.

Before Audrey could pull Maggie away, her attention was diverted to her mother, Jill, who was standing near the coffee station—clearly trapped in conversation with Mark Haskell.

Mark had leaned in slightly, his expression half amusement, half challenge.

"You keep saying this isn't a good idea," he said, "but I think we both know otherwise."

Jill sighed, stirring her coffee with unnecessary force. "Mark, I don't have time for romance right now."

Mark grinned. "You make time for things that matter."

Maggie, never one to miss an opportunity to meddle, suddenly appeared at Jill's side and patted Mark's arm approvingly.

"That's right! Listen to Mark."

Jill shot her mother a murderous glare. "I don't need my family ganging up on me right now."

Audrey smirked, taking a sip of her own coffee. "I like Mark. You should stop monkeying around and just say yes."

Jill scoffed. "To what?"

Maggie gave Mark a playful wink. "To whatever he's asking."

Jill groaned. "This is an ambush."

Mark looked pleased. "A well-executed one." He turned to Maggie. "I like your daughter, but I gotta say, Maggie—you might be my favorite Holbrook."

Maggie beamed. "Mark, you flatterer. If Jill doesn't want you, I'll adopt you myself."

Jill pinched the bridge of her nose. "I swear to God, if you don't stop—"

Audrey leaned toward Mark conspiratorially. "I think she's warming up to you."

Jill let out a sharp exhale. "I'm leaving before one of you tries to officiate something."

Mark chuckled as she stormed off. "She's feisty. I like that."

Maggie watched Jill's retreating figure and sighed dramatically. "Impossible."

Mark, finishing his coffee, gave Maggie a wink before heading toward the exit. "I'll see you ladies around."

Shaking off the entertainment of Jill's romantic troubles, Audrey turned her attention back to the mystery at hand.

"Nana," she said, grabbing her grandmother's arm before she could get pulled back into more gossip, "I need your help."

Maggie sighed but followed her anyway. "Let me guess. You're on a mission."

Audrey scanned the room. "There was a man talking to Bradley earlier. Tall, suit jacket, very businessy."

Maggie frowned. "Yes, I saw him walking around. I didn't recognize him."

At that moment, the smitten fire chief conveniently materialized beside them, eager for another chance to chat with Maggie.

Audrey seized the opportunity. "Chief, do you know who that man was talking to Dr. Comstock earlier?"

The fire chief brightened at the chance to be helpful. "Yes, that's Fred Grindle."

Maggie's brow furrowed. "Grindle . . . Grindle . . . Nope, not ringing a bell."

The fire chief leaned in slightly, clearly enjoying Maggie's undivided attention. "Big property developer out of Bangor. Owns a bunch of real estate up and down the coast."

Audrey and Maggie exchanged a look.

Fred Grindle.

Maggie shrugged. "Never heard of him."

"Yeah, he comes to Halibut Cove quite a lot with his eye toward buying up properties. Last I heard, he was trying to get his hands on Chips Hogan's property to turn into a bed and breakfast, but you know how stubborn Chips was, he refused.

Now, suddenly, this Grindle guy was in cahoots with Bradley?

Alarm bells began ringing in Audrey's head.

Something wasn't adding up.

Chapter Thirty-six

Maggie pulled into the driveway just as the mailman, Tom Jenkins, was stepping out of his truck, a bundle of envelopes in hand. He was a familiar sight, his uniform slightly rumpled, the logo on his cap faded from years of service. He was one of the good ones—always had time for a quick chat, always knew what was going on around town.

"Morning, Tom," Maggie called, stepping out of her car.

Tom looked up and grinned. "Morning, Maggie. Just about to drop this off for you."

Maggie took the stack of mail and tilted her head. "How's your mother? I heard she had a fall."

Tom let out a sigh but nodded. "She's resting, on the mend. Stubborn as ever. You know how it is."

Maggie chuckled. "Oh, yes. Stubbornness runs deep in some families."

Tom smirked. "Speaking of family—my oldest got into Bowdoin."

Maggie beamed. "No! That's wonderful news, Tom! I always knew that boy would make something of himself."

Tom puffed up with pride. "Yeah, I'm pretty proud.

Gonna have a little celebration this weekend at my parents' in Pittsfield, nothing fancy."

Maggie squeezed his arm. "You should be proud. Give my congratulations to Luke and the rest of your family."

Tom tipped his cap. "Will do. And tell your crew to behave themselves."

Maggie snorted. "I can't make any promises."

Maggie had always wondered why Tom and his wife had divorced soon after their youngest son Tucker was born. She didn't want to pry, but she never understood it. Tom was so handsome and charming, not to mention a real looker.

Tom laughed, climbed back into his truck, and drove off.

As Maggie walked toward the house, Flounder, her ever-loyal Golden Retriever, came bounding down the hill, tail wagging furiously.

"All right, all right, I'm home," she said, ruffling his fur. "No need to act like I've been gone for weeks."

She shuffled through the mail—a few flyers, a couple of stray bills she hadn't switched over to paperless yet, nothing of real interest—until she reached a white envelope.

The handwriting was childlike, scrawled and uneven, barely legible. No return address. Postmarked Halibut Cove.

Maggie's brows knit together.

She carried the stack inside, fed Flounder, and then sat at the kitchen table, staring at the odd envelope.

Something about it prickled the back of her neck.

She opened it carefully and pulled out a single sheet of paper.

Her stomach turned to ice.

The message was computer-generated, the letters mimicking an old ransom note, as if they had been cut from a magazine but clearly printed from a modern program.

> *Maggie Holbrook,*
> *You're asking too many questions.*
> *Let sleeping dogs lie.*
> *Your meddling is dangerous.*
> *Not just for you, but for your family.*

Maggie's grip on the paper tightened.

Her heart pounded, but not with fear—no, this was something else.

Rage.

Threaten her? Fine.

Threaten her *family*?

That was a whole different story.

She snatched her phone off the table and sent out a group text.

Holbrooks. Family meeting. ASAP.

Fifteen minutes later, everyone was gathered in the Holbrook living room.

Jill stood with her arms crossed, her expression tight with frustration.

Audrey sat forward on the couch, brow furrowed in concern.

Cord and Sandy leaned against the mantle, tense and alert.

Oliver, arms crossed, let out a slow breath. "All right, what's this about?"

Maggie held up the ransom-style note.

Jill's face darkened. She grabbed the letter and scanned it, her jaw clenching as she read.

"This is insane," she muttered. "Mom, this is a direct threat. You need to back off."

Her mother, her brothers, her daughter—all too damn stubborn.

"Fine," she said begrudgingly. "You want to keep at this? Knock yourselves out. But don't get in my way. And for God's sake, don't do anything stupid."

Maggie smiled sweetly. "Define 'stupid.' "

Jill let out a sharp breath and stood. "I hate this family."

Cord smirked. "No, you don't."

Jill threw him a look. "Right now, I really do."

As Jill grabbed her keys and headed out the door, Maggie turned to her sons and granddaughter.

"Well," she said, tapping the ransom note against her palm, "it looks like we have a puzzle to solve."

Cord cracked his knuckles. "Damn right we do. And if I have to bust a few heads to get to the truth, so be it."

"I draw the line at violence, Cord. This is the twenty-first century, not the old west," Maggie said sharply.

"Sorry, Ma, you're right. As always."

She could tell he was just appeasing her.

Cord was mad as hell about the warning note.

He was itching for revenge.

And justice.

She just hoped his more sensible younger brother, Sandy, would be able to keep him in line and out of trouble.

Chapter Thirty-seven

The wooded trail stretched ahead of them, winding through the towering pines. The late morning sunlight filtered through the branches, dappling the dirt path with shifting patches of gold. Audrey inhaled deeply, the crisp scent of pine and salt from the distant cove filling her lungs.

"Beautiful morning," Isabella said, adjusting the straps on her backpack.

"Perfect hiking weather," Audrey agreed.

They had been walking for a while, their boots crunching over fallen leaves, when Isabella hesitated before speaking again. "You know, your mother asked me to come along with you today."

Audrey snapped her head toward her. "What?"

Isabella gave her a sheepish look. "She's worried about you. Ever since your grandmother got that note . . . well, let's just say she's not keen on you wandering around alone these days."

Audrey let out an exasperated sigh. "Of course. I should have known. She still thinks of me as a kid."

"Cut her some slack," Isabella said, nudging her with

an elbow. "It's not every day your family gets a ransom-style death threat."

Audrey crossed her arms. "It's just frustrating. She never stops worrying. I mean, I get it—she's a cop, it's her job to be paranoid—but come on. I can take care of myself."

Isabella smirked. "Can you, though? I seem to recall someone face planting into a tide pool last summer."

Audrey groaned. "That was one time."

Isabella chuckled, shaking her head.

They walked in comfortable silence for a while before Isabella changed the subject. "So . . . I got a question for you."

Audrey glanced at her, curious. "Shoot."

Isabella paused, as if gathering courage, and then spoke. "Would you mind if I went out with Mason?"

Audrey nearly tripped. "What? Mason, as in my mother's deputy, Mason?"

"There aren't that many Masons in town as far as I know, Audrey."

Audrey's mouth dropped open. "I just thought . . . I mean, is he even your type? I did not pick up on any kind of attraction between you two. It's fine, you just took me by surprise—"

Isabella laughed. "Relax. I was just thinking about asking him out. I happen to think he's cute."

Audrey's stomach tightened unexpectedly. "You do?"

Isabella gave her a knowing look. "You're not into him, are you?"

Audrey scoffed. "No! Of course not. I mean, he's *Mason.*"

"So you wouldn't mind?" Isabella pressed.

"Nope."

"Are you sure?"

"Yes. I'm sure."

Isabella tried reading Audrey's tight expression.

Audrey reassured her. "Totally. One hundred percent."

Isabella nodded. "Okay."

A moment passed, then, to Audrey's own horror, she blurted out, "Actually . . . yes, I do mind."

Isabella stopped walking. "Excuse me?"

Audrey clamped her mouth shut.

What the hell was that?

"I thought you said you didn't like him," Isabella said, her arms crossed.

"I—" Audrey floundered, feeling her face heat up. "I don't! I just . . . I don't know!"

Isabella grinned. "So you *do* like him."

"No! I mean . . . I don't know!"

Isabella laughed. "Relax. I won't ask him out. But you might want to figure out your feelings before someone else does."

Audrey groaned. "I hate you."

"You love me."

They continued on the trail in silence, Audrey's mind racing, when a figure emerged ahead of them on the path.

Audrey's stomach clenched.

Evan Barker.

He stood leaning against a tree, arms crossed over his chest, in sweats and wearing hiking boots, looking as if he had all the time in the world.

Audrey immediately stiffened, exchanging a glance with Isabella, who raised an eyebrow.

"Well, well," Evan said, his lips curving into a smirk. "Fancy meeting you two out here."

Audrey narrowed her eyes. "What are you doing here, Evan?"

Evan let out a mocking laugh. "It's a public trail, sweetheart. Last I checked, even a Barker can take a walk in the woods. Or do the Holbrooks own this too?"

Audrey's hands clenched into fists. "It's just a coincidence that you're here at the same time as us?"

Evan's smirk widened. "Paranoid much?"

Audrey took a step forward, her voice cold. "If you're trying to intimidate us, it's not working."

Evan chuckled. "Now why would I want to do that? I'm just being friendly." His gaze flicked toward Isabella, who had remained silent so far. "Speaking of friendly . . . Isabella, right?"

Isabella stiffened. "Yeah."

Evan's expression softened just a fraction, his tone turning smooth. "You know, I don't think we've ever had the pleasure of getting to know each other properly."

Audrey bristled. "She's not interested."

Evan ignored her, keeping his lazy, amused gaze on Isabella. "I'd rather hear that from her."

There was a tense pause, and then Isabella squared her shoulders, her voice steady.

"No."

Evan blinked, then let out a low chuckle, shaking his head. "Damn. Didn't even let me finish my pitch."

Audrey took Isabella's arm, stepping protectively closer. "We're leaving."

Evan held up his hands. "Hey, no need to get all worked up. Like I said, it's a public trail."

Audrey gritted her teeth. "Let's go."

They brushed past him, Isabella keeping her head high, and Audrey could feel Evan's eyes burning into her back.

She risked a glance over her shoulder.

He was still watching them with a menacing glare.

"Isabella," she whispered. "Stay away from Evan. There's something dangerous about him."

Isabella nodded. "Don't worry. That guy gives me the creeps."

Audrey looked back again.

Evan was gone.

They continued on for another thirty minutes and had almost forgotten about Evan when Flounder, who had been trotting ahead of them off leash, suddenly spotted a squirrel.

With a thrilled bark, he took off into the trees.

"Flounder!" Audrey shouted, breaking into a jog.

"Do you want me to come?" Isabella asked.

Audrey shook her head. "No. Stay on the trail. I'll catch up."

She raced after Flounder, weaving through trees, dodging roots, branches snagging at her jacket, her breath coming fast.

She skidded to a halt in a small clearing, scanning the trees.

"Flounder? Come here, boy!"

Silence.

Then—

A shadow moved behind her.

Before Audrey could turn, a force slammed into her back, sending her sprawling forward.

She barely had time to react before rough hands grabbed her, yanking her up and shoving her forward.

Audrey gasped as her foot hit open air.

The ground vanished beneath her.

She teetered on the edge of a rocky cliff, her arms flailing. Panic flooded her.

Before she could fall, her hands shot out, gripping onto a jagged rock ledge.

She dangled over the precipice, her feet kicking at nothing but empty space.

Audrey's chest heaved as she looked down. The drop below was sickeningly far, the jagged rocks unforgiving.

Above her, a figure loomed.

Dressed in dark clothing, their face obscured by a black ski mask.

Audrey's heart pounded wildly.

"Help me!" she gasped, trying to haul herself up.

The masked figure crouched down, resting one knee on the ground.

For a horrifying moment, Audrey thought they were going to pull her up.

But then—

They pried one of her fingers loose.

Audrey screamed.

"No! Please! Don't do this!"

Another finger.

Her grip weakened.

Her arms trembled.

The masked figure leaned closer, voice low and almost amused.

"Let go."

Audrey gritted her teeth, clawing at the rock with her free hand, desperately trying to find a new hold.

But her fingers were slipping.

She was seconds from falling.

Suddenly—

A furious snarl.

A blur of golden fur launched itself at her attacker.

Flounder.

The dog sank his teeth into the figure's arm, growling ferociously.

The attacker let out a sharp cry, stumbling backward.

Flounder held on, shaking his head violently, his teeth dug deep into the fabric of their jacket.

There was blood.

The attacker kicked out at Flounder, wrenching their arm free, and bolted away in the woods.

Flounder turned his attention to Audrey, gazing down at her helplessly, barking wildly.

Audrey clung to the ledge, her arms burning, her fingers slipping.

She couldn't hold on.

She was going to fall.

"Audrey!"

Isabella's voice rang through the trees.

Suddenly, strong hands gripped her wrists.

Audrey sucked in a breath, eyes flying open to see Isabella kneeling above her, straining to pull her up.

"Hold on!" Isabella gritted through her teeth.

Audrey scrambled, using what little strength she had left to push up with her legs, desperate to get away from the ledge.

With a final heave, Isabella yanked her over the edge, and they collapsed onto the dirt together, panting.

Audrey pressed a shaking hand to her forehead, her pulse still racing.

Isabella knelt beside her, eyes wild with concern.

"What the hell just happened?!"

Audrey took a deep breath, trying to steady herself.

"Someone—someone tried to kill me."

Isabella looked ready to explode. "Then we need to tell your mother. Right now."

"No."

Isabella blinked. "Excuse me?"

Audrey shook her head firmly. "Not a word. To anyone."

Isabella gawked at her. "Are you out of your mind?! Your mom is the police chief! She's supposed to handle things like this!"

Audrey swallowed, her hands still trembling. "If Mom or Nana find out . . . they'll lose their minds, they'll never let me out of their sight again. And I can't afford that."

Isabella crossed her arms. "You almost got killed, Audrey."

Audrey nodded, breathing deeply. "I know. Which is exactly why I need to find out who's behind this before they try again."

Isabella groaned. "I really hate this plan."

Audrey forced a weak smile. "Welcome to my life."

Isabella exhaled heavily. "Fine. But you need to watch your back."

Audrey looked toward the woods, her pulse steadying but her mind still racing.

Someone wanted her out of the picture.

And now, more than ever—

She needed to find out who and why.

Chapter Thirty-eight

Jill took a slow sip of her coffee, her gaze locked on the mist rolling over the water beyond the kitchen window. Across the table, Maggie methodically spread jam over a thick slice of toast, her expression thoughtful.

"We need to talk about Fred Grindle," Maggie said finally, setting down her knife with a decisive clink.

Jill exhaled through her nose. "You think he's tied to Bradley?"

Maggie nodded. "I think he was always part of this plan. We just didn't see him."

Before Jill could respond, Audrey walked in, looking for coffee. She moved slower than usual, shoulders a little tight, her mouth a fraction too forced in its casual smile. She grabbed a mug and poured herself some coffee, her movements overly deliberate.

Jill instantly clocked it. Something was off.

"You're up early," Jill noted, watching her carefully.

Audrey took a sip of coffee and reached for a muffin. "Busy day."

Jill studied her daughter. Something wasn't right. But Audrey shrugged it off, too easily, and Jill knew better than to push. She let it slide—for now.

She took a final sip of her coffee, then stood. "I've got to get to the station."

Maggie smirked. "Go keep the town safe, Chief."

Jill smirked and headed out to the car, already reaching for her phone to call Mason.

Her pockets were empty.

She frowned, checked her bag—nothing.

"Dammit."

She sighed and turned back toward the house, retracing her steps to the kitchen. As she approached the doorway, she heard Maggie's voice.

". . . stopped by The Chowder House this morning to grab fresh muffins, and Isabella was acting strangely."

Jill froze just outside the room.

"She's usually a morning person, cheerful, always so chatty," Maggie continued. "But today? She barely smiled. Kept her head down."

Audrey hesitated. "She's probably just tired."

Maggie wasn't buying it. "Or maybe something happened between you two."

Audrey sighed. "It's nothing, really. She just—well, she asked me if I liked Mason before she made a move. It caught me off guard, that's all. Made things a little awkward."

Maggie hummed, tapping her nails against the table. "That's not it."

Audrey stiffened. "What do you mean?"

Maggie's voice softened, carrying just enough for Jill to catch through the doorway. "Something happened yesterday, didn't it?"

Audrey's fingers tightened around her coffee mug. "No."

Maggie just stared at her.

Waiting.

Audrey huffed. "I mean—yes, something happened. But it's not a big deal."

Maggie folded her arms. "What kind of something?"

Audrey swallowed, looking down at her muffin as if it could offer an escape. "Isabella and I went for a hike with Flounder . . ."

Maggie's eyes narrowed. "*And*?"

Audrey hesitated again.

Jill leaned in against the doorway, unseen, her pulse quickening.

"And," Audrey finally muttered, "I was attacked."

Jill stepped into the room like a storm cloud rolling in. "*What*?"

Audrey's head snapped up, her face going pale.

Maggie sighed. "And here we go."

Jill's expression was pure fire. "Someone attacked you?! And you didn't tell me?!"

Audrey closed her eyes briefly, cursing under her breath.

Jill advanced on her, hands on her hips. "Why am I just now hearing about this?"

Audrey set down her coffee mug with a little too much force. "Because, Mom, this is exactly the reaction I was trying to avoid."

Jill's nostrils flared. "Someone tried to hurt you. That's not a reaction to avoid!"

Maggie rubbed her temples. "For the love of God, Jillian, let her speak."

Jill turned back to Audrey. "Start from the beginning. And don't leave out a single detail."

Audrey sighed, knowing there was no way out of this now. She began to talk.

Jill and Mason stood outside the Barker house, pounding on the door.

Nothing.

Finally, the door creaked open, and Evan Barker leaned against the frame, his red-rimmed eyes and rumpled T-shirt suggested he hadn't seen a bed before dawn.

Jill eyed him. "Late night?"

Evan yawned, stretching an arm over the door frame. "What can I say? Good whiskey, bad decisions."

Mason sighed. "Are your parents home?"

Evan snorted. "They're with the family lawyer." He sneered. "Your brother."

Jill's lips pressed into a firm line. "And what do you think of that?"

"I think they shouldn't trust a Holbrook." Evan rubbed his eyes. "But they won't listen to me. So . . . you got something to say, or are you just here because you want to admire my handsome face?"

"I need to know where you were yesterday."

Evan's laziness vanished. "Why?"

Jill stepped forward. "Because Audrey was attacked."

"I was hiking. We ran into each other. But you know that already, don't you? I'm sure she told you. Why don't you just go ahead and arrest me? You already think I did it."

Mason tensed beside her. "Wouldn't be the first time you've tried to intimidate her."

Evan rolled his shoulders, giving a slow grin. "I intimidate a lot of people, Barney Fife."

"But trying to push her off a cliff, that's just next-level crazy," Mason seethed.

Evan faltered a bit.

As if he hadn't expected to hear that.

Or perhaps he was just acting surprised.

Jill crossed her arms. "Take your shirt off."

Evan blinked, then let out a bark of laughter. "Now, Chief, I had no idea you were into me. I've never really had a thing for older women before, but hey, if you try hard enough, I could be convinced to play ball."

Jill gritted her teeth. "Just do it."

Evan glanced at Mason. "You too, Deputy? Didn't peg you for the jealous type."

Mason's jaw clenched. "Take off the shirt, or I do it for you."

Evan grinned. "If you wanted me naked, all you had to do was ask."

Jill was seconds from throwing him through a wall. "Now."

With a sigh, Evan peeled off his shirt.

No dog bite on the left arm.

Audrey had been very specific about that.

Jill's stomach sank.

Evan raised an eyebrow. "Satisfied?"

Jill gritted her teeth. "For now."

The Halibut Cove Inn was a charming white clapboard building with a wide porch that overlooked the harbor.

Inside, the morning crowd had settled in the dining room for breakfast. Fred Grindle sat at a corner table near the bay window, leisurely cutting into a stack of blueberry pancakes. He was a broad-shouldered man in his early fifties with graying hair, sharp eyes, and an air of self-importance. His gold watch gleamed under the morning light, and his neatly pressed button-down suggested he was a man who preferred things a certain way—clean, orderly, and entirely under his control.

Jill and Mason stepped inside, the small bell over the door announcing their arrival.

"Chief! Deputy!" A warm voice greeted them. Penny Campbell, the owner of the inn, bustled over, wiping her hands on her apron. She was a woman in her late sixties, round-faced, with the kind of energy that could put a caffeinated squirrel to shame. "You two here for breakfast? Law enforcement eats for free."

Mason perked up.

"Just here on business, Penny," Jill said, flashing a polite smile. "But thanks for the offer."

"Well, at least let me get you a cup of coffee!" Penny insisted, already reaching for a pot.

Mason looked hopeful, but Jill cut in quickly. "We're good, thanks."

Penny sighed dramatically. "A crying shame. You're missing out on my cinnamon rolls. Fresh out of the oven."

Fred, still chewing a bite of pancake, dabbed his mouth with a linen napkin and sat back in his chair as they approached. "Good morning, officers," he greeted smoothly. "What can I do for you?"

Jill pulled out a chair across from him but didn't sit. "I'm Chief Holbrook, this is Deputy Dooley. We have a few questions."

Fred gestured to his plate. "Do you mind if I finish my breakfast first?"

Mason raised an eyebrow. "That depends. You planning on taking your sweet time?"

Fred chuckled, picking up his coffee cup. "You law enforcement types are always in such a hurry."

Jill leaned in slightly. "Do you know Chips Hogan or Griffin Mead?"

Fred didn't even pause to think. "Never heard of them."

Jill tilted her head. "Strange. You seem to know quite a few people in town."

Fred set down his cup. "My business brings me to a lot of places, Chief, but I don't usually concern myself with the affairs of the locals."

Jill studied him. "And what business is that, exactly?"

Fred wiped his mouth again and smiled. "That would be confidential."

Mason crossed his arms. "Let me guess—if we want more details, we should talk to your lawyer?"

Fred pointed at him approvingly with his fork. "Now you're catching on."

Jill's patience thinned. "Two people are dead, Grindle." She didn't know him well enough to call him by his first name. "And you just happen to show up, getting cozy with Bradley Comstock. That doesn't strike you as a little . . . suspicious?"

Fred set down his fork, meeting her gaze without a hint of concern. "Not in the slightest. As far as I know, Dr. Comstock is a fine, upstanding citizen who is beloved by many people in this town in need of dental care. We just happen to be doing a little business together, which as I said before, is confidential. You're barking up the wrong tree, Chief. If you want to know my business, get a warrant."

Before Jill could press him further, the front door of the inn swung open.

Melanie Blaisdell breezed in, her heels clicking on the wooden floor, a bright smile on her face.

She wore a fitted sweater and a pencil skirt, her hair perfectly curled, lipstick freshly applied. She walked straight up to Fred and kissed him lightly on the cheek.

"Morning, handsome," she purred, running a manicured hand down his arm.

Jill and Mason exchanged a look.

Melanie finally turned to them, grinning. "Chief, Mason. What a surprise!"

Mason's mouth nearly fell open.

Fred stood up from the table and wrapped an arm around her waist. "Melanie's taking the morning off to show me around your charming little town."

Melanie giggled, playfully swatting his shoulder. "Fred's been so busy with business, I figured he needed a proper tour. I mean, what kind of host would I be otherwise?"

Jill's jaw tightened.

Mason's eyebrows shot up to his hairline. "Wait, so . . . you two are . . . ?"

Melanie laughed lightly. "Oh, Mason, don't look so shocked. Fred and I get along splendidly even though we've only known each other a few weeks."

Fred winked at her. "I'm just lucky she has good taste."

Jill clenched her teeth. "Right. Well, don't let us keep you from your . . . tour."

Fred chuckled and picked up his napkin. "Wouldn't dream of it."

Melanie smiled sweetly. "You both have a wonderful day."

Jill and Mason turned and walked out of the inn, stepping onto the porch.

Mason exhaled loudly, shaking his head. "What the hell was that?"

Jill pulled out her sunglasses and put them on. "You tell me, Deputy. You're the one with all the observations."

Mason scratched his head, still dumbfounded. "I mean, is Melanie really interested in Grindle, or is she using him?"

Jill sighed. "Considering she's spent the last few months pining over Bradley Comstock, I'd say this whole thing smells of revenge dating."

Mason whistled. "She sure sold it well."

Jill glanced at him. "Getting better at spotting things, aren't you?"

Mason grinned, pleased with himself. "I try."

Jill clapped a hand on his shoulder. "Keep up the good work, Deputy."

* * *

Jill sat in her cruiser, parked across the street from Comstock Dental, her fingers drumming idly against the steering wheel. The late afternoon sun had begun its slow descent, casting long golden shadows along the quiet streets of Halibut Cove. A few stragglers still wandered in and out of nearby shops, but for the most part, the workday was winding down.

She'd been waiting for nearly twenty minutes, watching the door of the dental office like a hawk.

Finally, the door swung open, and Melanie stepped out and locked up for the night.

Melanie was meticulously put together, as always—her blouse tucked perfectly into her tailored skirt, her auburn hair still in flawless curls despite a full day at work. She exhaled, yawning as she dropped her keys into her purse.

Jill pushed open the cruiser door and stepped out.

"Long day?" she asked casually.

Melanie whipped around, startled, her expression quickly shifting to irritation.

"Yes, as a matter of fact, I had loads to do this afternoon after taking the whole morning off, as you already know," she said, shouldering her bag defensively. "How can I help you, Chief?"

Jill took her time, leaning against the hood of her car, arms crossed.

"I'm just tying up some loose ends," she said. "Thought I'd have a little chat with you before you head off for the night."

Melanie huffed out a laugh, and adjusted the strap of her purse. "If this is about Fred, I don't see how that's any of your business. Fred and I are just having fun. If you must know, I enjoy his company."

Jill nodded slowly, watching her. "Is that right? And Bradley?"

Something flashed across Melanie's face, something she tried to mask with a smirk.

"Bradley is my boss," she said, a little too flippantly.

Jill stepped forward, her voice lowering. "You know, I get it. Unrequited love is a real bitch."

Melanie's shoulders tensed.

Jill tilted her head, assessing her reaction. "You've been carrying a torch for Bradley ever since you started working for him, I imagine."

Melanie stiffened. "This is ridiculous."

Jill continued, her tone soft but relentless. "And what did you get for it? A pat on the head? Him using you when it was convenient? And then, when you tried to make him jealous, what did he do?"

Melanie's jaw clenched.

Jill leaned in, voice gentle now. "He encouraged it, didn't he?"

Melanie inhaled sharply, looking away.

Jill didn't let up.

"You wanted Bradley to notice you, so you dated Fred," she said matter-of-factly. "But instead of getting jealous, Bradley thought it was a great business move."

Melanie let out a shaky breath, her carefully constructed mask crumbling.

"Yeah," she whispered. "That's exactly what happened."

Jill waited.

Melanie crossed her arms, hugging herself. "I thought if he saw me with someone else, maybe he'd—" She broke off, shaking her head. "But he didn't care. He *wanted* me to date Fred. Said it would be 'strategically beneficial' for him."

Jill's stomach tightened.

"That was the moment I realized," Melanie continued bitterly. "Bradley never felt anything for me." She laughed hollowly. "And now I can't even stand to be around him. I'm looking for another job. I just . . . I can't do it anymore."

Jill studied her, searching for any sign of dishonesty. "And the night Griffin Mead was killed? You're his airtight alibi. Was that just a made-up story to protect him?"

Melanie shook her head, adamant now. "I swear, I was with Bradley that night. He didn't kill Griffin. I wouldn't lie about that, Chief. But there was no love lost there, to be honest. I know there was something that happened between Griffin and Bradley's father. He just didn't want to talk about it."

Jill didn't respond right away. She wanted to believe her, but her gut told her there was still more to this story.

"So you admit Bradley has deep resentment about what happened to his father," Jill pressed.

Melanie sighed. "Yes. He's never been able to let it go. But that doesn't mean he killed anyone."

Jill took a step back, processing. "And Fred? What's his angle?"

Melanie hesitated, then shook her head. "I don't know. He and Bradley were definitely working on something big, but I never got the full details."

Jill nodded slowly.

If Fred was involved in Bradley's business dealings, and those dealings somehow involved the Barkers' land, then maybe there was a reason both Chips Hogan and Griffin Mead had to go.

The question was, What exactly were they covering up?

Melanie shifted uncomfortably. "Are we done here?"

Jill studied her one last time, then gave a slow nod. "For now."

Melanie turned on her heel and hurried to her car, the usual self-assured strut missing from her step.

Jill watched her go, feeling like they were finally getting close.

Maybe too close.

Chapter Thirty-nine

Maggie pushed open the glass door to Dr. Comstock's dental office. Antiseptic and mint lingered in the air, clashing unpleasantly with the memory of the warm blueberry muffin she'd eaten earlier.

At the front desk, Melanie looked about as miserable as a woman could get while still being conscious. She barely glanced up from her computer, sighing heavily as she tapped at the keyboard.

"Mrs. Holbrook," she said dully, not bothering to feign enthusiasm. "You're early for your root canal."

Maggie arched a brow, setting her purse on the counter. "I'm not here for that."

Melanie double-checked her desktop screen and finally looked at her. "You're . . . not? But it says right here—"

"I happened to be running some errands here in town when I got your text confirming the appointment, so I decided to just drop by in person and cancel it."

"But what about your tooth?"

"Feels fine to me. And if any problems do come up, I'd rather get dentures."

Melanie still appeared confused. "I-I really don't understand why—"

Maggie leaned in slightly. "There was never any reason for me to write that appointment down in my calendar because I never had any intention of allowing myself in that man's chair with him hovering over me with a drill." She waved a dismissive hand. "Never going to happen."

Melanie's shoulders sagged, looking relieved to have one less thing to deal with today. "Okay, well, I guess I'll—"

Before she could finish, Bradley emerged from his office, walking side by side with Fred Grindle, the developer's ever-present smirk firmly in place.

Fred was all smiles, clearly pleased with whatever business they had just concluded.

Maggie turned, giving Fred a once-over. "Well, Mr. Grindle, I didn't know dental offices doubled as investment hubs. Did you get your teeth polished while you were here?"

Fred flashed her a grin so white it was nearly blinding. "My teeth are already perfect," he said, tapping one with his index finger.

Maggie tilted her head. "Sharp white teeth. Like a shark."

Fred chuckled. "I do have a taste for seafood."

"Careful." Maggie smirked. "You don't want to bite off more than you can chew."

Fred winked, clearly enjoying the banter, then turned back to Bradley. "I'll catch up with you later." With that, he strolled out the door.

Bradley turned to Maggie, eyes narrowing slightly. "Mrs. Holbrook. Ready for your root canal?"

Melanie, still at the desk, quickly interjected. "She, uh, she just canceled."

Bradley's jaw ticked. "May I ask why?"

Maggie gave him a slow smile. "You're too young to remember a movie called *Marathon Man*, aren't you?"

Bradley's expression remained blank.

Maggie sighed, feigning disappointment. "Sir Laurence Olivier? Dustin Hoffman? The scene with the drill?"

Still nothing.

She gave him a pitying look. "I'll leave you to look it up. Enjoy your day, Dr. Comstock."

And with that, she turned and sauntered out, leaving Bradley stewing. The late-morning sun hit her face as she crossed town, her thoughts still circling the conversation. By the time she pushed open the door of The Chowder House, the warm, familiar space was buzzing—Audrey, Isabella, and Ethel bustled about in the thick of the lunch rush. The aroma of clam chowder and freshly baked bread made her stomach growl. So much nicer than Dr. Comstock's antiseptic-smelling office.

In the corner booth, Fred Grindle sat hunched over a steaming bowl of chowder, spooning it into his mouth with obvious pleasure.

Maggie watched him for a moment before turning to Audrey, who was wiping down the counter.

"Tell Isabella to ask Mason out," Maggie said, eyeing the younger woman across the room.

Audrey sighed. "I already did. She's hesitant because of how I reacted when she asked me about it."

Maggie smirked. "Then tell her again that you're not interested in Mason."

Audrey didn't respond right away, instead watching Isabella as she worked. "Yeah, I know. I don't want a potential relationship to ever come between us."

"You're not interested, are you?"

Audrey hesitated again. "No, Nana, I'm not."

"Then tell her. She won't wait forever, you know," Maggie said.

Audrey sighed, then gave a nod. "Okay. I'll talk to her again."

Maggie patted her granddaughter's hand. "Good girl."

She turned toward Fred's booth, grabbing a napkin from the counter before sliding into the seat across from him.

Fred, clearly not expecting company, jumped slightly, spilling a dribble of chowder down his chin and onto his tie.

Maggie handed him the napkin. "Careful, Fred. Can't have you ruining that fancy tie."

Fred dabbed at himself, frowning. "Mrs. Holbrook. To what do I owe the pleasure?"

Maggie folded her hands on the table, smiling sweetly. "I just thought we could have a chat. I know my daughter Jill's been giving you a hard time, but that's her job. Me, on the other hand?" She leaned in. "I'm just a friendly investor looking for the next big thing."

Fred hesitated, but curiosity won out. "Go on."

Maggie launched into a quick history of the Holbrooks, their success in real estate, fishing, even canned chowder. "And I have a rather large sum of money I'd like to put into something worthwhile."

Fred's eyes gleamed with interest. "Well, I might have a few opportunities in mind."

Maggie waved a dismissive hand. "I'm not interested in just anything. I want in on your deal with Dr. Comstock."

Fred's posture stiffened. "That's not really—"

"Come on, Fred." Maggie smiled. "You're an opportunist. You wouldn't turn away someone with deeper pockets than Bradley, would you?"

Fred considered this, then sighed. "Look, it's not what you think. Bradley had some property in New Hampshire he needed help selling. That's it."

Maggie narrowed her eyes. "I wouldn't expect you—someone of your stature and reputation, although I'm not suggesting it's a good reputation—to be so willing to slum it as a simple real estate agent. Too small potatoes."

"Maybe I like doing nice things for people?"

"So you just happened to be doing this out of the kindness of your heart?"

Fred chuckled. "Let's just say I was close with Bradley's father once upon a time. I wanted to help the kid out."

Maggie studied him. "So Chips Hogan and Griffin Mead had nothing to do with this deal?"

Fred blinked. "Who?"

Maggie leaned back, watching him closely. "You must have heard of them."

"Come to think of it, yes. Your daughter, the Chief, mentioned those names to me." Fred shook his head. "I'll tell you what I told her, I never heard those names before I came to town."

Maggie's mind raced.

She believed him.

Then what was Bradley's real angle?

Fred cleared his throat. "So, how much are you looking to invest?"

Maggie smiled, grabbed her purse, and slid out of the booth.

"Oh, zero."

Fred frowned. "Excuse me?"

Maggie patted his shoulder. "I don't do business with crooked investors." She leaned down, whispering in his ear. "Enjoy your chowder."

Fred watched her walk away, his face twisting in frustration.

She'd just outplayed him.

Got the information she needed at no cost.

Maggie strolled over to the register, where Audrey was ringing up a customer.

Audrey arched a brow. "That looked like fun."

"Oh, it was." Maggie smirked.

Audrey handed the customer their change, then turned back to her grandmother. "So?"

Maggie sighed, crossing her arms. "Fred's not tied to Chips or Griffin. So getting ahold of his property was definitely not the motive. Where does that leave us?"

Audrey frowned. "The only thing Bradley had in common with the victims was the failed deal with Ed Comstock. Both Chips and Griffin, and if Grandpa was still alive, I'm sure he would be the next target. It's been right in front of us since the beginning."

Maggie nodded. "It's the reason he moved here in the first place and set up his practice."

Audrey exhaled. "So it was revenge all along."

Maggie tapped her fingers against the counter. "But he was out of town when Chips was poisoned."

"And Mom says Melanie's still sticking to her alibi," Audrey said.

Maggie's eyes darkened. "Then who the hell helped him?"

They exchanged a glance, the pieces of the puzzle coming together, but one crucial question still unanswered.

Who else wanted these men dead?

Chapter Forty

The Holbrook house was eerily quiet when Audrey descended the stairs early the next morning. The scent of brewed coffee and toasted bread that usually signaled her grandmother's presence in the kitchen was conspicuously absent.

That was odd.

Maggie was an early riser, always the first to claim the newspaper, usually with a knowing smirk as if she'd gotten to the day's gossip before anyone else.

Audrey poked her head into the kitchen. The coffeepot sat untouched, the chairs still neatly pushed in, and the morning paper was still folded on the counter.

Frowning, Audrey moved to the stove, cracking eggs into a pan, flipping toast onto plates. Maggie loved a proper breakfast, and maybe the smell would lure her down. But when the food was plated and growing cold, Audrey finally decided to go upstairs and check on her.

She knocked softly.

No answer.

"Nana?" she called, pushing the door open.

The sight that met her made her stomach drop.

Maggie lay sprawled across her bed, barely conscious,

her face damp with sweat, her breathing labored. She moaned softly, turning her head but not really looking at Audrey.

Panic gripped Audrey's chest. "Nana!" She rushed to the bedside, grabbing her grandmother's clammy hand. "What's wrong? Are you sick? I'm calling an ambulance—"

Maggie weakly batted her hand away. "No. Don't be ridiculous." Her voice was hoarse, barely above a whisper. "It's just the flu. Or something. Probably a twenty-four-hour thing."

Audrey's heart pounded. Maggie looked awful—her skin was pale, her pulse faint, her usually bright eyes dull and unfocused.

"This isn't the flu," Audrey said firmly. "I'm calling 911."

Maggie tried to sit up but immediately swayed, her body trembling with the effort. "Don't fuss, dear. Just get me some coffee. That'll fix me right up."

Audrey hesitated, torn between arguing and racing for the phone. But Maggie, stubborn as ever, fixed her with a look that told her this battle wouldn't be won easily.

Audrey gritted her teeth. "Fine. Stay put. I'll get you coffee."

She hurried down the stairs, shakily pouring a cup, adding a splash of cream, and rushing back up, determined to force Maggie into reason.

But the moment she pushed the door open, her world tilted.

Maggie was no longer in bed.

She had collapsed on the floor, convulsing.

Audrey's scream pierced the silence.

She dropped the coffee, ceramic shattering on the hardwood as she lunged toward her grandmother, grabbing her shoulders, shaking her.

"Nana! Hold on!"

Fumbling, hands trembling, Audrey snatched her phone from her pocket, dialing 911.

"911, what's your emergency?"

"I need an ambulance—now! My grandmother—she's having a seizure!"

The operator's voice was calm, giving her instructions, but Audrey barely processed them. She was too busy holding Maggie, whispering, "It's going to be okay, Nana, everything's going to be okay."

Audrey's heart pounded in her ears as she crouched beside her grandmother's trembling body. Maggie—her stubborn, tough-as-nails Nana—was sprawled on the floor, her lips chalky, her breathing shallow and erratic.

Audrey had never seen her like this.

"Hang on, Nana," Audrey whispered, clutching her hand, which was clammy and weak.

The sound of wailing sirens filled the air as the paramedics burst through the door, their presence both a relief and a gut-wrenching confirmation that this was serious.

"What do we got?" one of them asked, kneeling beside Maggie and checking her pulse.

"She—she was fine last night," Audrey stammered. "This morning, she wouldn't wake up, she was sweating, then—then she just collapsed."

A second paramedic pulled out a blood pressure cuff, wrapping it around Maggie's arm. "Does she have any pre-existing conditions? Medications?"

"She takes blood pressure medicine, but she's otherwise healthy. Really healthy." Audrey's voice cracked, desperation clawing at her throat. "I can't understand what's going on. I mean, it happened so suddenly. No warning whatsoever."

The paramedic frowned as he checked Maggie's pulse again. "Her pressure's dangerously low."

They lifted Maggie onto the gurney, securing straps around her frail frame. Her head lolled slightly, and a fresh wave of panic crashed over Audrey.

"Nana?" she whispered, gripping her grandmother's hand. It was cold, still very clammy, slipping away from her grasp. "Please, please stay with me."

Maggie's eyelids fluttered, then stilled.

Audrey felt like she'd been punched in the stomach.

"Let's go!" the lead paramedic barked, wheeling Maggie out the door.

Audrey ran alongside the gurney, her mind screaming the same words on repeat.

Don't let this be the last time I see her awake.

The Holbrooks gathered in the sterile hospital waiting room, tense and silent, the air thick with worry.

Jill stood rigid, arms crossed, her cop's mask firmly in place, but Audrey knew her mother well enough to see the cracks underneath.

Cord paced like a caged animal, jaw clenched, fists tight. "What the hell is taking so long?"

Sandy sat slumped forward, elbows on his knees, shaking his head. "I don't get it. I stopped by the house last night, and she was having a glass of wine by the fire, regaling me with how many steps she got in yesterday."

Oliver arrived last, his face pinched with concern. "Sorry I'm late. I was in the middle of my closing argument and suddenly had to request a recess in Clyde Peterson's trial," he muttered, running a hand through his hair. "Tell me what's going on."

Before anyone could answer, Katie, in her nurse's uniform, stepped into the room.

Audrey knew instantly—before Katie even said a word—that something was seriously wrong.

Katie wasn't sugarcoating anything.

"This is bad," she said, keeping her voice low but firm.

The room stilled.

Audrey's chest tightened.

"What does that mean?" Cord demanded. "What's wrong with her?"

Katie glanced at the floor almost as if she was trying to hide her worry. "We don't know yet. Her blood pressure is frighteningly low, and she's barely responsive."

"Food poisoning?" Sandy suggested, looking desperate for an easy answer.

Katie shook her head. "No. The symptoms don't fit."

"Then what?" Oliver asked.

Katie shrugged. "They really don't know yet."

Cord, already a bull in a china shop, slammed his fist against the counter. "Well, why can't these damn doctors figure it out?"

Oliver shot him a sharp look. "Cord. Losing your temper isn't going to help."

Cord exhaled hard, pacing. "She was fine yesterday."

Katie touched Cord's arm. "They're working as fast as they can, but—" Katie stopped herself, not sure if she should divulge what she was about to say.

Sandy stepped forward, curious. "But what, Katie?"

Audrey felt the words before Katie spoke them. Felt the realization crash into her like an icy wave.

Katie hesitated. Then, lowering her voice, she said, "One of the doctors thinks she might have been poisoned."

The words landed like a bomb.

Cord's head snapped up. "Poisoned?" he bellowed.

Oliver grabbed his arm. "Shut up!" he hissed. "Do you want to get Katie in trouble?"

Cord swore under his breath, pacing faster, hands on his hips.

Oliver exhaled, rubbing a hand over his face.

Audrey felt like she'd been punched again.

Jill turned to her, eyes narrowing. "Audrey—"

"He poisoned Chips Hogan, Mom." Audrey's voice was stronger now, more certain. "He drugged Griffin Mead, setting him up for drowning." She looked her mother straight in the eyes. "And now that Grandpa Wes is gone, he's coming for Nana instead."

Katie glanced toward the hallway, lowering her voice even more. "I shouldn't have said anything. We don't have proof yet. We've sent her blood for testing."

"Who the hell would do this?" Cord seethed.

Audrey met Jill's gaze. "Bradley Comstock. We both know it."

Cord cocked an eyebrow. "The new dentist? Why would he—?"

Jill clenched her jaw. "We have no evidence."

Audrey didn't blink. "Then I'll get some."

The Holbrook house felt wrong when Audrey stepped inside.

Her grandmother should be here. Instead, she was fighting for her life in a hospital bed.

Audrey swallowed down the fear and moved quickly.

She stormed upstairs, heading straight for Maggie's room. If her grandmother had been poisoned, then there had to be something here—some clue.

She tore through the nightstand drawers, flipped through papers, and checked the closet. Nothing.

Then she stepped into the bathroom.

The gift bag from Dr. Comstock's office sat on the sink counter.

Audrey's pulse pounded.

She grabbed it, heart racing, and pulled out the travel-sized toothpaste.

The seal was broken.

Her stomach dropped.

Oh my God.

This was how he did it.

Audrey's hands shook as she stuffed the toothpaste into a plastic bag.

She had the proof she needed to prove Bradley had poisoned her grandmother.

Audrey returned to the hospital, her heart in her throat.

She found Jill standing near the nurses' station, talking in hushed tones with Oliver.

Audrey didn't hesitate.

She shoved the plastic bag into her mother's hand.

Jill frowned. "What is this?"

Audrey lowered her voice. "You need to get this tested."

Jill looked down at the bag, then back at Audrey.

For the first time that day, Jill's face went pale.

Audrey turned on her heel and walked away.

She'd done what she could.

Now it was up to Jill to prove it.

And arrest Comstock for two murders and one attempted murder.

At least that's what she prayed would be the outcome.

It was still a question mark whether Maggie was going to even make it.

Chapter Forty-one

Jill had slept in a chair at the hospital, her arms crossed, chin tucked to her chest, the tension in her body refusing to unwind even in exhaustion. She had barely shut her eyes before footsteps approached, and she snapped awake.

Katie stood before her, a clipboard in hand, a weary but relieved expression on her face.

"She had a rough night," Katie said in a hushed tone, casting a glance at the others scattered around the waiting room—Cord, Sandy, Oliver, and Audrey—all looking ragged from worry. "It was touch and go for a while, but this morning she's stabilizing."

Jill exhaled, releasing a breath she hadn't realized she was holding.

"She's not out of the woods yet," Katie added, "but the doctors are optimistic."

Sandy slumped back in his chair, rubbing his face. Cord let out an audible breath, his jaw tight, as if forcing himself not to break something. Audrey pressed her palms together, closing her eyes for a second in silent gratitude.

"Mom's always been a fighter," Jill said, her voice rough from exhaustion.

Katie nodded, but then, after a quick scan of the room, she lowered her voice.

"There's something else."

Everyone went still.

Jill straightened in her seat, sensing the weight in Katie's words.

"The toxicology report came back."

The room seemed to shrink.

"She tested positive for dimethylmercury."

Jill's stomach dropped.

Cord's hands balled into fists. "What the hell is that?"

"Extremely toxic," Katie said grimly. "A few drops absorbed through the skin can be lethal within weeks."

A cold chill ran down Jill's spine.

Cord was out of his chair in an instant. "I'm going to kill him."

Jill grabbed his arm, hard. "No, you're not."

"Jill—"

"No, Cord." Jill's voice was steel. "You're going to let me handle this. I promise you—" She met his furious gaze. "I will nail him for this."

Cord's chest heaved, but he stepped back, shaking his head in rage.

Jill turned, grabbed her coat, and headed straight for the station.

Jill sat at her desk, flipping through the toxicology report again, as if staring at it hard enough would make the missing pieces magically fall into place.

Dimethylmercury.

The poison was lethal.

A drop or two absorbed through the skin could take

weeks to manifest, but once symptoms appeared, it was often too late.

She knew Bradley Comstock was behind this.

She just didn't know for certain how he'd delivered it.

She was banking on the toothpaste Audrey had given her.

Mason walked into her office, file in hand, his face grim.

"Well?" Jill demanded, sitting up straight.

Mason sighed, tossing the folder onto her desk. "Toothpaste came back clean. No trace of mercury or anything remotely toxic."

Jill gritted her teeth.

"Damn it."

Mason slumped into the chair across from her. "You really thought that was it, huh?"

Jill pressed her fingers to her temple, thinking fast. "It made sense. Bradley, somehow with help, poisoned Chips Hogan's clam chowder. Probably drugged Griffin Mead in his dental chair. Why not do the same to my mother?"

Mason shook his head. "Maybe it wasn't the toothpaste, but what about the rest of that gift bag?"

Jill's gaze snapped up.

Mason nodded toward her. "She probably used everything in that bag, right? The toothbrush? The mouthwash? I mean, I would. Save me from having to go buy it at the drugstore."

Jill's eyes widened.

She shot up from her chair. "We need to go back to the house. Now."

Mason blinked, scrambling to his feet. "Wait, what? Right now?"

"Right now, Dooley." Jill was already grabbing her jacket. "We missed something. I know it."

Mason sighed, grabbing the car keys. "Guess I shouldn't have ordered lunch, huh?"

Jill strode past him toward the exit.

"You can eat when we have our damn evidence."

The ride to the Holbrook house was silent, except for the occasional grumble from Mason's stomach.

"God, I'm starving," he muttered.

Jill barely heard him. Her mind was racing, going over every interaction she'd had with Bradley Comstock.

He was confident.

Too confident.

He knew she didn't have a smoking gun.

But that meant one thing—he thought he'd covered his tracks.

And that? That meant there was something still there.

She gripped the steering wheel tighter.

She'd find it.

She'd bury him with it.

Mason sat up straighter as they pulled into the Holbrook driveway.

"All right," he said, stretching. "Let's go hunt for poison."

Jill threw the car into park.

And together, they headed inside.

Jill flung open the door to Maggie's bathroom, Mason right on her heels. The small space was pristine, except for the faint scent of lavender from Maggie's usual soap and the neatly arranged toiletries on the counter. But Jill wasn't here to admire Maggie's impeccable housekeeping skills—she was here to find out how Bradley Comstock had tried to kill her mother.

She turned to Mason, who had already pulled on a pair of latex gloves.

"All right," Jill said, rolling up her sleeves. "We tear this place apart."

Mason cracked his knuckles. "And here I thought I was just gonna be solving parking disputes today."

Jill ignored him and reached for the small white gift bag from Comstock Dental, sitting by the sink. She turned it over, examining it carefully before dumping the contents onto the counter.

Out spilled:

A mini bottle of mouthwash
A pack of floss
A brand-new toothbrush still in its plastic packaging
A second tube of toothpaste, not the one Audrey had given her to get tested.

There must have been two in the bag.

Jill picked up the toothpaste first, unscrewed the cap, and sniffed it. Nothing unusual. She squeezed the tube slightly, watching the paste ooze onto her glove.

Mason peered over her shoulder. "What, you think he dabbed it on there like some Cold War spy?"

Jill scowled. "I don't know. I thought maybe he laced it with something."

She turned to Mason, holding out the tube. "Bag it."

Mason took out an evidence bag, sliding the toothpaste inside before sealing it.

Jill reached for the mouthwash next. It was one of those small, single-use bottles, the kind you could toss in a travel bag. She unscrewed the top, giving it a cautious sniff.

Mason watched her warily.

"Uh, should you really be sniffing a bottle that might be laced with a neurotoxin?"

Jill shot him a glare. "What do you suggest? Taking a swig?"

Mason put his hands up. "Hey, I'm just saying, let's not be the next two victims here."

Jill rolled her eyes and poured a tiny drop of the mouthwash onto a paper towel, rubbing it between her fingers.

Nothing.

She sighed, tossing it aside. "Bag this one too."

Mason obliged, muttering under his breath. "Gonna need to order more evidence bags at this rate."

Jill turned her attention to the floss, pulling the tab and unraveling a few inches. She ran it between her gloved fingers, feeling for anything unusual—a residue, a powder, anything that might explain what had made Maggie so sick.

On the sink, Mason spotted another toothbrush resting in a ceramic holder. He picked it up carefully. "This one looks used," he observed, examining it under the bathroom light.

"Check the bristles," Jill said.

Mason frowned, holding it closer. The blue-and-white bristles looked normal at first glance, but as he turned it, something glimmered faintly under the light.

"Uh . . . Chief?"

She looked up from the floss.

Mason tilted the toothbrush toward her. "Tell me that's just the light playing tricks."

Jill snatched the brush from his hand, holding it up. There was an unusual, silvery sheen to the bristles—barely noticeable unless you were really looking.

Her pulse kicked up.

Mason exhaled sharply. "Son of a bitch."

Jill met his gaze, her jaw tightening. "Bag it. Now."

Mason carefully slipped the toothbrush into an evidence bag, sealing it with a decisive snap.

Mason hesitated. "You think that's it?"

Jill let out a breath. "I don't know. But if Comstock poisoned Mom, and she used this toothbrush every day . . ." She didn't need to finish the sentence.

Mason sealed the toothbrush in an evidence bag, his face tense.

Jill stared at the evidence bags lined up on the counter—the second tube of toothpaste, the mouthwash, the floss, and now the toothbrush.

If Bradley had poisoned her mother, this was the proof they needed.

She turned toward Mason.

"Let's get this tested," she said. "And if this is what I think it is . . . Comstock is going down."

Jill stormed into Comstock Dental, sending a ripple of alarm through the waiting room.

A woman clutching a magazine peered up, wide-eyed. A man who'd been flipping through his phone froze mid-scroll.

Melanie looked up from the reception desk, her face pale. "Dr. Comstock is with a patient."

Jill's voice sliced through the office.

"Get him out here. I need to talk to him."

Melanie hesitated.

"I'm not playing around," Jill growled.

Melanie jumped. Bradley's office door swung open violently, and Comstock stormed out, his irritation barely concealed.

"Chief Holbrook," he said, coldly, glancing at the patients now nervously watching. "Are you seriously disrupting my patients again?"

Jill ignored the growing tension. "Office. Now."

With a sharp glare, Bradley motioned for her to follow him inside.

Jill shut the door firmly behind them.

She leaned over his desk, voice low but lethal.

"Maggie Holbrook was poisoned."

Bradley's expression didn't flicker.

Jill kept going. "Just like Chips Hogan. Just like Griffin Mead, who was likely drugged in your chair and later pushed into the water and left to drown."

She leaned in closer, eyes narrowing.

"I know what this is about," she said, her voice razor-sharp.

Bradley's lips twitched, but he said nothing.

"Revenge."

Still, he remained cool.

Jill pushed harder.

"You blame Hogan, Mead, and my father for your father's death. For the failed deal. You wanted payback."

Bradley let out a slow, measured breath. "That's a fascinating theory, Chief."

Jill's fists clenched.

Bradley leaned back in his chair. "So where's the poison?"

Jill hesitated—too long.

A slow smirk curled at the corners of his mouth.

"You don't know."

Jill's blood boiled.

"It's only a matter of time, Bradley," she spit out.

"Test everything," he offered, spreading his arms in an almost mocking invitation. "My novocaine, my toothpaste—whatever you need. I have nothing to hide."

Jill's teeth gritted.

Bradley tilted his head. "You have no evidence."

Jill's jaw locked.

Bradley leaned forward. "So unless you're here to arrest me, Chief, I have patients to see."

He was cool and collected, but she noticed his hand shaking slightly.

"I'll be back," Jill said before turning sharply and storming out.

She was fuming as she climbed into her cruiser. She knew she didn't have enough to hand off to the DA yet—not the kind of airtight proof that would hold up in court. But rattling Comstock had its own purpose. If he felt the walls closing in, maybe he'd make a mistake, slip up, and give her what she needed. She relished the thought of throwing him off his game, watching him squirm.

Of course, it was a gamble—one she might regret if he clammed up instead of cracking under pressure. Still, she was so close.

Her phone buzzed.

A text from Sandy.

Get to the hospital.

Jill had never driven so fast in her life.

The moment she'd gotten Sandy's frantic text, she'd floored it, racing through town toward the hospital, heart pounding in her chest. She didn't know what she was walking into—another emergency? Worse? By the time she screeched into the parking lot, her own hands were shaking, her knuckles white on the steering wheel.

She rushed through the automatic doors, her boots clacking against the linoleum floor as she darted past the nurses' station and into the waiting room.

But where was everyone?

The usual group of Holbrooks wasn't huddled in the uncomfortable hospital chairs. No Cord pacing like a caged tiger. No Sandy fidgeting in the corner. No Oliver sitting with his arms crossed, trying to look calm but failing miserably.

A deep pit settled in Jill's stomach.

She turned sharply, ready to grab the nearest nurse and demand answers, but before she could, a familiar figure appeared in the hallway—Katie.

Jill felt the blood drain from her face.

The nurse's uniform, the serious look on her sister-in-law's face—it didn't help calm the storm raging inside Jill's chest.

"Where is she?" Jill demanded.

Katie gave her a sympathetic smile. "Come on, she's awake. The family's with her."

Jill didn't hesitate. She followed Katie down the hall, past closed doors and busy nurses, until she reached Maggie's room.

Inside, the entire family was gathered, surrounding Maggie's hospital bed like a protective circle. Cord stood closest, his arms crossed but relief evident in his tense shoulders. Oliver sat in the chair beside Maggie, looking both exhausted and relieved. Sandy leaned against the wall, hands shoved in his pockets, watching their mother with a cautious, almost childlike worry. And Audrey—Audrey was at Maggie's side, clutching her hand.

And then there was Maggie sitting up in bed.

Her cheeks had color.

Her eyes were open.

And when she saw Jill, she smirked.

"Damn, kid," Maggie rasped, voice hoarse but strong. "You look like hell."

Jill let out a shaky laugh, blinking back tears.

She rushed forward, grabbing Maggie's hand—warm, solid.

Jill choked on a breath, relief rushing through her.

Maggie squeezed her fingers.

"Don't let that bastard get away with it."

Jill's eyes darkened.

"I won't."

Chapter Forty-two

The diner was quiet, save for the rhythmic hum of the overhead fans and the occasional clang of silverware against ceramic plates. Audrey wiped down the counter, glancing at the clock. Almost closing time.

Ethel emerged from the kitchen, drying her hands on her apron. "How's your Nana doing?"

Audrey smiled, the worry in her chest loosening just a bit. "She's stable. Doctors are keeping her one more night for observation, but she should be home tomorrow."

Ethel nodded. "That woman's tougher than a two-dollar steak." She motioned toward a booth. "Customer at table seven."

Audrey turned and saw Mason, casually seated with a menu in hand. He lit up when he saw her approaching.

"My lucky night," he quipped, setting the menu aside.

Audrey rolled her eyes but couldn't help smiling. "You're here awfully late for dinner."

Mason smirked. "Late-night stakeouts require fuel."

Audrey raised a brow. "Are you working a case or just here to inhale an obscene amount of fries?"

He shrugged. "Why not both?"

Audrey jotted down his order and slid it into the kitchen window. Since Mason was their last customer, the cook had his dinner ready within minutes. Audrey delivered his bowl of clam chowder and side of fries.

"Last of the clam chowder. Enjoy."

Mason nodded. "Thank you."

"Living dangerously?"

Mason gave her a quizzical look before realizing. "Oh, you mean the chowder?" He shrugged. "I have no enemies." Then he thought about it some more. "Not that I know of."

Audrey smiled.

He opened his mouth to say something, paused as if working up the courage, but Audrey didn't give him the chance.

"Let me know if you need anything else."

She made a beeline back to the register.

Across the counter, Isabella watched, arms folded.

"Take my shift," Audrey said, pointing at Mason.

Isabella snorted. "No thanks. I already gave up on that dream."

Audrey blinked. "What dream?"

Isabella motioned toward Mason slurping his chowder and then munching on a handful of fries. "Look at him. The man chews like a lawnmower. Mouth half-open. We'll be divorced in a week."

Audrey bit back a laugh. "So that's why you're suddenly 'over it'?"

Isabella shrugged. "That, and it's plain as day he's more into you."

Audrey almost choked on air. "Excuse me?"

Isabella rolled her eyes. "Please. The way he looks at you? It's like a Golden Retriever waiting for a treat."

Audrey brushed it off, scribbling on Mason's bill. "You're imagining things."

"Mm-hmm." Isabella leaned in. "So why do you look so flustered?"

Audrey ignored her, delivering Mason's check. He seemed like he was working up the nerve to say something, but before he could, she cut him off again.

"Clocking out. If you want dessert, Isabella's got you covered."

Mason offered a disappointed smile. "Good night, then."

Audrey nodded, stepping outside into the crisp night air.

The walk home should have been straightforward, but Audrey's feet had a mind of their own. Before she realized it, she stood in front of Bradley Comstock's house.

All the lights were off.

The place looked empty.

Her gut told her the poison had to be somewhere in that house. If he didn't keep it at his office, he had to store it at home.

Screw it.

Audrey crept toward the back, testing the doors.

Locked.

The windows?

Locked.

Then, bingo. She remembered the bathroom window she had unlocked the last time she was in the house. It took some effort, but she managed to pry it open and wiggle inside, nearly getting stuck in the process.

As she twisted her way through, movement in her peripheral vision caught her attention. A neighbor strolled by on the sidewalk.

Audrey ducked down.

The neighbor paused, frowning toward the house.

Audrey's heart slammed against her ribs.

Keep walking.

Please keep walking.

After a tense moment, the neighbor moved on.

Audrey exhaled, then got to work.

She started in the bathroom, rummaging through drawers and medicine cabinets.

Nothing.

No mysterious vials.

No suspicious pill bottles.

Carefully, she slipped into the hallway, scanning the house. Photos lined the walls.

Bradley's father.

Everywhere.

Framed pictures of Ed Comstock, smiling, fishing, shaking hands in business deals.

A shrine.

Yeah, this guy's revenge plot checks out.

Audrey searched the living room, the kitchen, even the study. Nothing.

She was about to call it quits when—

A key turned in the front door lock.

Audrey's blood turned to ice.

Bradley was home.

She scurried down the hall, slipping into a closet, pressing herself into the farthest corner.

The front door clicked open.

Footsteps.

She saw the closet knob twitch.

Audrey held her breath.

Bradley hung up his coat, then moved toward the bathroom. A second later, she heard the shower start.

She was halfway to the door when she froze.

She needed to see his arm.

Whoever had attacked her in the woods had been bitten by Flounder. If Bradley had a bandage, she'd have her proof.

Carefully, she crept toward the bathroom door, peeking through the crack.

The room steamed up.

Bradley stepped out of the shower, towel-drying his hair.

No bandage.

No bite marks on his left arm.

No injury whatsoever.

Not even a scratch.

It wasn't him.

She turned toward the front door, reaching for the handle—

Ding-dong.

Audrey froze.

Footsteps down the hall.

She panicked, darting toward the kitchen as Bradley opened the door.

"Clyde." Bradley's tone was clipped.

Clyde Peterson stepped inside, agitated. "Cops have been sniffing around."

Bradley sighed. "So?"

Clyde scowled. "So? They're trying to link me to you. I can't afford that. My trial's already on thin ice."

Bradley rolled his eyes. "Relax."

Clyde gritted his teeth. "I'm not going down for someone I barely know."

Bradley studied him, then smiled coldly. "Then maybe I will make it worth your while to keep your mouth shut."

Clyde hesitated. "I need to think."

Bradley's eyes darkened. "Don't make my life difficult. Or yours."

"Just so you know, I don't respond very well to threats," Clyde huffed before storming out.

Bradley slammed the door.

Then, he snapped.

He knocked over a lamp, sending it crashing to the floor.

Muttered to himself, pacing, completely unraveling.

Audrey watched in horror.

Then, Bradley cut his hand on the broken glass. He cursed, storming off toward the bathroom.

Audrey didn't wait.

She darted for the door, flinging it open, slipping into the night.

As soon as she was a safe distance away, she pulled out her phone.

Dialed Jill.

"Mom," she whispered. "Did you get the test results back on the contents of the gift bag?"

"Still waiting. Why?"

"I may know of another way we can nail him."

Chapter Forty-three

Jill sat at the head of the long wooden table in the courthouse conference room, arms crossed, face set in stone. The air was tense. Across from her sat Clyde Peterson, looking like a man who had just realized he might be out of options. Mark Haskell, the DA, sat beside Jill, his legal pad lined with notes, while Oliver Holbrook, Clyde's defense attorney, adjusted his tie, preparing for what was sure to be an interesting negotiation.

Mark leaned forward, tapping his pen against the table. "Clyde, let's cut to the chase. The jury is still deliberating, but my gut tells me they're not going to take your side. This is a way out—plead guilty, take probation, no jail time. You'll have to complete anger management courses and pay restitution, but you won't spend the next nine to twelve months in a six by eight cell."

Clyde raised an eyebrow. "That's it?"

Mark nodded. "That's it. If you answer every single one of our questions truthfully regarding Bradley Comstock."

Jill watched Clyde carefully as his expression shifted. She could see the gears turning in his head.

"Comstock?" Clyde finally said. "Really?"

Jill leaned in. "Yes. But if you lie to us, the deal is off the table."

Clyde let out a breath, rubbing the back of his neck. He turned to Oliver. "What do you think?"

Oliver sighed. "The evidence against you isn't great, Clyde. But I have a bad feeling about this jury. If you take this deal, you get to go home. If you roll the dice, you might not."

Clyde exhaled sharply. "Fine. But just so we're clear—this deal only covers my current assault trial, right? Not anything else?"

Mark folded his hands on the table. "Correct. Any other crimes are not included in this plea agreement."

Jill narrowed her eyes. If Clyde had anything to do with Comstock's scheme, this deal could backfire spectacularly.

Oliver gave Clyde a meaningful look. "If you've done something worse, Clyde, you better think long and hard before opening your mouth."

Clyde hesitated, then nodded. "I'll take the deal."

Mark slid a document across the table, and Clyde signed his name at the bottom.

Mark turned to Jill. "He's all yours."

Jill sat forward, locking eyes with Clyde. "Have you done any work for Bradley Comstock?"

Clyde shook his head immediately. "Nope."

Jill didn't believe him. "Are you sure about that?"

Clyde smirked. "I don't work for dentists."

Jill crossed her arms. "Then let's talk about the deadly nightshade. We know you ordered it."

Clyde leaned back in his chair, looking relaxed. "I don't deny that."

"Did you give it to Bradley Comstock?"

"Nope."

Mark narrowed his eyes. "Clyde, you remember the deal, right? If we find out you're lying, we void this agreement, and you're back in front of that jury."

Clyde held up a hand. "I'm telling you the truth."

Jill's jaw tightened. "Did you use the nightshade to poison Chips Hogan?"

"No."

"Did you push Griffin Mead into the water while he was under the influence of a drug?"

"Absolutely not."

Jill studied him.

He wasn't squirming.

He wasn't sweating.

For the first time, she believed him.

"Then why were you at Bradley Comstock's house last night, talking about the murders?"

Clyde's head snapped up. "How the hell do you know about that?"

Jill didn't answer.

Clyde sighed. "I kept hearing my name being thrown around with Comstock's, and I wanted to know what was going on. I don't need cops knocking on my door when I'm already on trial for assault."

Jill leaned in. "So he wasn't buying your silence because you were his accomplice?"

Clyde snorted. "Nope. But it sure sounds like he's got one."

Jill frowned. "If you didn't order the nightshade for Comstock, then who was it for?"

Clyde hesitated.

Jill tapped her fingers on the table. "Come on, Clyde. We made a deal. Talk."

Clyde chuckled. "You're not going to believe me."

Jill rapped sharply on the front door.

A moment later, Melanie Blaisdell swung it open, looking startled. "Chief Holbrook?"

Jill folded her arms. "We need to talk."

Melanie stepped back warily. "About what?"

Jill crossed the threshold, not waiting for an invitation. "About the nightshade plant you bought."

Melanie's eyes widened, but she quickly recovered. "That's ridiculous."

Jill's voice was cool but steady. "Clyde Peterson admitted he ordered the nightshade. For you."

Melanie swallowed. "Look, I ordered it because it's—" she sighed. "It's got beautiful flowers. I thought it would look nice in my garden next spring."

Jill wasn't buying it. "Not because you wanted to help Bradley frame Waldo Duggan for murder?"

Melanie looked horrified. "What? No!"

"What I can't figure is—if it was really for your own use, why go through Clyde? Why the post office box?"

Melanie's lips thinned. For a moment she looked cornered, then she let out a sharp breath.

"Because I didn't want my name attached to it, all right? Belladonna isn't illegal, but it sounds bad. One person at that nursery gossips, and suddenly everyone in Halibut Cove thinks I'm stirring poison in my teapot. Around here, I've already got a reputation for being odd, and I don't need to feed it. Clyde owed me a favor, so I asked him to handle the order. That's all there was to it."

Jill studied her. The explanation was neat, maybe a little too neat. "So, where is the plant now?"

Melanie hesitated. "It's . . . gone."

Jill's stomach sank. "Gone?"

Melanie nodded slowly. "I came home one day, and it was missing from my greenhouse."

Jill's mind raced. "And before it went missing, you told Bradley about it at work, didn't you?"

Melanie looked away. "Maybe."

That was it.

Bradley had stolen the plant and used it to kill Chips.

"Why didn't you say anything when we found the plant in Waldo Duggan's house?"

"I—I don't know, I guess I thought I might not be the only one who has that plant."

Jill stepped back. "I need you to think very carefully, Melanie. Are you absolutely certain Bradley was with you the night Griffin Mead drowned?"

Melanie lifted her chin defiantly. "Yes. We were working late. I swear."

Jill exhaled slowly. Bradley had to have an accomplice. But if it wasn't Clyde or Melanie . . . who was it?

Jill pushed through the front door of The Chowder House, scanning the room for Mason. The diner was still busy with late-morning regulars, the usual crowd of fishermen and shop owners finishing their breakfasts. She spotted Mason at a booth, hunched over an overflowing plate of food, eating like a man who hadn't seen a meal in a week. Across from him, Isabella watched in disgust, arms crossed as she stared at him with barely concealed horror.

"You do realize that food isn't trying to run away from you, right?" Isabella deadpanned, watching Mason shovel forkfuls of eggs, bacon, and pancakes into his mouth like a human vacuum.

Mason barely looked up. "I'm a growing boy."

"You're a grown man," Isabella countered. "And you eat like a raccoon that just found an open dumpster."

Before Mason could retort, Audrey slid into the booth next to Isabella, rolling her eyes at their bickering.

"Give him a break," Audrey said, nudging Isabella with her elbow. "He's got a point. Growing boy and all."

Mason perked up, swallowing his bite of pancake with visible effort. "Thank you! See? Audrey gets it."

Audrey shrugged. "Besides, I'd rather listen to him eat than hear you lecture him about it."

Mason beamed, clearly touched Audrey had come to his defense.

Jill marched up to their booth, interrupting the moment. "Mason, let's go."

Mason froze mid-bite, looking between Jill and the remainder of his breakfast. "I still have hash browns left."

"You'll survive."

"But they're crispy," Mason argued, fork hovering dramatically.

Jill let out a long, slow breath. "Mason, I swear to God."

Mason groaned but reluctantly waved down Ethel, who had been watching with amusement from behind the counter.

"Can I get a to-go box?" Mason asked hopefully.

Ethel smirked. "I'd say yes, but I think the chief might physically remove you from the booth before you get a chance to use it."

Before Mason could argue further, Jill's phone buzzed in her pocket. She pulled it out and checked the text.

Her entire posture stiffened.

Lab results back. Dimethylmercury detected in toothbrush bristles.

Jill exhaled slowly, gripping her phone tighter.

This was it.

Finally.

The proof they needed.

Audrey noticed the sudden change in her mother's demeanor and narrowed her eyes. "What?"

Jill shoved the phone back into her pocket, masking her expression. "Nothing. Let's go, Mason."

Audrey didn't buy it. "Mom, what is it?"

"Audrey, drop it," Jill warned, but Audrey wasn't backing down.

She leaned in, lowering her voice. "Is it about Nana?"

Jill clenched her jaw, then, with a reluctant sigh, leaned toward Audrey and whispered, "The test results came back."

Audrey's heart kicked into high gear. "And?"

Jill hesitated before whispering, "It was the toothbrush. That's how he poisoned her."

Audrey sat back, stunned, the weight of the revelation settling over her.

"You're sure?"

"Positive."

Audrey exhaled sharply. She turned to Ethel, Isabella, and Jimmy, who were watching the exchange with confused curiosity.

"We got him," Audrey announced.

Ethel straightened immediately. "You mean Comstock?"

Audrey nodded grimly. "We have proof. He tampered with the toothbrush in that stupid dental gift bag. That's how he poisoned Nana."

A collective gasp rippled through the group.

"That son of a—" Ethel caught herself, shaking her head.

Isabella's hands clenched into fists. "I knew he was creepy, but this is next level."

Jimmy looked downright pale and stopped clearing plates from a nearby table. "He tried to kill your grandmother over some grudge?"

Jill cut in. "We need to move. Now."

Audrey's voice turned sharp. "I want to be there when you arrest him."

Jill shook her head firmly. "Absolutely not."

"Mom—"

"Audrey, I mean it," Jill snapped. "This is a police matter now. Mason and I will handle it."

Audrey didn't like it, but she knew better than to push.

Mason finally threw his napkin down, standing up with a heavy sigh. "Well, there go my hash browns."

Jill ignored him. "Let's go."

With that, she turned on her heel, Mason following behind as they stormed out of The Chowder House and straight toward Comstock Dental.

Jill strode purposefully into Comstock Dental, Mason right behind her. The waiting room was full of patients. A young mother was trying to keep her toddler entertained with a set of plastic dinosaur figurines, while an older gentleman in a flannel jacket checked his watch impatiently.

Melanie sat behind the reception desk, fidgeting with a pen, looking bored as she scrolled through something on her computer screen.

Jill didn't waste time. She marched straight up to the desk and tapped her badge on the counter.

"Where is he?" Jill demanded.

Melanie's brows furrowed, glancing up. She wasn't happy to see Jill twice in one day. "Who?"

Jill leveled her with a look.

Melanie stilled, realizing. "Dr. Comstock?"

Mason crossed his arms beside Jill. "Yeah. That guy. Where is he?"

Melanie rolled her chair back, hesitating. "He's—he's with a patient."

"Get him out here," Jill ordered.

A tense silence settled over the room. A woman in the waiting area lowered her magazine, eyes flickering between Jill and Melanie.

Melanie swallowed hard, standing up. "I—Um—Okay, just a sec." She hurried toward the hallway, where the exam rooms were located.

Jill and Mason exchanged a glance.

They waited.

And waited.

The longer the silence stretched, the more a sinking feeling settled in Jill's gut.

Melanie finally reappeared, but she was alone.

Her face had drained of all color. She looked panicked, hands twisting together in front of her.

Jill's stomach dropped.

"He's not there, is he?" Jill said, her voice eerily calm.

Melanie blinked rapidly, her mouth opening and closing. "He must have—"

Mason stepped up next to Jill, voice sharp. "Where is he, Melanie?"

"I—I don't know!" Melanie stammered. "He was here this morning. I confirmed his appointments, he even had a patient in the chair—but there's no one back there . . ."

Jill turned on her heel.

"Let's go," she snapped at Mason.

Mason bolted after her. "I knew it. I freaking knew it—"

They raced out of the office, nearly barreling into a delivery man coming in with a package. Jill ignored his startled protest, her boots hitting the pavement hard as she and Mason rushed to the cruiser.

"Someone tipped him off," Jill muttered, throwing the car into drive so fast the tires squealed.

"Melanie?" Mason guessed.

"Maybe." Jill's jaw clenched. "Or someone else. Either way, Comstock knows we're coming for him."

They sped toward Bradley's house, the cruiser kicking up dust as Jill pushed the speed limit on the narrow roads.

When they finally pulled up to Comstock's driveway, Jill's worst fears were confirmed.

His car was gone.

The house was dark.

Too dark.

Jill threw the car into park, jumped out, and stalked up the front steps. She banged on the door with enough force to rattle the hinges.

"Bradley Comstock! Halibut Cove Police Department! Open up!"

Silence.

Mason stepped up beside her, peering through the nearest window.

"Place looks empty," he muttered.

Jill ground her teeth together.

She knew he was already gone.

"Damn it!" She slammed her palm against the doorframe, stepping back to take in the house. "He's on the run."

Mason exhaled sharply, raking a hand through his hair. "Who could have warned him?"

Jill turned back toward the cruiser, already thinking, already planning.

"We need to get an APB out on his car," she said. "Call the state police, the sheriff's department, hell, the Coast Guard if we have to. Comstock is not slipping away from us."

Mason nodded, pulling out his phone. "I'll get on it."

Jill took one last look at the empty house, her fingers curling into fists at her sides.

Bradley Comstock might have gotten away for now.

But Chief Jill Holbrook wasn't about to let him disappear forever.

Chapter Forty-four

Audrey hovered as Maggie settled into her favorite chair by the fireplace, a thick quilt draped over her legs. The moment they'd arrived home from the hospital, Cord and Sandy had started buzzing around her like nervous bees, fetching her pillows, adjusting the lighting, making sure she was comfortable.

"You two are worse than a pair of mother hens," Maggie grumbled, batting Cord's hand away as he attempted to fluff her pillow for the third time. "I appreciate the attention, but I'm not an invalid."

"We just want to make sure you're okay, Nana," Audrey said, setting a cup of tea on the side table.

"I'll be better once you all stop smothering me," Maggie huffed. "Cord, Sandy, go check your lobster traps, do something useful."

Cord checked his phone. "Too foggy today, anyway. Forecast says it'll be better in the morning."

Maggie let out an exaggerated sigh. "Fine. But if you're going to slack off today, at least do it at the tavern where I don't have to watch you watching me."

Cord and Sandy exchanged a look before grinning.

"She's kicking us out," Sandy said.

Cord smirked. "Four o'clock is close enough to happy hour, I guess."

"Go," Maggie said, waving a hand dismissively. "Drink your terrible beer and tell your fishing stories. Just leave me in peace."

Audrey watched her uncles amble out the door, chuckling to themselves.

"I don't need a babysitter, you know," Maggie said pointedly, narrowing her eyes at Audrey.

"I'm not leaving you alone," Audrey said firmly.

Maggie huffed but didn't argue. "Fine. But if you're staying, I'm putting you to work. I need my prescription picked up."

Audrey grabbed her coat. "I'll go right now."

"And grab some groceries while you're out," Maggie added. "You might as well cook me a nice dinner."

Audrey smirked, grabbed the keys, and headed out.

By the time she stepped out of the pharmacy, a thick fog had settled over town, rolling in from the harbor like a heavy wool blanket. The streetlights glowed eerily through the mist, elongated shadows stretching across the pavement.

Audrey hugged her coat tighter around her as she walked to her car, balancing a grocery bag in one hand, Maggie's prescription in the other.

That's when it happened.

That prickle at the back of her neck.

The sensation that someone was watching her.

She froze, glancing around the parking lot.

No one.

Only the fog shifting through the dimly lit lot, swallowing the outlines of parked cars.

Audrey shook her head, forcing herself to breathe.

You're being paranoid.

She reached for the car door.

A strong arm suddenly grabbed her from behind.

A damp cloth clamped over her nose and mouth.

Chloroform.

She kicked, struggled, but the world around her blurred.

Then, everything went dark.

Audrey drifted in and out of consciousness, her head throbbing like a drumbeat.

The world around her was cold, metal, and suffocatingly small.

It took her a few seconds to realize she was moving—the steady hum of an engine vibrating beneath her. Her body shifted and jostled with every bump in the road.

A car.

She was in a trunk.

Panic flooded her chest.

She tried to move, but her arms and legs felt heavy, sluggish, like her body wasn't fully cooperating. The chloroform still had its cloying grip on her senses.

Breathe, Audrey.

Think.

She pressed her hands against the cool metal walls, feeling for seams, a latch, anything.

Nothing.

She was locked in.

The car slowed, took a turn, then picked up speed again.

Audrey forced herself to listen—the rhythm of the tires on the road, the occasional splash of water from puddles, the faint sound of rain tapping against the roof.

Then she heard something else.

A police siren.

The car screeched to a halt.

Audrey's heart pounded. Was this her chance?

Muffled voices.

A radio crackling.

She started kicking the trunk lid with her feet.

Desperate to make enough noise to be heard.

A moment later, the car lurched forward again.

Faster now.

Reckless.

Audrey bit her lip, frustration rising.

Must have been a roadblock.

The cops were out looking for him.

But Bradley had somehow gotten through.

She scrambled for her phone in her back pocket, but it had no signal.

The car weaved back and forth, twisting through side streets. He was taking back roads.

Avoiding checkpoints.

Her breath came faster, the trunk feeling smaller, tighter.

She tried to keep her fear in check, but the reality of her situation pressed in on her from all sides.

Then, the car slowed again.

Came to a stop.

A door opened.

Boots crunched against gravel.

Then, the trunk popped open.

Bradley Comstock's face hovered above her, his expression eerily calm, but his eyes blazing with something darker.

"Rise and shine," he murmured.

Audrey glared up at him, forcing steel into her voice. "Kidnapping now? That part of your grand plan?"

Bradley sighed theatrically. "Not my first choice, believe

me. But I ran out of options thanks to your mother and her merry band of idiots." He leaned against the car, rolling his shoulders. "Had to dodge roadblocks. They're looking for me everywhere."

Audrey's stomach clenched.

He really was running out of time.

Bradley shook his head, as if disappointed by the entire situation. "I had a nice, quiet exit planned. But no . . . now I'm forced to improvise."

Audrey held her breath slightly.

She was not going to die here.

Bradley exhaled sharply. "So, change of plans." His lips curved into a slow, smug smile. "Since the roads are no good . . . I figured I'd take the scenic route."

Audrey's whole body quivered.

She knew what that meant.

The boats.

Bradley grabbed her arm, yanking her up roughly.

Audrey dug her heels into the trunk's lining, twisting to try and break free, but Bradley's grip was like iron.

"Easy now," he warned. "I'd rather not have to knock you out again."

Audrey glared. "My brothers are out lobstering. You won't find a boat to steal."

Bradley chuckled, eyes gleaming with amusement. "Nice try, sweetheart. I already know the fleet's docked." He shoved her forward, stepping aside to let her stumble out of the trunk.

The moment her feet hit the ground, the trunk slammed shut behind her.

Audrey flinched, the sound reverberating through the quiet, foggy night.

She stared at the closed trunk, a sense of hopelessness creeping in.

No one knew where she was.

She was at Bradley's mercy.

And if he got her on a boat . . .

She wasn't coming back.

Audrey's pulse pounded in her ears as she stumbled toward the dock, Bradley's vise-like grip digging into her arm. The fog had thickened, clinging to the air like a suffocating blanket, muting every sound except for the rhythmic slap of water against the pilings. The docks were nearly empty this time of night—no fishermen unloading the day's catch, no workers securing lines or stacking crates. Just darkness, the eerie glow of the harbor lights, and her captor, marching her straight toward the boats.

Think, Audrey. Think.

Bradley nudged her forward with a gun, his breath warm against the back of her neck. "Keep moving," he ordered, voice eerily calm. "No sudden moves, or I won't hesitate to put a bullet in you."

Audrey gritted her teeth, her mind racing. She had to get out of this.

They reached the dock where her family's boats were moored, their names painted in bold script on the sides. If she got on one of those boats, she was dead.

Bradley shoved her forward.

Audrey took a deep breath.

She had only one shot.

At the last possible second, she threw herself sideways, kicking out as hard as she could, striking Bradley's wrist.

The gun clattered to the dock, spinning away.

Bradley cursed, momentarily stunned, and Audrey didn't waste a second. She spun on her heel, slammed both hands into his chest, and shoved him with everything she had.

Bradley staggered backward.

His foot slipped on the wet dock.

His eyes went wide with shock.

Then—with a sickening splash—he toppled over the edge and into the freezing water below.

Audrey didn't stop to watch him struggle.

She ran.

Her lungs burned as she tore down the dock, her boots pounding against the wooden planks. The fog was so thick she could barely see, but she knew these docks better than anyone. If she could just make it to Main Street, she had a chance.

Just keep running.

Don't look back.

She darted between stacks of lobster traps, her breath coming in sharp gasps. She risked a glance behind her, but there was no sign of Bradley.

For a brief, flickering moment, she thought she was in the clear.

Then, a hand shot out of the darkness and yanked her backward.

Audrey let out a strangled gasp as a strong arm wrapped around her waist, dragging her into the shadows of an alley between two buildings. A hand clamped over her mouth, muffling her scream.

Her heart nearly stopped.

Then, a voice—low, urgent—whispered in her ear.

"Shhh. It's me."

Audrey's body went rigid.

Jimmy.

She twisted, trying to get a better look at him, relief flooding through her.

"Jimmy," she gasped, voice muffled against his palm.

He slowly loosened his grip, and she whirled to face

him, her breath coming fast. "Bradley kidnapped me. I need help. He's—"

"I know," Jimmy interrupted, eyes darting around the foggy street. "He's looking for you. We don't have much time."

Audrey clutched his arm. "You have to help me get to the police. My mom—"

Jimmy hesitated.

Audrey froze, suddenly realizing something was off.

His expression wasn't right. There was no urgency, no real concern.

His gaze flicked past her—not at her, but over her shoulder, toward the docks.

And that's when Audrey felt it—the slow, creeping dread curling in her stomach.

No.

She took a tiny step back, her voice barely above a whisper.

"You knew."

Jimmy sighed. "I didn't want it to come to this."

Audrey's breath hitched.

He wasn't here to help her.

He was here to give her back.

Bradley's mystery accomplice.

Of all the people in town . . .

Jimmy?

Her mind raced. How had she missed the signs?

Jimmy gave her a pleading look, like he wanted her to understand. "I didn't have a choice, Audrey. He—"

"Shut up," she hissed, taking another step back.

Jimmy reached for her, but she slapped his hand away.

That's when she heard the footsteps—heavy, fast, coming up behind her.

Before she could react, a strong arm wrapped around her throat, jerking her backward.

Bradley.

Soaked, furious, his breath ragged with rage.

"You just couldn't make this easy, could you?" he snarled in her ear.

Audrey fought back, kicking wildly, but Bradley tightened his grip, pressing the barrel of the gun against her ribs.

Jimmy stood frozen, his expression a mixture of guilt and fear.

Audrey locked eyes with him.

"Don't do this," she whispered. "You don't have to do this."

Jimmy's jaw clenched.

For a moment, just a moment, Audrey thought maybe—maybe—he would change his mind.

Then, he turned away.

Bradley shoved her forward.

"Back to the boat," he growled.

Audrey stumbled, her mind spinning.

She had been so close to getting away.

Now, she was trapped again.

And this time—

She might not get another chance.

Bradley shoved Audrey down into the cabin, the boat still docked, rocking slightly beneath her. She caught herself against the wall as Jimmy hovered by the doorway, his eyes darting between her and Bradley.

Her mind raced.

The Coast Guard would be monitoring the harbor exits. If Bradley was on the run, where could he possibly go?

Bradley ran a shaky hand through his damp hair, his jaw clenched in frustration. "We need to move. Now."

Jimmy shifted uncomfortably. "Where are we gonna go?"

Bradley spun toward him, his voice sharp. "We head toward Yarmouth."

Audrey gasped.

Nova Scotia. They were planning to disappear in Canada.

She needed to act fast.

As Bradley stalked toward the helm, she stealthily pulled out her phone.

The Holbrooks all had a boating app that linked their vessels to a shared GPS system. Audrey quickly navigated to the emergency distress beacon, her hands shaking as she sent the signal.

A confirmation blinked on the screen.

Help was on the way.

Before Bradley turned back around, she slipped the phone behind a pillow on the cabin bench.

Bradley exhaled sharply. "Jimmy, untie the ropes. We need to get out of here."

Jimmy hesitated. "Bradley, maybe we should—"

A voice boomed through the night.

"This is Chief Jill Holbrook. Step away from the boat and put your hands in the air!"

Audrey's stomach flipped.

They came.

Jimmy froze.

Bradley's head snapped up as the glow of flashing red and blue lights reflected off the water.

"No, no, no!" Bradley whirled on Jimmy, shoving him toward the cabin wall. "How the hell did they find us?"

Audrey stayed silent.

She knew exactly how.

Jill's bullhorn crackled again. "Bradley Comstock, you are surrounded. Do not try to escape."

Jimmy swallowed hard, his Adam's apple bobbing. "Bradley, we need to give this up."

Bradley's eyes flashed with fury. He grabbed Audrey by the arm and hauled her up the stairs onto the deck.

"You let me go," he growled at Jill and the other officers, pressing the barrel of his gun against Audrey's temple, "or she dies."

Everything stopped.

Jill stood at the dock, her hands clenched into fists, Cord and Sandy behind her.

Mason was there, too, standing just a step away from Jill.

Bradley tightened his grip around Audrey, dragging her closer to the edge of the boat.

"I *will* shoot her, Holbrook," Bradley snarled.

Jill's expression hardened. "We're not letting you leave, Bradley."

Bradley pressed the gun harder against Audrey's temple. "Then you're saying goodbye to your daughter."

Audrey could barely breathe.

Her gaze flickered to Mason.

Wait.

Audrey did a double take.

He wasn't there anymore.

One second Mason was standing next to Jill.

The next, he was gone.

Jill turned slightly, as if realizing it, too.

"What happened to Mason?" she whispered to one of the officers.

But Audrey knew.

She glanced over the side of the boat, the faint ripples of water barely visible in the moonlight.

Mason was in the water. Clinging to something.

Bradley, too distracted by the stand-off, didn't notice.

Seconds passed like hours.

Jimmy's hands were trembling. "Bradley, please, we have to stop this—"

"Shut up!" Bradley barked. "Jimmy, get us out of here. Now."

Jimmy hesitated, then obeyed, rushing to the helm and revving the engine.

The boat lurched forward, cutting through the dark water.

"No!" Jill's voice boomed from the dock.

Audrey's heart pounded as she turned back to the water.

Mason was gone.

No.

Not gone.

Climbing.

She barely made out the shape of his hand gripping a loose rope on the side of the boat, hoisting himself up.

They weren't out of this yet.

Bradley dragged her back down below deck as the boat picked up speed.

"We're almost clear of the harbor," Jimmy called from the helm. "But the Coast Guard is trailing us—"

Then—

A loud thump.

Audrey's heart leapt.

Mason was on board.

Bradley turned, his brows furrowed. "What was that?"

Audrey played dumb and just shrugged.

Bradley grabbed her by the collar, shoving her to the floor. "Stay down, or I'll put a bullet in your leg."

Audrey's mind reeled.

Mason was here.

She just had to wait.

Then, all at once—chaos erupted.

Mason burst through the cabin door, tackling Bradley with a force that sent them both crashing against the wall.

Bradley yelled, his gun skidding across the floor.

"Jimmy!" he roared.

But Jimmy hesitated.

Mason swung, landing a punch across Bradley's jaw.

Bradley staggered but recovered too fast.

He grabbed the discarded gun.

And fired.

The gunshot ripped through the cabin.

Mason jerked, a pained grunt escaping his lips.

"No!" Audrey screamed, rushing to his side.

Mason slumped against the wall, gripping his side. Blood soaked his shirt.

Bradley smirked.

Audrey's vision blurred with fury.

She lunged, shoving Bradley backward, using every ounce of her strength.

Bradley stumbled, hitting his head against the table, stunned just long enough for Audrey to grab Mason's fallen gun.

"Move, and I swear to God I will shoot you," she snapped, aiming it at Bradley's chest.

A beat of silence.

Then—

"Coast Guard! Hands up!"

Relief flooded Audrey's body.

They were saved.

Officers stormed the boat, guns raised, forcing Bradley to the ground as he screamed and thrashed.

Audrey rushed to Mason, her hands pressing against his wound.

"You're gonna be okay," she said, her voice shaking.

Mason gritted his teeth, his face pale. "Holbrook, you're—you're a terrible liar."

Audrey choked on a laugh, tears burning her eyes.

Without thinking, she leaned down—

And kissed him.

A real, desperate, heart-pounding kiss.

When she pulled back, Mason blinked, dazed.

Then, with a weak grin, he murmured,

"Finally."

Chapter Forty-five

Jill stormed into the small, cramped interrogation room of the Halibut Cove Police Station, her expression dark as a brewing nor'easter. She planted her hands on the metal table, leaning in so close that Jimmy Beckett had nowhere to look but into her piercing blue eyes.

"Let's not waste time," she said coolly. "We both know you're in deep. You poisoned Chips Hogan. You pushed Griffin Mead into the water. And you helped Bradley Comstock kidnap my daughter."

Jimmy sat motionless, his fingers laced together in his lap. His eyes flicked to the mirrored window, probably wondering if someone—anyone—was coming to save him.

But no one was.

Jill had made damn sure of that.

Bradley had already lawyered up, his fancy Boston attorney arriving at the police station within hours of his arrest.

But Jimmy?

Jimmy had no lawyer.

No high-priced defense team working to spin the narrative.

No safety net.

Just him and the hard, cold truth.

"I've got nothing to say," Jimmy muttered, staring at the tabletop.

Jill let out a sharp, humorless laugh. "That's cute. You think staying silent is gonna save you? You think Bradley's gonna swoop in and take the fall for you?" She shook her head, tapping the table for emphasis. "Let me tell you something, kid. Bradley doesn't give a damn about you."

Jimmy's jaw twitched, but he said nothing.

Jill straightened. "All right. Have it your way." She turned on her heel and stalked out of the room, slamming the door behind her.

Now it was Audrey's turn.

Time for Good Cop, Bad Cop.

She knew this was unprofessional.

Using her daughter like this.

But with Mason in the hospital fighting for his life, she needed someone Jimmy knew well, someone he was comfortable around, near his own age, to get him to open up.

Jill watched from the video feed outside the interrogation room, arms crossed tightly over her chest.

She knew Audrey had a shot at getting through to Jimmy. They had history—both born and raised in Halibut Cove. Went to high school together. Audrey knew Jimmy before he got in over his head, back when he was just a kid bussing tables at The Chowder House, dreaming of something bigger.

Audrey pulled out the chair across from Jimmy, leaning back in a relaxed posture. "I get it, Jimmy," she said, voice low and conversational. "I really do."

Jimmy snorted, still staring at the table. "Yeah? What exactly do you get, Audrey?"

"That Bradley sold you a dream," Audrey replied. "Made

you feel like you were finally getting out of this town. That you were gonna be more than just a guy scraping plates and wiping down tables."

Jimmy's hands clenched into fists.

Audrey tilted her head, watching him. "He played you. Convinced you this was about justice, when really? It was just about his own twisted revenge."

Jimmy's throat bobbed as he swallowed.

"He's got a top-notch lawyer," Audrey continued, voice softer now. "You don't. You really think he's gonna go down for this? Or do you think he's gonna pin everything on you?"

Jimmy's breathing turned shallow.

Audrey leaned in, her voice dropping to barely a whisper. "Bradley is gonna walk, Jimmy. And you? You're gonna take the fall for everything."

Jimmy looked up sharply, his eyes wide. "No. He—he wouldn't do that."

"I think you know he would. I don't want to see that happen. Neither does Ethel or Isabella. We're like a family at The Chowder House. I've always liked you, Jimmy."

"Not enough to go out with me!" Jimmy snapped.

"No, but that doesn't mean I don't care for you."

Jimmy didn't say anything.

Just let the silence stretch.

And then, finally, Jimmy exhaled shakily, his body sagging like a balloon losing air.

He opened his mouth.

He was finally ready to talk.

Jill burst back into the room, not bothering to sit. "Tell me everything," she demanded.

Jimmy ran a hand down his face, his fingers trembling. "Bradley planned it all," he said, voice hoarse.

"How'd you two meet?"

Jimmy explained that they had met nearly six months ago at a fundraising dinner catered by the inn where Jimmy worked an occasional second job as a busboy. He was young, broke, and desperate for a way out of his dead-end life. Bradley, new to town, saw the hunger in his eyes and took him under his wing—offering advice, encouragement, the occasional expensive gift. To Jimmy, he was a mentor. A savior. By the time Bradley finally laid out the plan, Jimmy wasn't just willing—he was convinced he was helping the only person who had ever believed in him.

Jill nodded silently as Jimmy finished. Then took a breath. "And the nightshade?"

Jimmy looked down at the table. "That was all Bradley. He stole it from Melanie."

Jill nodded, already aware of this information.

Jimmy nodded. "She had one in her greenhouse—just for decoration or whatever. She liked the weird-looking plants. One day, Bradley just took it. He told me to crush up the berries and put them in Chips Hogan's chowder at The Chowder House."

Jill felt a cold rush of anger. "So you poisoned Chips."

Jimmy nodded miserably. "Yeah."

"Why?" Audrey pressed.

Jimmy's gaze dropped. "Bradley told me that Chips—along with Griffin and Wes Holbrook—destroyed his father. Took everything from him. Made him lose his business. Drove him to suicide."

Audrey nudged Jimmy. "And Griffin Mead? How'd you drug him?"

Jimmy exhaled shakily. "It wasn't at the dentist's office like you thought," he admitted. "Bradley gave me Clonidine and told me to slip it into Griffin's drink at the Thirsty Gull that night. Griffin had no idea what was happening—one minute he was fine, the next he was woozy, stumbling. I followed him when he left the bar, waited till he got down to the docks, then . . . Once he was drugged up and weak, it was easy to . . ."

He trailed off, but Jill already knew the answer.

Griffin had been too disoriented to fight back when Jimmy shoved him into the water. He'd drowned, just as Bradley intended.

"You murdered him," Jill growled.

Jimmy's voice broke. "I didn't want to. But Bradley—he kept saying this was justice. That these people had to pay. That I'd be nothing forever if I didn't see this through."

"And Audrey?" Jill's voice shook with fury.

Jimmy squeezed his eyes shut. "Bradley thought she was on to him. She was asking too many questions, getting too close. He told me to get rid of her."

Jill's hands clenched into fists. "So you tried to kill my daughter."

Audrey touched Jill's arm. "Mom . . ."

Jimmy's head snapped up, his face pale. "I wasn't gonna do it! I mean—I tried, but—I don't know, I freaked out. That damn dog got in the way, and then Isabella came, and—"

"You nearly threw her off a cliff."

Jimmy flinched. "I know." His voice cracked. "I know."

Audrey swallowed hard. "Then who was it trailing me down on the pier? The tall, broad-shouldered man—that wasn't you."

Jimmy shook his head quickly. "No. That was Bradley. I bumped into you first, but when you took off, he followed. He wanted to make sure you didn't get away."

Audrey's breath caught. She remembered the sound of footsteps behind her, the looming shadow, the bulk of a man closing in. Jimmy hadn't fit that silhouette. But Bradley had. The pieces clicked together, cold and certain.

The room went silent.

Finally, Jill let out a slow breath. "Here's what's gonna happen."

Jimmy looked up warily.

"You're facing two counts of murder, one count of attempted murder, kidnapping, and God knows how many other additional charges," Jill said, voice steely. "But . . . maybe, just maybe, the DA will cut you a deal—if you testify against Bradley."

Jimmy blinked.

Jill leaned forward, her tone calm but firm. "This is your one shot, Jimmy. You help us bring him down, and maybe you don't spend the rest of your life in a prison cell."

Although given the severity of his crimes, she knew that was probably a long shot.

She just needed him to cooperate.

"Please, Jimmy," Audrey pleaded.

Jimmy hesitated.

Then, finally, he nodded.

"I'll testify."

Jill exchanged a glance with Audrey before reaching for her phone.

She had a district attorney to call.

And Bradley Comstock's days were officially numbered.

Chapter Forty-six

Maggie adjusted the cuffs of her tailored coat as she stepped into the county courthouse. The hallways were crowded with lawyers in pressed suits, clerks with stacks of files, and a few familiar faces from Halibut Cove who had undoubtedly come to witness the proceedings.

Beside her, Audrey walked with quiet determination, her shoulders squared, her chin lifted. Maggie squeezed her granddaughter's arm reassuringly, though she could tell Audrey's mind was elsewhere—likely replaying every terrifying moment from her kidnapping.

They entered the courtroom, finding seats in the front row, and settled in for the show.

Bradley Comstock was led into the courtroom in an orange jumpsuit, his wrists shackled together, his expression a mask of cool detachment.

Maggie took a long, satisfied breath.

He wasn't so smug now.

The defense attorney leaned toward him, whispering something. Bradley's eyes flickered with irritation, and when he saw Maggie and Audrey sitting front and center, his face darkened with anger.

He turned to his lawyer and muttered something sharply, but the attorney only sighed and shook his head.

"It's a public courtroom," the lawyer said in a low, exasperated voice. "They have every right to be here."

Bradley's eyes narrowed.

Maggie smirked.

Judge Marla Baxley, a no-nonsense woman with silver-streaked hair pulled into a tight bun, took her seat at the bench and banged her gavel once, calling the court to order.

"Case Number 24-7859," the bailiff announced. "The State of Maine versus Bradley Comstock."

Bradley's lawyer stood. "Your Honor, my client pleads not guilty to all charges."

A murmur rippled through the courtroom.

Maggie leaned toward Audrey and whispered. "He still thinks he can weasel his way out of this."

Audrey frowned. "Typical."

Mark Haskell, the district attorney, rose from his chair. "Your Honor, given the severity of the charges—two counts of first-degree murder, attempted murder, kidnapping, and conspiracy—the state is seeking a substantial bail amount for the defendant, if not a denial of bail altogether."

Bradley's lawyer shot to his feet, adjusting his tie. "Your Honor, my client is a pillar of the community—a well-respected dentist, a business owner. He has deep ties to Halibut Cove and is no flight risk."

Judge Baxley's brows lifted slightly, unimpressed with the defense's argument.

Mark scoffed. "Not a flight risk?" He turned to the judge. "Your Honor, the defendant was literally on the run when he was apprehended—after taking a hostage. That alone should be enough to deny bail outright."

The judge adjusted her glasses, flipping through the case file. "I agree with the prosecution," she said firmly. "Bail is set at two million dollars."

The gasp that rippled through the room was almost satisfying.

Bradley stiffened, his cool composure cracking ever so slightly. He turned to glare at Mark, but the DA merely folded his arms, satisfied.

Maggie smiled.

This was going exactly as it should.

As the courtroom began to empty, Bradley remained seated, his lawyer whispering furiously in his ear. Jill entered and approached, hands on her hips, her badge gleaming in the fluorescent lights.

Bradley smirked, though it was far weaker than before.

"Chief Holbrook," he drawled, his voice still clinging to some false confidence. "Here to pin more imaginary crimes on me?"

Jill didn't blink. "Oh, they're not imaginary, Comstock."

Bradley chuckled, shaking his head. "You're blaming me for everything, but Jimmy was the one who poisoned Chips Hogan. Jimmy was the one who drugged Griffin Mead and pushed him into the water. I had nothing to do with any of it."

Jill leaned in slightly, her voice cold as steel. "Jimmy was your pawn. You played him like a fool, but he's not the one who masterminded this whole revenge plot." She tilted her head, watching Bradley's reaction. "You gave Jimmy the nightshade you stole from Melanie. You planted the belladonna plant in Waldo Duggan's pantry to frame him. You fed Jimmy every lie in the book to make him do your dirty work."

Bradley stayed silent, his expression unreadable.

Maggie stepped forward, arms crossed. "You've been obsessed with revenge for years, haven't you? Blaming Chips, Griffin, and my late husband, Wes, for your father's failures."

Bradley finally turned toward her, and for the first time, there was real hatred in his eyes.

"You think this is funny, Mrs. Holbrook?" he said, his voice low and full of venom.

Maggie tilted her head, unbothered. "Not funny. Sad."

She could see it now—the desperation, the years of resentment, the way he'd spent decades fueling his hatred, all for this moment.

And now, it was over.

"You must be disappointed," Maggie continued, her voice dripping with false sympathy. "I survived."

Bradley's lip curled, his fingers clenching into fists.

Audrey leaned in, voice sharp as glass. "Oh, and by the way, Jimmy took a plea deal. He's going to be the star witness against you at your trial."

For the first time, Bradley faltered. His eyes flickered, his cheeks paling slightly.

Jill nodded slowly, enjoying the moment. "That's right. Jimmy agreed to testify about everything. The nightshade. The Clonidine. The kidnapping. All of it."

"I'll be taking the stand too," Audrey said sharply. "Recounting my whole ordeal with you."

"You're no victim!" Bradley spit out. "You were obsessed with me—always snooping, following me around, basically stalking me!"

"Well, I guess we'll just have to see who the jury believes," Audrey said with a confident smile.

Maggie watched with satisfaction as Bradley's mask slipped entirely.

He knew.

He knew he was done for.

As they exited the courthouse, Maggie held her head high, breathing in the crisp autumn air.

Audrey grinned at her. "Well, that was satisfying."

Maggie chuckled, linking arms with her granddaughter. "The only thing that would've made it better is if they gave me five minutes alone with him and a rolling pin."

Audrey laughed. "Mom would've arrested you."

"Totally worth it."

"I thought you said violence was never the answer."

"It's not. But I can dream, can't I?"

Jill joined them, hands on her hips. "We've still got a long road ahead," she said. "The trial. The sentencing. But one thing's for sure . . ."

Maggie smiled knowingly. "Bradley Comstock is never going to see the outside of a prison cell again."

And with that, they walked down the courthouse steps—one battle-scarred family, but stronger than ever.

Chapter Forty-seven

The moment Maggie walked inside The Chowder House, she saw the entire staff gathered in a half-circle near the counter, clapping and grinning at none other than Waldo Duggan.

The grizzled old cook, looking a little thinner but no less ornery, stood with his arms folded across his chest, trying to look as if he didn't appreciate the attention. But Maggie could see it—the slight quirk of his mouth, the way his eyes softened just a little.

Waldo cleared his throat gruffly. "All right, all right. Enough of this nonsense. It's just my first day. No need to make such a fuss."

Ethel, standing beside Audrey and Isabella, smirked. "Well, to be fair, Waldo, I've been wanting to steal you away from the Seaview for years. I've been just waiting for the right opportunity."

The Seaview had been slow in bringing back Waldo after his name was cleared in the Chips Hogan murder, so Ethel stepped in, hiring him on the spot.

The kitchen crew cheered, and Ethel wiped her hands on her apron, stepping forward. "I always knew the only thing you could murder was a medium rare steak, Duggan. And you know damn well you love the attention."

Waldo grumbled something unintelligible but didn't argue.

Maggie walked over to the group, her presence immediately drawing Waldo's attention. He gave her a slow nod, his way of acknowledging what she'd done for him without getting too sentimental about it.

Maggie tilted her head. "Welcome to The Chowder House, Waldo."

"Didn't have much of a choice," he muttered, rubbing the back of his neck. "Figured it was better than sitting at home, listening to my neighbor yammer on about lobster quotas."

Laughter rippled through the crowd, but Maggie's focus shifted to Ethel, who looked more worn-out than usual.

As Waldo shook hands with a few of the kitchen staff greeting him, Maggie walked over to Ethel and lowered her voice. "You okay?"

Ethel sighed, rubbing her temples. "I don't know, Maggie. The past few weeks have been a nightmare. Waldo getting arrested. And that poison scare? Half the regulars who did show up here wouldn't touch the chowder for a while. Every time I turned around, someone was whispering about it."

Maggie nodded. She'd seen firsthand how much of a toll it had taken.

Ethel exhaled deeply, as if finally admitting it to herself. "I'm tired, Maggie. I've been thinking . . . maybe it's time to step away."

Maggie studied her friend carefully. This wasn't just a passing thought. Ethel was really considering retirement.

She placed a hand on Ethel's arm. "Let's talk later. I've got a few ideas."

Ethel nodded, looking relieved.

Maggie turned back to Waldo. "How about a cup of coffee?"

Waldo gave her a wary look. "What's the catch?"

"No catch," Maggie said innocently. "Just a little chat."

With a long-suffering sigh, Waldo muttered, "I haven't even started yet, and you want me to take a break already?"

"I'm sure Ethel won't mind."

Waldo sighed. "Fine. Ten minutes."

Maggie and Waldo slid into a corner booth, as Isabella placed two mugs of hot coffee in front of them.

Waldo stirred in a spoonful of sugar, eyeing Maggie suspiciously. "All right, Maggie. What's this about?"

Maggie took her time, blowing lightly on her coffee before taking a sip.

"I wanted to talk about the Holbrook–Duggan feud," she said finally.

Waldo snorted. "Feud's over. You proved I wasn't guilty. I'm grateful, even if I don't say it."

Maggie smirked. "You just said it."

Waldo grumbled into his coffee.

Maggie reached into her purse, pulling out a few old recipe cards, yellowed with age.

"I've been going through some old family records," she said, spreading the cards out on the table. "Turns out, the Holbrook and Duggan chowder recipes? Almost the same—just a few different spices here and there. Close enough that most folks would never know the difference."

Maggie gave a small, knowing smile. "I could still taste it, of course. But to everyone else? It might as well be the same bowl of chowder."

Waldo bristled, his jaw tightening. "Maybe to some people," he muttered. "But mine's still better."

Maggie chuckled. "Waldo, it's ridiculous that we've spent all these years pretending there was some big secret between them when they're practically the same."

Waldo rubbed his jaw, looking conflicted. "You saying your husband and my father were fighting over nothing?"

Maggie leaned back, giving him a knowing look. "I'm saying it was never about the chowder."

Waldo was silent, staring at the recipe cards. "So what now? You want me to admit the Duggan chowder's not as special as we always thought?"

Maggie laughed. "Not at all. I want us to work together."

Waldo narrowed his eyes. "What do you mean?"

"I'm offering you a stake in the Holbrook chowder business."

Waldo's mouth fell open slightly before he snapped it shut. "You're joking."

"I don't joke about chowder," Maggie said seriously.

Waldo sat back, his fingers drumming against the tabletop. "You really want me to partner with you? After all these years?"

Maggie nodded. "It's time we put all this behind us. We can have the best damn chowder in all of Maine—Holbrook and Duggan, together."

Waldo shook his head, a slow grin creeping onto his face. "You Holbrooks. Always gotta make everything a big deal."

"Damn right," Maggie said cheerfully.

Maggie stood up, brushing imaginary crumbs off her skirt.

"Now," she said, grinning mischievously, "since we're doing this, we're going to celebrate properly."

Waldo groaned. "Oh, hell. What are you planning?"

"A big event," Maggie declared. "The whole town. A celebration of our new partnership."

Waldo held up a hand. "No big speeches. No banners. No fancy nonsense."

Maggie pretended to consider. "Fine. Minimal banners."

"Maggie," Waldo said warningly.

Maggie laughed. "Relax. It'll be great for business. And besides," she added, nudging his arm, "it's about time people saw us working together instead of against each other."

Waldo sighed. "If I say yes, will you stop pestering me?"

"Absolutely not," Maggie said cheerfully.

Waldo shook his head, but Maggie could see it—the small smile, the acceptance.

It had taken decades, but finally, the feud was over.

And in its place?

A brand-new beginning.

Chapter Forty-eight

Audrey tapped lightly on the hospital room door before stepping inside.

Mason lay propped up against a stack of pillows, looking better than she had expected. His shoulder was bandaged, his color had returned, and there was a distinct look of boredom on his face as he flipped through the TV channels with the remote in his good hand.

"Which *Housewives* are you bingeing?" Audrey asked, crossing her arms and leaning against the doorframe.

Mason looked over and immediately brightened. "Holbrook." He clicked the remote, silencing the TV. "Finally, someone with a brain. I was about to throw myself out the window if I had to watch one more episode of *Antiques Roadshow*."

"Wow. Strong feelings about appraised furniture."

Mason grinned. "Turns out, I prefer actual crime to old people selling clocks."

Nurse Katie, who was in the room, smirked as she jotted something down on his chart. "I'll leave you two alone," she said knowingly. "Just don't stress him out too much, Audrey. He's still recovering."

Audrey rolled her eyes. "I'll do my best."

Katie gave Mason a pointed look. "No funny business, Dooley."

Mason smirked. "Wouldn't dream of it."

Katie snorted and walked out, leaving them in silence.

Audrey pulled up a chair and sat down. "So. You got shot."

Mason snorted. "Yeah. I was there."

"Feels like I should be thanking you," Audrey admitted. "You saved my life."

Mason waved it off. "Eh, you did most of the work. I just bled dramatically for effect."

Audrey rolled her eyes. "Don't downplay it. You risked your life for me, Mason."

Mason held her gaze, his usual smirk fading. "I'd do it again."

Audrey glanced at his IV, at the machines beeping softly beside his bed. "So how long until you're back on your feet?"

Mason sighed dramatically. "I'd say a week, but Jill's being a real hard-ass about it. Says I need to fully heal before she lets me back in the field."

Audrey raised a brow. "My mother? Cautious?"

Mason laughed. "I know, right? But she's looking out for me." He paused. "She's a damn good cop."

Audrey blinked, not expecting the sudden earnestness in his tone.

Mason shifted slightly, wincing as he adjusted his injured shoulder. "She's one of the best I've ever worked for," he continued. "Tough as hell, but fair. And she actually gives a damn. I've learned more from her in the last year than I did the whole time I was at the academy."

Audrey stared at him. "You actually admire her."

Chapter Forty-nine

Jill leaned against the wall of Oliver's office, arms crossed, watching as Rhonda and Bert Barker sat across from Oliver and DA Mark Haskell. The tension in the room was thick, despite the fact that they all knew what was coming.

Cord stood near the door, his jaw set, clearly struggling with the reality of the situation. He had come to show support, but Jill could tell he wasn't sure what to say.

Mark cleared his throat, placing a file on the desk. "Given the evidence, the history of abuse, and the mitigating circumstances, we're prepared to offer a deal."

Bert immediately stiffened. "No. She's not taking any deal."

Rhonda placed a calming hand on his arm. "Let's hear it first."

Mark continued. "If you plead guilty to second-degree manslaughter, the sentence will be six months in prison, with time served counting toward that total. No additional charges."

Bert's face turned red. "Absolutely not! She was defending herself! She should walk free!"

Oliver held up a hand. "Bert, sit down."

Rhonda, calm and composed, looked at Mark. "And after that? Will this finally be over?"

Mark nodded. "After that, you're free to go home. No parole, no probation. Just six months, then you can put this behind you."

Bert shook his head vehemently. "This isn't justice."

Rhonda gently squeezed his hand. "Bert, listen to me. I want this behind me, no matter what. I don't want to fight anymore."

Bert looked at his wife, desperation in his eyes. "But six months—"

Rhonda cut him off softly. "It's six months. I can do that. I need to take responsibility for what I did. I need this done."

Phoebe, standing behind her mother, wiped at her eyes, her voice thick with emotion. "Mom, are you sure?"

Rhonda nodded, a weight seemingly lifting from her shoulders. "Yes. It's time."

Mark slid the plea deal across the table, and Rhonda, without hesitation, picked up the pen and signed her name.

Bert exhaled sharply, looking defeated. Phoebe moved beside him, placing a hand on his shoulder.

Rhonda looked at Oliver, gratitude in her eyes. "Thank you—for everything. I can finally stop looking over my shoulder."

Oliver nodded and offered her an encouraging smile.

Jill watched as the reality of the moment sank in for everyone. This was truly the end of a decades-old nightmare.

As the legal proceedings wrapped up, Jill lingered outside Oliver's office.

She didn't intend to eavesdrop, but when Cord and Phoebe stepped into the hallway, their voices carried.

Phoebe forced a small smile. "I know why you wanted to talk to me, Cord."

Cord looked away, clearly uncomfortable. "I don't want to hurt you."

Phoebe laughed quietly, but it sounded hollow. "We both know this isn't working."

Cord hesitated. "I care about you, Phoebe. But I—"

Phoebe cut him off gently. "You don't love me enough."

Cord flinched. "I thought I did."

Phoebe nodded, blinking back tears. "I get it. Really, I do."

Cord sighed. "I still want to be there for you. As a friend."

Phoebe hesitated, then offered a weak smile. "I'll hold you to that."

Cord nodded, looking like he wanted to say more but couldn't find the words.

Jill waited until Cord walked away before stepping outside. Phoebe stood in place for a moment before steeling herself and heading out the opposite way.

As Jill slid into the driver's seat of her car, her phone buzzed.

It was a text from Audrey.

Can you pick me up at the hospital?

Jill responded.

On my way.

When she pulled into the hospital parking lot ten minutes later, Audrey was already outside, waiting. She slid into the passenger seat, fastening her seatbelt.

Jill glanced at her daughter. "Mason doing okay?"

Audrey nodded, staring out the window. "Yeah. He's recovering. Still restless."

Jill smirked. "Of course he is."

They drove in silence for a few minutes, the coastal road stretching ahead of them.

Finally, Jill sighed. "I know I can be . . . overbearing."

Audrey arched a brow. "You don't say."

Jill rolled her eyes. "All right, all right. But look, I just—" She gripped the wheel. "I worry about you."

Audrey softened. "I know. But I'm not a kid anymore."

Jill glanced at her, then nodded slowly. "I know that now."

Another beat of silence.

Then Audrey smirked. "So, Mark Haskell, huh?"

Jill groaned. "I am not having this conversation with you again."

Audrey grinned. "Come on, Mom. He's clearly into you."

Jill shook her head. "I don't have time for this."

Audrey shrugged. "You make time to interrogate criminals. You can make time for a dinner date."

Jill sighed dramatically, gripping the wheel. "Fine. One more date. But if he starts talking about court filings, I'm out."

Audrey laughed, feeling something lighter between them.

For the first time in a long time, they weren't fighting.

And maybe, just maybe, things were finally falling into place.

Chapter Fifty

Maggie had always believed in the power of Sunday dinner. No matter how chaotic life became, no matter the fights, the murders, the near-death experiences—this family always gathered around the table. And tonight, with her famous chowder steaming in the center, fresh baked bread, and a platter of seafood, the Holbrook family was ready to celebrate surviving the last few months of insanity.

As usual, Cord and Sandy bickered over who got the last crab cake, Jill attempted to keep the peace, and Audrey teased Mason—who was now a permanent fixture at family gatherings. Even Oliver had joined them, pouring himself a generous glass of wine. Katie was working a night shift at the hospital, so Oliver had come solo, though he insisted he was under strict orders to report back on everything that happened at dinner.

Maggie, seated at the head of the table, lifted her spoon and took a slow, satisfying sip of chowder. Perfect. No deadly nightshade, no poison, no crime scene investigators lurking outside. Just a normal, peaceful meal.

Imagine that.

The table was alive with conversation, everyone lighter,

the burdens of the past few months finally easing off their shoulders.

Then, Sandy cleared his throat.

The table fell quiet, all eyes turning to him. Sandy was never the one to command attention. He was steady, dependable, but rarely outspoken.

"There's, uh . . . something I want to say," Sandy started, rubbing the back of his neck. "I've been doing a lot of thinking lately. About my life. My future."

Cord, ever the protective big brother, raised a brow. "You okay, bud?"

Sandy nodded. "Yeah. Actually . . . I think I am." He took a breath. "I've been talking to Tom Jenkins—you know, the mailman?"

Cord, clueless, took a bite of a dinner roll. "About what?"

The rest of the family burst into laughter.

Cord chewed with his mouth open. "What am I missing?"

Audrey reached over and squeezed her Uncle Sandy's hand. "Tom's a great catch. I'm happy for you."

Cord blinked. "Wait. Tom Jenkins is gay?"

Audrey shook her head. "Uncle Cord, you miss everything! You worked with Sandy every day and didn't even know he was gay. This is classic."

Cord grumbled but shook his head with a chuckle. "Guess I'm just oblivious."

Maggie smiled proudly. "Tom's a good man."

Sandy relaxed at the support. "Yeah. And, well . . . I don't know where things are headed yet, but I'd like to find out."

Audrey clinked her glass. "To Sandy and Tom!"

The family raised their glasses, and even Cord, still processing, muttered, "Yeah. To Sandy and Tom."

"Okay, that's enough," Sandy said. "No more fuss."

Cord scratched his head. "You know, if I was going to fix up Sandy, I'd go for that new pharmacist at the drugstore, the one who works out at the gym all the time, with the abs?"

Oliver slurped some chowder and then set his spoon down. "Married to a woman. With five kids."

"Seriously? I would've bet money he had a little sugar in his tank," Cord said, wide-eyed.

"Did you really just say that, Uncle Cord? You're so getting canceled if you don't watch it," Audrey giggled.

Cord looked around the room. "Canceled? What the hell's she talking about?"

Maggie smiled. "I always worried he spent too much time out on that boat."

With the focus shifted from Sandy, Audrey leaned forward, excitement practically radiating off her.

"So," she started, "I have an announcement too."

Maggie cocked an eyebrow. "You're not running off with Mason to become a detective, are you?"

Audrey snorted. "No. But I am taking over The Chowder House."

Silence.

Then chaos.

Cord nearly choked on his drink. Sandy's jaw dropped. Jill blinked in surprise, and Oliver let out a low whistle.

"Wait, wait," Jill finally said. "You're what?"

Audrey grinned. "Ethel's retiring. She's been through too much with all the drama surrounding the restaurant, and she's ready to step away. I'm buying it from her."

Jill's brow furrowed. "How exactly are you going to afford to buy a restaurant?"

Audrey glanced at Maggie, who simply smiled and lifted her glass.

Jill's eyes widened. "Mom?"

Maggie shrugged. "She needed an investor. I had the means. Seemed like a good fit."

Jill let out a breathless laugh, shaking her head. "You two . . . you really don't do things small, do you?"

Maggie smirked. "Wouldn't be Holbrooks if we did."

Audrey laughed, and Maggie saw tears of gratitude in her granddaughter's eyes.

The family raised their glasses again, this time to new beginnings.

"To Audrey," Oliver toasted. "The next great Holbrook entrepreneur."

"To Audrey!" they all echoed, clinking their glasses together.

Later that evening, with the house finally quiet, Maggie sat on her porch, Flounder curled up at her feet, as the sun sank into the horizon. The ocean stretched out before her, calm, steady, just like it had always been.

For the first time in months, she felt peaceful.

The family had survived.

They had faced murder, betrayal, old ghosts, and dangerous men—and yet, here they were. Stronger than ever.

She took a deep breath, the salt air crisp and cool.

The Holbrook name had weathered many storms, but it wasn't going anywhere.

Neither was she.

As Flounder let out a contented sigh, Maggie leaned back in her chair, watching the final streaks of sunlight fade into twilight, and smiled.

Because, despite all the chaos, all the danger, all the uncertainty—

They had come out on top.

And that was something worth celebrating.